# Exile

Aimée Walsh

# Exile

JOHN MURRAY

*For survivors, the diaspora, and my friends and family.*

First published in Great Britain in 2024 by John Murray (Publishers)

1

Copyright © Aimée Walsh 2024

The right of Aimée Walsh to be identified as the Author of the Work has been asserted by her in accordance with the Copyright, Designs and Patents Act 1988.

All rights reserved. No part of this publication may be reproduced, stored in a retrieval system, or transmitted, in any form or by any means without the prior written permission of the publisher, nor be otherwise circulated in any form of binding or cover other than that in which it is published and without a similar condition being imposed on the subsequent purchaser.

The extract from *Milkman* by Anna Burns has been reproduced with permission from Faber and Faber Ltd.

All characters in this publication are fictitious and any resemblance to real persons, living or dead, is purely coincidental.

A CIP catalogue record for this title is available from the British Library

Hardback ISBN 9781399815857
Trade Paperback ISBN 9781399815864
ebook ISBN 9781399815888

Typeset in Sabon MT by Hewer Text UK Ltd, Edinburgh
Printed and bound in Great Britain by Clays Ltd, Elcograf S.p.A.

John Murray policy is to use papers that are natural, renewable and recyclable products and made from wood grown in sustainable forests. The logging and manufacturing processes are expected to conform to the environmental regulations of the country of origin.

Carmelite House
50 Victoria Embankment
London EC4Y 0DZ

www.johnmurraypress.co.uk

John Murray Press, part of Hodder & Stoughton Limited
An Hachette UK company

The truth was dawning on me of how terrifying it was not to be numb, but to be aware, to have facts, retain facts, be adult.

Anna Burns, *Milkman*

# Part One

# I

It happens just as it did every weekend, more or less, since I hit puberty. The sun is beginning to dip below the horizon for the night, transforming the sky to a deep purple. Our car turns the corner onto Donegall Square North, with the back of City Hall looming large. Saturday night traffic moves slowly, as if each of the drivers is in awe of the architecture. Its grandness sharp against the gummed footpath beneath. Red brake lights shine on our faces, as taxi drivers pull into the tight space in front of our car. Ma says nothing, happy to let them out in the hope that by that time I will change my mind and make the return journey home with her, to hot chocolates and matching jammies on the sofa, spooning melted marshmallows around big, bowled mugs. This is her fantasy. We don't even speak when we're in the gaff. No chance of change now though; my stomach has already begun to feel that nervy flutter, the ripple moves up from the seat to my belly. I try my best to ignore the sensation, hoping that it's not a bout of the runs after the feed of Chinese food I shovelled into me earlier. Swear, lining my stomach never does any actual good; it is inevitable that the girls will get a visual of my dinner as it makes its second coming into some pish-splashed bog at 2 a.m.

In my hands, the papery foil of Wrigley's Extra unwraps easily from its wee silvery jacket. Like Eucharist, the gum is placed into my mouth to avoid disturbing my freshly Juicy-Tubed lips. I move my arm to extend the packet across the car. Ma shakes her head. It'll put her off her dinner, she tells me.

—And have you your taxi booked? Ma asks into the silence.

—I'll book one when my free calls come through tonight. I'll be grand. Aisling will have minutes on her phone anyway.

—Will you be sure to call me if you have any trouble getting home?

A light flickers on, bringing a yellow glow to my face. Blue glitter on my eyelids glints like a disco ball. I lean towards it, pushing my chin to my chest to assess the hastily streaked eyeliner, before adding another confident swoop of deep black kohl to the waterline. The visor bangs shut, like an oyster slamming its shell together in escape of some nearby danger. Swivelling to fully turn in my seat, I watch my ma's face as she drives through the city, her hands at ten and two, her back straight as a board. After a moment or so, I test my luck.

—No, sure, I thought I'd take my chances sitting around City Hall until the buses start.

She doesn't even let her eyes twitch in recognition.

—Fine, yes, I'll text you.

—Call me. My phone will be on loud.

—OK, I said yes already!

Ma doesn't say a word. It falls on deaf ears.

Finally, I admit defeat and say, —Will you ever just give over? I'll be alright.

—And are you wearing socks, love?

—Excuse me?

—Socks, she said, giving me that infuriating look, where she tilts her jaw into herself and does a wee smile. —So, your feet aren't all exposed to those rental gutties. Lord knows whose trotters have been in there first.

Aye, right enough, I did tell her we're for the bowling alley. I can barely keep on top of the story we're all running with for our mas these days. There's no real reason to be spoofing at this stage, it's our big blow out after our exams finishing earlier in the week. As if she thinks we're shaking off our school years in a bowling alley. Rubbery skids from our borrowed shoes up and down the lanes. I'd honestly rather die. But I'm not ready to tell her any different, out of habit more than anything else.

Headlights pass by in the opposite direction, away from town, striping the inside of the car. Her eyes narrow, while her lips dance around the words she wants to say but will not come. I can't look at her when she's like this, so I pull the magnet hidden under a black patent bow on my handbag, tipping out high street make-up, a provisional driving licence that has seen better days, and finally my phone into my lap. There are no new messages, so I shove it into the depths of my bag again. The atmosphere feels heavy with the quiet between us.

Belfast is a small enough city that everybody knows somebody who knows who you are after. It's one of those places. But for all its size, travelling across the city feels crawling. The silence inside the car only seems to move things slower, so when I see where I'm for, I'm half out of the door before the car has stopped.

—Will you wait in the car until you can see them? Fiadh? Did you hear me?

—Don't wait up, I shout, as the door slams.

The car doesn't move at first, but as I'm making my way towards the bowling alley, I peer over my shoulder. When our wee car turns the corner, I double back on myself. The screen of my phone lights up: 'Aisling.' A shriek slices through the street before I can answer.

—FEE-AH!

The sound of it could make glass shatter. Danielle's holding the second syllable like her life depends on it. She is tottering towards me at high speed, wobbling from foot to foot, each step a marvel of nature and science. When she reaches me, her arms latch to my neck, slightly overshooting the mark, pulling me along with her. A stream of giggles and the acrid smell of vodka lingers on my kissed cheek.

—Where have you *been*?! I've been waiting on *you*!

Before I can tell her that I've just been dropped off, she shouts, —Come on already, I'm busting for a pint.

While I was lining my stomach with a chow mein, Danielle opted for a half bottle of Glen's vodka with her older sister. Passed down like a family heirloom, 'Eating's cheating' is her night out mantra. Together we walk up towards the Dublin Road, swapping gossip from the days before: who was said to be riding who; who was dumped by her boy in public; did you hear who was fingered on a bin? Aisling rings again. This time I answer. She doesn't get a word in.

—We're on our way past the cinema now. We'll not be long, love.

Snapping the phone shut, I roll my eyes, —Worse than my ma, swear!

After a brief stop at the shop for fegs, the two of us light up outside, stilling our nerves for the final, albeit small, ascent up the road to the summit, Lavery's backbar.

—Who all's out thenight, then? I ask.

—If you're asking if your boy is coming, it'll be a bit later on he says.

After a minute of silent walking, she crumbles, —Ah for fuck's sake, when'll you and him just get together? It's been forever. You must know he likes you.

—Ah, I don't know about that.

I crush the spent feg end under my platform, kicking the ground to unstick it from my shoe.

—We're just mates. Sure, I've known him since I had the tits of a wee boy.

—Aye, but you're a ride now, love.

—Stop that now. Mon, we get ourselves in for a pint before you start asking when I'll see you too.

The bouncers on the door know us. They'd seen us regularly most Saturday nights since we were fifteen, and in some instances, during the week too when we were after a hassle-free weekday entry to the nightclub upstairs. Now that we were all of legal drinking age and free from the shackles of exams, we approached the doors with the confidence of a Victoria's Secret model heading down the runway in those giant wings: assured in the knowledge that absolutely everybody thought we were rides. In the early years of us heading out out, Danielle was one of those girls co-opted into showing the bouncers her tits in lieu of ID. Approaching the entrance, the doorman stands feet spread wide, getting a good look of her; his eyes scanning up and down, committing the outline to memory.

—Bout ye, girls? Yous having a good night? he says as we get near him.

—All the better for seeing you, love, Danielle flirts as we sail past and into the bar.

Once the door swings shut between us, she sticks her tongue out and gags, —He's a fuckin' rotter. Boke.

Like Russian dolls, Lavery's opens out from bar to bar, always revealing a smaller more compact version of itself the further you descend. Opening the doors to the back bar, I am overwhelmed by a cacophony of chat, the slight vibration of those attempting to get a dance going, and huddles of people putting wrongs to right around small tables filled with empty pint glasses. An arm juts out of the crowd, high in the air, waving and jumping, as Aisling signals our arrival. Literally everybody from school is out, but because we've planned to be out together, The Girls, it doesn't really matter.

Sure, we wouldn't know half of these people's names in a month. It was only the other week when we'd been sat in the exam room, a bitter coldness to the sports hall on that last morning. It's the type of chill which long distance drivers welcome in the car window as they're heading down the motorway. Pastel coloured papers piled on each desk, text facing downward. Everybody was exchanging raised eyebrows and taut smiles, not quite well wishes. Nerves swelled up in my stomach. At the side of the room, Aisling was stuffing her bag with colour-coded revision notes, milking every single second. She would kill us if we ever touted on her, that she had spent months tucked in an alcove in the music section of Belfast Central Library drawing miniature diagrams of the heart onto those cards. Testing and retesting her recall by sketching out the ventricles again and again and again. She made a beeline for her desk, just in time for the head examiner to announce the start.

—The time is now nine-thirty. You may begin.

A flutter of pages. Silence. The examiners' feet echoed up and down the hall as they paced like guards. I opened the first page: *What is a prokaryote?* My eyes glazed over with tiredness. Trying to recall anything from the substitute Biology teacher's class. All I could remember is Danielle turning to me mid-class and saying she's 'pro-carry out'. Over at her desk, she was writing furiously.

A steady stream of my classmates began to hand in their papers early. Bouncing out the room with a kick of freedom in their step. Just as I was conjuring the last answers to write into the booklet, one of the invigilators told the room that no more early hand ins would be accepted. We were too near the end. Each minute eked out, stretched beyond its limit, snapping the fabric of time from the room. Old socks haunted the hall, wafting with every movement. I could see myself and Danielle skiving off in the corner, while Aisling did the beep test, racing up and down the room. The P.E. teacher Ms Finley shouting *Go*. Faster and faster. Shoes squeaking up the polished floors. *Go*. Two girls neck and neck, running against each other. Everything else fading around them. The whole gym fell away as we focused on the pair of them. *Go*. Aisling's shoes didn't quite touch the line before she turned. The other clocked it, barrelling straight into her. Hair was torn on the floor. Ms Finley was over between them like a bolt. Pulling the two apart. All she said was *Go*.

Aisling's enthusiasm for cheap and nasty drinks brings me back.

She pulls Danielle's arm to the bar.

I follow close behind, squishing between the two to hear what's happening. They face forward, leaning across the deep wooden bar slicked with remnants of tequila and sambuca, the smell pungent and uninviting.

—THREE TEQUILAS PLEASE, Aisling screams across to the barman, who winces at the volume, loud with sheer proximity.

Salt and lemon are set out without ceremony to all but us three. The additional tools needed to take our shots gave us a joy which is only experienced by the inexperienced. We throw the golden liquid down our gullets, wince, and gag. Aisling screams across the bar for three Carlsbergs to wash the taste of regrets away.

Crossing back towards the crowd, we huddle together to convene a plan of action for the night: dancing or sitting listening to self-indulgent blokes debate the intricacies of things which are in equal parts eye-wateringly boring and irrelevant. With a knowing look between us, then back over the pack of boys, we turn on our heels and head back through the maze of bar rooms towards the stairs at the front. The pervert bouncer greets Danielle with a Cheshire cat grin.

—Alright, sexy? Couldn't resist?

Turning the corner on the stairs, Danielle leans into us.

—The Brook should have that on tap. Best contraception out there.

I answer, —My vagina would up and leave.

—Aye, the band would have to split up due to creative differences, Aisling laughs.

At the top of the stairs, we can feel the music vibrating out from the club and up through our legs to our stomachs. A tired-looking girl is staring through the window down to the street below. One arm perched on a table, a lonely pint and a metal petty-cash box are all that's in front of her. With half-opened eyes, she takes in the sight of us.

—Having a good night, girls?

Soon as we've parted ways with our fivers, she's slapped the three bands on our wrists. It's as if we were never there. She's back to looking out the window, down onto the street, a pint held close to her lips.

We make our way inside the nightclub, red beams bouncing around the room, momentarily lighting up the couples hidden in dark corners, converging bodies melting into one shining orb.

The uncovered bulbs had been buried by the darkness, but now they shine into life, bringing an interrogative brightness to the room, shining on all our sins we hoped to hide. The bar clears quickly, with the bouncers marching between the tables shouting, —Drink up! That's it! On you go home!

And for those already on their feet and making their way to the exit, a firm hand appears at their back to usher them out. Like herded cattle, we push out the back door, and emerge in the alley behind, where people gather in groups, indiscreetly concealing pint glasses filled with amber-gold liquids. In the recesses, men lean against the walls, holding themselves or another, it's often hard to tell which.

On Bradbury Place, we take it in turns to call what feels like the only two taxi companies serving the whole city.

—Sorry, nothing for forty minutes, love. Ring back then, we are told over and over.

—Fuck, I'm starving.

—Mon, says Danielle, leading the way to Bright's chippy just up from the bar.

The green and gold sign gives a regal air, often amiss in other late-night chippies, but truth be told, the inside is like a military operation. People and chips made sloppy by a feed of drink are dripped around the walls of the takeaway. A formidable woman behind the counter shouts order numbers out to the crowd, and then again with an increasingly admonishing tone with every time she repeats the number.

—Nai, one of yous ordered a curry chip, number SEVENTY-SIX! NUMBER SEVENTY-SIX. SEVEN-SIX.

When the person eventually approaches the counter, she asks —Were you asleep, love? Her tone now much softer, while sliding a warm paper package, wrapped like a newborn, across to him. He accepts it like a gift from God. Staggering away, across the tiled floor, he pushes him and his bounty out the door and into the night.

—Will you get me a cheesy curry chip, if I get the taxi? Danielle asks me.

—I'm not ordering that. You can have cheesy or curry. Both is madness.

—Swear you're ordering a half and half? At least my combo isn't two carbs.

—Right enough, Aisling says, as if she's emerging for the first time from her beer-fog.

When I get to the counter, I order the cheesy curry chip and two half-and-halfs, while the other two grab a table laden with old wrappers and spilt Fanta. I don't leave the counter until I've arms full of polystyrene boxes filled to the brim with the cure.

—Andy's texted that he's in the new pizza place down the street.

—Boke.

—Is he going back with you? Danielle says, as she shovels chips covered in globs of curry and cheese into her mouth.

Reared on rom-coms, Danielle and Aisling let their minds run riot when it comes to Andy. I have known him for what feels like forever; we have been friends since we were little. When the girls see him, worlds of possibilities unfurl before their eyes. He has come out with us in the past, and Aisling can't help herself, alternating between nauseating flirting and trying to play matchmaker. I often think she does the latter to force him into admitting undying love for her, mind. I keep the two distinct, especially during these sacred Girls' Nights.

—Nah, love. Just me and the cat thenight. You know, preppin' for my life of singledom forever.

I laugh, but it sounds more like an inward sniff, convincing nobody.

Aisling's phone drills against the table. An automated voice lets us know *your taxi has arrived*.

The street outside the chippy is a warzone: there is a girl sat on the kerb, her heels piled beside her. Her bodycon skirt is rolled up on her hips. Bare arse on kerb stone. She's none the wiser though, her head is between her legs as she spews. One person is scooping her hair from her face, while another rubs her back. Beyond, a fella stumbles in the opposite direction, wide-legged like a cowboy. In the distance, the sound of chanting what is probably a rendition of 'Wonderwall'.

Aisling's judiciously scanning the number plates of all the parked cars. Her eyes darting back from phone to car every few seconds. Once a match has been confirmed, she yells over to Danielle and I, —Mon, yous.

We bundle our chips into our coats, pressed up against our tits.

—I fuckin' see that. Drop it and yous will be paying for a clean.

—No flies on you! Danielle slurs.

—Fuck up or you're going nowhere, wee love.

The car juts off towards North Belfast. Roads blur past, as rain slicked tarmac reflects the streetlights. Danielle is holding in either a laugh or a boke. It's hard to tell at this time of the evening, so I keep the chat with the taxi man going until we are near enough to home.

# 2

As if through back-lit windows their eyes stare out at me, watching me take the whole scene in. Their motionless faces have faded in the sunlight. The transparent film is only a few millimetres thick, each holding a new universe on its surface. Each rectangle lights up into the Dublin Road like little television sets. These images, no matter what they show, appear drab. Tucked under the plastic casings, the corners of the posters curl, as if recoiling from the cold. I pull my jumper closer around myself. In the left top-corner, there are explosions as scenes of war-torn countries rage in the background. Another poster shows some woman, her gold dress like liquid dripping off her, pooling at her feet. Half-closed eyes give her the appearance of tiredness, as if waking from a deep sleep to find you are being held up by some bloke leaning on your shoulder. To the right, a cartoon cat is shown mid-leap. The furry face caught beaming about the attempt at escape.

Da bounces up the road, stuffing a battered wallet back into his pocket. He tells me that the parking meter's sorted for a few hours. Enough time to watch whatever is on. Every month, we make a pilgrimage into the city centre to see a movie together. Our only time out of the house just the two of us. I used to think of these ventures as loathsome, dragging my feet, shoes not quite put on the back of my heels. Tonight, I've come straight from the coffee shop up the road, where I'd holed up with a Scandi crime book. It was a ritual of mine to head into No Alibis bookshop without anything particular in mind. The bookseller drew me further into the sanctuary amongst the stacks, guiding me to exactly what I needed. After, with a paper parcel tucked under my arm, I walked down Botanic Avenue, as I had done so many times before, to the coffee shop with the biggest armchairs. It had been daylight when I arrived, but now as I dander down the street, the streetlamps are glowing.

Stood together, Da and I look at the tattered posters. He has his hands on his hips, assessing what's changed since our last trip. It's usually all much the same. He always tells me a rough biography of every actor he recognises, which to be fair, isn't many these days. His favourite stories begin when he recognises an old Hollywood classic. One look at a poster for *Casablanca* or *It Happened One Night* and it all comes back to him. In these moments, it's like he leaves his body, returning to a time before me, before ma. He tells me of the dates he came on with a girl who emigrated to Australia. Her bag filled with confectionary to be snuck in. The excitement of it all. Purging himself of the memory, his head shakes into a frown.

He ushers me inside, holding the door open to let me walk in first. Years of people have streamed in through these doors. The entryway holds infinite imaginations within itself, projected onto the minds of those who enter. Fantasies of groups fill my mind, as if even this was a movie. They'd be coming in arms linked, laughing surreptitiously. But in reality, everybody scuttles in hunched over, holding the rain up and away from themselves. Inside the entrance, they shake like dogs. The carpet, like every other visit, is sticky with trodden popcorn, gripping our trainers as we make our way to the ticket desk. We're here for *Psycho*. A surly teenager's hand cradles the paper slips as they fall from the machine.

Inside the theatre, it's always the usual suspects who haunt the Classic Movie Nights. There's the old bloke in the back, dressed to the nines in tweeds and slacks. Shined shoes. Tucked in the front corner, a couple, no older than my da's age, beginning to divvy out a bag full of store-bought snacks. Briny olives in a plastic container are passed back and forth. The smell floats through the whole cinema, giving everything that salt-watery scent. I feel I know these people like the back of my hand, having sat in dark rooms with them for hours and hours of my life. Our own little commune. The lights begin to dim. Confectionary packets crinkle. There's no shushing here though.

Rain streams down onto the city, with a motorway underpass now becoming a bowl to catch the flood. News reports flash up warnings of dangerous driving conditions and the millions of pounds in wasted public spending in construction costs. My ma is furious when she spots Andy pull up outside. She jumps out of her armchair to twitch the net curtains back, to get a good gawp at the red clapped out car, vibrating with music in the street.

—And you're going to battle the elements in that? Oh, Fiadh, you'd be better in a boat in this weather.

I'm shrugging to free my hair caught between my coat and shoulders. A quick tap of my pockets releases a jingle that lets me know I've my keys on me; I'm free to go.

—Awk Mummy, it'll be alright. Sure, it can't be wet everywhere, can it?

—You better take a jumper too love. You don't want to be catching your death!

—I'll be back soon, don't worry!

Before I can reach the front door, Ma steps out and pulls her cardigan tighter around her. Like night and day, her face morphs into a beaming smile. One arm raised, she leans out the door frame, —Awk, how are you Andrew, love? And your mother?

Our families have been intertwined since primary school, when both me and Ma saw Andy being scolded by his ma for taking too long to get off the school-trip bus. He was scooped, his tie ragged to the side like a cartoon businessman caught in a blizzard.

—Look at the state of ya, son! Come on, get yourself in the car now so we can get you home and sorted! His ma shouted across towards him, standing just beyond the bus steps. —I'll be seeing you, Marie, she said as she moved away from my ma and the other mothers waiting for their kids to appear.

Andy and I had met earlier that day on a cross-community field trip, paired together for our shared interest in animals, which at that age only extended to our own pets. We sat next to each other on the bus, hoping for the world to swallow us up and spit us back in our own homes.

Then in the leisure centre, the floor squeaked underfoot as the two school groups moved across the sports hall, creating a sound like a flock of birds. On a padded gym mat, we sat side by side, heads turned to the walls, trying to catch the eye of any of our respective pals.

—Chris! Here, Chris! What flavour of crisps do you have? Swap?

My supplied lunch was arranged around me: sweaty cellophaned cheese sandwiches, a Fruit Shoot, and a packet of Golden Wonder. I opened the green packet and potent onion floated out of the bag.

Andy turned around, —Did you get the cheese and onion ones?
—Yeah.

A silence slipped between us. The crisp packet crinkled in my fist.

—Want one?
—Mine are prawn cocktail. Rotten, he said as he put his hand out for one, a smile communicating the thanks he could not yet say.

Now, he drives us towards Jordanstown, to see the sea we know is nearby. On the stereo, he's playing Bloc Party's *A Weekend in the City*. A sharp turn of the wheel pulls us into the car park which faces out towards the water, to the other side of the lough. We both get out of the car, pushing the doors against the sea breeze, arms bent like bows to protect against the bounce back. Anaconda-like, my scarf is hooped around my throat, tucked into the front of a khaki green parka. There's one of those coffee stands fashioned out of an old horse trailer. Andy gets us two teas, watery despite the teabag still swimming in the cup. Further along Loughshore, we walk past a monument to joy, twisted and tied, like a bungee-rope replica of the pyramids of Giza. Children climb and cascade from the top, trusting that no hurt will come from their descent. For a moment, Andy and I stop, watching the fun that the weeuns are having.

Like a confession, a long sigh is released from my body as I hug the takeaway cup to my chest. The liquid tastes more like the insides of a kettle than anything resembling tea. Still I drink on for the sheer pleasure of heat. The path ahead stretches as far as our gaze can go, back towards the cranes of the docks towering in the skyline. The dishwater sea thrashes against the shore, sandwiching us between it and the motorway traffic. Only a chain-link fence holds us secure between the two dangers.

I turn to face Andy, with the wind lapping hair around my face, one side flipping to the other like a Kate Bush tribute act. An oversized black patent bag hooks over my arm, an anchor for fidgeting hands, which repeatedly pass the cup from one to the other to avoid a scalding.

After a few minutes of staring towards the city, he says —Are you going out to Sketchy then?

—Ah, I might. Who all's going?

—Does that mean you aren't happy enough to go with just me?

—Sure, it'd be like this, but I wouldn't be able to hear you. If that's what you're after, let's just go back to the car and blast the radio.

He doesn't laugh. Instead he takes a sip out of a bottle of Sukie, before stretching out his arm. His head twitches, then a flicker of the eyebrow. All of this in lieu of words. We have this language between us which does not require words, a shorthand of gestures, an electric current flowing directly from one to the other. We are two parts of the same entity, predicting the other's thoughts in symbiosis. People in school joked that we are like twins separated at birth, a mirror of the other. I shake my head. Further up the path, he breaks the silence —Have you spoken to any of the others from school?

—Nah, not today, I say before putting a chewing gum in my mouth.

—Yeah, well I was going to say Aisling and Danielle fancy tonight. You could come to mine for pre-drinks?

—Aye, maybe. I'll see what's on the telly sure first and let you know.

He pushes my shoulder —Mon, we get you back to the *Radio Times*.

We both retrace our steps back towards the play area, the coffee cart and finally the little car which carried us here. Slamming the door closed, he starts the engine, turns up the volume on his radio, and lets out a howl as he revs the engine with the brake still on.

The queue for the club snakes from the entrance, along the park towards the UGC Cinema. In twos and threes, groups of people huddle together against the biting wind. The rain drizzles down, sticking to the recently sun-shimmered legs of the girls in the queue, each bouncing from one platform heel to the other to maintain body heat. I cup my hand into a fist, hugging it with the other, blowing air into the entanglement of frozen fingers. Danielle and I line up against the brick wall, both dreaming that we are home in our pyjamas instead of standing in the cold in minidresses. A flurry of stamps of Danielle's heels on the ground chorus a sharp exhale of breath, as she says —Isn't it meant to be summer?!

I fumble around in my clutch for my ID, shaking it like a snow globe to move my lip gloss and a tester bottle of DKNY perfume. As we approach the entrance, we recognise the bouncer as a man who lives in the same apartment block as Aisling. There he is. Big Dave. He dips his head at us in recognition. On Saturdays gone by, the lot of us shared a cigarette with him at Aisling's gaff. Her ma saying —Sure, isn't it better to know what they're up to? Better them doing it here than out there on street corners and park benches!

The off-duty bouncer always nodded sagely in agreement, as Aisling's ma gripped his leg.

Now, we pay a fiver into the club night, Sketchy. Strobe lights disorientate us as we walk across the dance floor. We try our best to give off an air of irresistible collectedness. As is ritual on our Saturday nights out, Danielle suddenly stops in front of me, leans into my ear and shouts — SAMBUCA!? The wide look in her eyes shows it is more of a call to arms than a question. Powerless to say no to that sort of persuasion, I follow her as she pushes her way through the throngs of people at the bar.

The barman slops two gloopy sambucas into neon thimbles on the counter. Clinked glasses, heads back, we neck the shots, feeling it slide down our throats. I order a blue alcopop, requesting a straw from behind the bar. I fancy myself the vision of a seductress, sucking on my straw while surveying the dance floor.

Assessing each boy who locks eyes with me, I do an internal evaluation of the likelihood of locking lips with a ride. There's the boy in a white diamanté slogan top; the one with 'surfer' hair, achieved through hours of having his ma do his frosted tips; the man who is far too old to be in this club, adorned with a tie and suit jacket; and of course, the group of lads from school, none of which I have ever spoken to for more than five minutes, except for Andy.

The intensity of the strobe light delivers me back into the room. Casting her gaze across the crowd, Danielle says —Slim pickings thenight isn't it?

She turns to the bar and asks for two double vodka Red Bulls. If nothing else, we'd make a quare go at the dance floor by ourselves. Daft Punk's 'One More Time' stutters through the speakers. We both down our WKDs, grab our freshly poured vodkas and head into the sea of people. As fast as we can walk without running, the two of us tear off towards the dance floor, spilling drinks as we go. In the middle of the crowd, we jump on the spot, bouncing off the people behind us. An arm is thrown around Danielle's shoulders, her pocket-sized height makes her the prime target for grab-and-dance moves. Through flickered lights, Andy comes into focus. He blankets himself around Danielle, and beams a smile towards me.

Outside, the smoking area heat lamp drapes us in sepia. When I close my eyes, the drink would have me believe I was anywhere else, a Spanish beach or a recently retubed sunbed. I approach anyone and everyone outside to ask for a lighter.

—I'm a social smoker, I joke. —So I don't carry one.

A woman in a leather jacket pulls one from her pocket and hands it over.

—I want that back, love, she spits out, without raising her eyes.

One long draw on the feg gets it going enough to sustain it for the whole smoke, and probably a headlight for another too. Andy stumbles over, grabs the cigarette from my mouth, inhaling deeply.

—Oi! Leave us some! Don't be a selfish wee prick!

He crosses his eyes while taking another draw, blowing the smoke onto my face. —Sure, I'm always thinking of you, Fiadh, he says while placing the cigarette between my lips.

—No, love, I say as I take the cigarette out of my mouth and crush it under my heel. —I'm alright, thanks.

# 3

The whole week was a complete wash-out, culminating in a weekend of rain pelting down sideways. It is one of those horribly wet Saturday nights. The type of evening where everybody says they want to be heading out, but you know deep down when you actually get all done up to go, there will be nobody out except the diehards. It's the kind of night where you have to turn your phone on silent so you don't feel like you are missing out, even though nothing is going on. This city has a knack of being able to do that, or maybe it's just that I'm single and newly eighteen. Ma always says, sure, what's for you won't pass you by. I'm taking that approach to nights out, though only when the weather is this fucking grim. The thought turns me that I'd spend ages tanning my legs just for it to drip off in the rain before I even leave the club queue. Instead, I'm curled up on the sofa in an oversized grey hoodie and tracksuit bottoms, the ones that are extra padded for hiking, but have the zips on the sides when you can't be holed changing into shorts. It has to be said: I'm living the life.

There's nothing on the telly though. I bounce through the channels, hoping that by the time I come full circle the programming will have had a word with itself. My ritual is disturbed by the doorbell ringing: once, twice, then held down to screech through the house. I've a fistful of the door handle and ready to rage, when I see it's just Andy being a wee dickhead. He's holding a big bag of cheese puffs and Rola Cola. Although he wasn't invited round, I can't be too annoyed as he must have gone to the big shop on the way to get the goods.

—Thought you would like some company if you are sitting in tonight. Can't have you being a loner, can I?

—How good of you, I say, standing to the side to let him in.

When he comes into the living room, he says —BBC News? Times are hard.

—I'll get a DVD, something more to your taste. *Mean Girls*? Seems very you.

My ma comes in just as we're settling in to pick the movie.

—Awk, what about ya Andrew love? How's your ma?

She's never done asking about his ma, as if they don't bump into each other down the shops every week. She knows more about what's going on with Andy's lot than he does, no doubt.

—Ah, you know, Marie. Same old.

Ma hovers in the doorway, watching the TV. She asks what we're for that night, and whether we'll be watching a movie. I tell her yes, but offer no more information. Internally I'm begging Andy not to take the bait. She'll be with us all night if he does. I can't have two gatecrashers in one night. I'll go spare.

She mumbles —Awk, sure, lookit, you two have fun. I'll leave you to it.

Once she's gone and there's no fear of her asking to watch yet another Marlon Brando film, I offer him the ceremonial honour of choosing the DVD for the night. He chooses something Da's had in the back of the cabinet for donkey's years. I'd be surprised if it actually works. Like a cupped hand accepting an offering, the DVD player retracts into itself, and begins to clunk into action. We settle back into the sofa, not saying much as we pretend to watch the film. The main actor is a ride, so there is that to keep me occupied. But the plot is lacking. Maybe the whole point is just that he's more than a pretty face, he's off out picking up his coffee, doing his errands, wearing a cosy jumper that his granny knitted him. All before he goes and batters some fellas. The man has range, it has to be said. Except I don't say it out loud. I couldn't, not to him. He goes all funny when I talk about lads I fancy. Instead, I pick up my phone and text Danielle. She'll not want to miss out on this vital information.

As soon as the phone is in my hand, he asks who I'm on the blower to. I tell him it's top secret and not to worry his head about it. He lunges over at me to grab my phone out of my hand. Reflexively, I stand up and hold the phone above me but he immediately tickles my armpit. This calls for the big guns, I jab two fingers into his ribs. That does the trick, and my phone drops to the floor. *Crack.* The screen shatters, leaving the outline of a snowflake across the glass.

—Ah, for fuck's sake, mate.

He stutters that he's sorry.

—You will be! Wait until Ma finds out it's broke. There'll be murder.

The laugh escapes me before I have a titter of wit to stop it. We're both in stitches. He says I can always just pick up pen and paper and write. Or carrier pigeons! Smoke signals! I have to sit down on the sofa to steady myself as the tears begin to stream.

—Nah, it's grand. Don't worry. Sure, I wanted a clear out of friends anyway. New number, who dis? You know.

He looks somehow offended.

—Obviously, I'm joking. Don't be a tit.

He is being a tit though. This I know. He's forever doing this. It puts me in mind of when we were knocking about the Abbey Centre years ago. We'd dander around the shops browsing in each of them, trying on clothes we couldn't afford. It was all a pantomime, really. His ma came bounding out of the BHS. Before she was even over at us, her arms were buried to the elbow in the big plastic bag. Out flapped pyjamas and cosy socks. She was over the moon by them. Holding them up to Andy's shoulder for sizing. He didn't hang around for the full fitting. For weeks after this, he ignored my calls to his door, as if I was somehow to blame for witnessing his own ma mothering him.

—Mate, I can't be dealing with this carry-on tonight. If I wanted to lose your number – or anybody's – I would have just done it. Trust me.

He is not soothed by this line of reasoning. We sit in silence. It's my house, so I'm used to the quiet, but I can see on Andy's face that he's gearing up to speak.

—What's the score then with September?

—Aye, think the girls are gonna try and find a flat somewhere around the university. Somewhere with a balcony and a bath, that's all we are after.

—A butler too while you're at it.

—We're not asking for much!

—You'll be hard pressed to find somewhere free from mould, never mind a balcony.

—Catch yourself on.

—Have you ever even been over to the Holylands, Fee? You're in for a shock.

—I've seen the brochure.

—Brochure?! Oh fuck. Here we go. It's only across the fucking city. Mon, I'll take ye. We can hunt out somewhere for a pint.

—I've been to Lavery's though!

—The great Belfast boundary: Lavery's back bar. As he says this, he sweeps his arm over the living room, scanning the great expanse. —There's more to it than that one bar.

—Way and shite. What're your plans for moving out? You gonna see what David's at?

He laughs into himself. He'd rather not be doing whatever his brother's at.

There's a buzz in the room, as we lean closer together, unfurling the future in our plans. Andy's hoping to live with some boys in our year, the ones he knows from his politics class. They are all dry shites, so I don't really know them. I'm sure I'm not missing out on too much though. Any time they've been out with us they end up in an argument about some long-dead bloke's voting records, or worse, the back catalogue of some obscure film director. More craic at a wake.

# 4

The roads spread long and wide before us. We have spent years dandering around them, trying to avoid a scrap, though that can't be said for Danielle. The streets are grey, reminiscent of sludge pulled from the drain or skies before a downpour. Walking up towards the shop feels like climbing Everest, the hills steep and burning on our calves. Danielle is wearing a thick loop of dusty pink lipstick, pilfered from her sister's make-up bag. Her hair is backcombed and held up in a bun. As we near our target, the Big Spar, Danielle tells us to fuck away off, we're cramping her style, as she heads in to flirt with the fella behind the counter. She tells us he looks like her first husband, then she swans away.

Aisling and I head down an entry between the pharmacy and somebody's gaff. We're doing anything to stave off the pre-carry-out jitters. The tingles are butterflying up my arms and legs. I'm bouncing from foot to foot like a wrestler waiting to be tapped into the ring.

—You need a shite or what? Stop it for fuck's sake.

Aisling gestures to my moving feet. I do a little tap jig with my feet, pumping my arms out. She's up off the wall and thumps my arm.

—You're a complete melter, wee girl.

I rub the sting from my arm.

—She's taking her time. She'll be in nattering the ear off that wee lad.

He could be anything from five years to two decades older than us, and the mystery has proven electrifying. The man has become a myth for us. We've spent hours scouring Facebook for any photos tagged at the Big Spar, trying to work out who he is, and who he was most likely to finger. His way of going gave off an air of classiness, so maybe he didn't even have Facebook. His polo shirts were blindingly white, ironed, fresh. We'd never see the likes of it.

—Aye, she'll be gabbing about *ski holidays, pensions,* and *the price of the school uniforms this year.*

Each word said as if passing directly out her nose, mocking those afeared of inhaling unrefined air. We both say 'terrible' at the same time, sucking in the words in one sharp inhalation.

A car horn screams us into silence. Danielle is running across the road, the olive-coloured bottle held to her chest. A banshee wail lets us know she's back with the goods.

Sat on the ground, we pass the cider between us. The first round of sips always tastes the worst. It's heavy with fizz as I swallow mostly foam. It's only five minutes before Aisling takes herself off for a piss down the alley. There's a low hiss of liquid meeting concrete, before she screams from down the entry—IS ANYBODY THERE?

She shakes off and runs back to us, arm outstretched for another swig.

—Should we head up the park? Bit of a nicer view than Mrs Pisses, Danielle says.

—Would you ever fuck up?

We're coming out of the entry when David saunters past. It's a strange one: David is the most ordinary looking guy round our parts, sort of somewhere between well-groomed and a chewed up pasty bap. His hair is always immaculate, each strand gelled into place on his forehead. You'd smell him a mile off too, in the best possible way, cologne wafting on the breeze announcing his presence before he arrives. But he's not a Calvin Klein model by any means, his skin is freckled, his body soft, but the way he carries himself ensures he gets a healthy dose of the girls round our way. He's got the attitude of somebody who knows all the world's secrets, an ability to crawl inside your head and peer out through your eyes back at himself. He knows what girls want to hear, always there with the right words.

—What's the craic girls? Where are we for then?

He stares right past Aisling and I straight to Danielle. His pink tongue wets his lips. Instead of saying a word, she pushes past and walks fast towards the park. We both follow her, breaking out into a run to keep up with her.

—Everything alright? Hold on, love.

My ballet flats are slapping from the sole of my foot to the ground. Water splashes onto my bare foot. Socks were a no-go zone. I wouldn't have been caught dead in a pair of socks. Ever since Danielle's big sister ripped her for having sock imprints on her ankles while she changed for swimming down the Valley Leisure Centre. The look on her face is burned into my mind. The realisation that the towel she had wouldn't cover both her tits and the ghost socks. It wasn't worth the risk. We were scundered for Danielle.

The three of us head up towards the park. We're all walking in silence as Danielle has a face on her like a slapped arse. Typical. She refuses to talk about it though, says Dee's a creep, and that's all there is to it. Aisling and I make eye contact behind her back. Since the three of us were wee, Danielle was always the most likely to go off the handle. As kids, Aisling took the longest learning to read the warning signs – the stomped feet, eyes rolled, the snaps – but now it came to her like an apparition, once seen it was impossible to ignore. Aisling had perfected the art of diffusing the situation with the care of a bomb disposal expert. Her arsenal: light humour and agreement. A slight nudge to the waist. Kindness and touch pulls Danielle back from the edge, from losing the run of herself.

The wind laps on the soaked cuffs of our jeans. Ragged threads are trailing behind us in the puddles. It's not even raining, but that's the way with Belfast. The ground is sodden even when the sun is shining.

Seen from the top, the hill is more of a huge artificial mound than anything else. There are two benches, sat back-to-back so you can get the perfect view over the terraced houses. To my eye, the grey tile streaking through the slate grey roads. We sit there passing the bottle between us as the city's lights twinkle on one after the other. Thick with drink, I try to express to the girls how much these streets mean to me, each one sprawling towards the centre, tangling together to create a knot in the middle. The greatest city I know. My brain and my lips are working different shifts, so I mumble out the words, —she's a grand wee place to be from, isn't she?

The girls break out into hysterics.

—She's the capital of fingering.

—More shades of shite than any other place in the world.

—Wonderful hospitality, Aisling says, pointing to the graffitied 'All Touts are Targets' on the side of the gable wall below.

Danielle holds the embers to the sky, puffs her back out, and exhales long plumes of smoke. We punctuate our glugs of cider with newly lit fegs, passed between us like a relay. Time trickles on as our words melt over us. The three of us are huddled together on a park bench. Aisling is sat on the back, and us at her feet on the seat.

Above us, Aisling breaks into song, which could have been anything from Billy Ray Cyrus to the Beatles; no discernible words are able to bubble through her liquor slicked voice. Just as quick as it begins, she's up on her feet and heading towards the bush.

—Nature calls. Broke my seal.

Danielle and I smoke on in silence. Our heads are lopped over the back of the bench at this stage, slugglish with the cider.

—What do you think of him? she says into the night.

—Wa?

—Of David.

—David? Andy's David?

—Yes, what other fucking David do you know, love?

—Beckham, for a start.

—A start? What others you got in your phonebook? Bowie? Schwimmer? Of course, Andy's David!

With eyes closed, I smile to myself. Happy at getting a rise out of her. It's easy when the drink's in.

—Well?

—Aye, he's David alright. He's OK enough, but I don't get it. The ones from round their way are mad for him. He's forever got a love bite. Says it's from a new one every time I'm round at theirs. Pure dirt. Has his ma's head away, I'm sure. Andy's always covering for him.

By the time I stop talking, I realise that Danielle hasn't made a sound throughout. I open my eyes, right my head and look at her. She's wiping her face, back turned towards me.

—Oh, love, what's up?

I'm reaching over to touch her back, but she's stood up and walked away. Aisling emerges from the bush with a bottle of vodka, covered in mud and leaves. She screeches as it waves over her head.

—Aw, what the fuck? What's happened? I found a ten glass! And yousins are off? Nah, you two are fucking frigids.

Aisling stamps her feet, giving a performance of huffing. We both follow Danielle down the hill, keeping a safe distance, but close enough to keep an eye on her. We stand sentry as she stumbles into an entry for a piss. She always had a thimble for a bladder. When she returns, the craic is zapped from her. Aisling and I give each other the nod: night's over, back to her gaff.

After drying off and putting on a selection of Aisling's T-shirts that she doesn't care for (she would never trust us with her good clothes, not in this state) we're settling into the front room, getting ourselves ready for a sleepover. We know that we have to look the part for fear her ma will pop her head in to check how we're all getting on. I'm at that stage of being blocked where looking around the room is a struggle, like staring through one of those wiggly window panes that every granny has in her house. My jeans are soaked to my thighs. It makes my teeth itch having them on for a second longer than needs be. Maybe it's the cider, or a test of our years of friendship, but I'm peeling off my clothes down to my kecks. The denim has left a faint blue stain on my legs. Or it could be the cold. It's often hard to tell.

# 5

Marching season comes around quicker every year. The July air is dense with the smell of burning tyres wafting through the house. Even with the windows closed it seems to seep in and stick to every surface. Ma is forever walking around with a bottle of spray, cleaning everything. I'm not sure if it's the nerves or the boredom that keeps her at it all day.

Our house is on the top of a hill, which looks down onto the loyalist estate below. We can see great big towers of pallets, tyres and effigies piling up for weeks before the event. During those two weeks when everything comes to a head, Aisling and I know not to expect too much from Danielle and Andy. They always head out to the parades and the bonfires, and conveniently know not to ask us what our plans are. It's easier this way. It works for us all to know that we can resume where we left off in a week or so, when the dust has settled.

Making our own traditions, Aisling and I hang out round at my house every year. Just trying our best to ignore what's going on down the hill. We make cocktails in all shades of green and gold: crème de menthe; rum; whiskey; an odd melon flavoured liqueur pilfered from Aisling's ma's cupboard. All in all, each ingredient is stinking, but together it's a crime against the taste buds. Still, we can't be seen to be Debbie Downers, so we grimace and sip away. Short sharp bursts to get through it all. I bet that the ones down the hill are having the best time. I purposely avoid Facebook for fear of seeing what I'm missing out on: craic by the fire, like in one of those American movies, except without the acoustic guitar sing-songs and with added undertones of sectarianism. It's a strange time.

I can't imagine Danielle running about banging her drum,

twirling a wee stick. The white hat and gloves. She'd nearly died off the time I suggested us wearing stone-washed denim out out. On any regular day she'd be scundered in that get-up. But this week she gives herself a pass: in her eyes there's not a single item of her usual wardrobe that can't be improved by the Union Jack. I don't have the heart to rip her for this next week.

Aisling sighs —Reckon they think of us at all?
—What, love? I say, without taking my eyes off the TV.
—Reckon Danielle wishes we were there?
—I'm sure she's gutted we're missing out on Costa del Loyalism.
—You know what I mean.

I do, to be fair, but I'm not ready to let Aisling know that.
—I don't actually.

We both say nothing as we watch the TV. An Olympic level of concentration goes into both of us pretending the silence is casual, normal.

—You need to take your face for a shite.
—Excuse me?
—You've a face like thunder, love. You're fumin'.

I'm not, but her saying it makes me raging. She's a nightmare sometimes, and I tell her so.

In other corners of the house, Ma and Da are both busying themselves around the gaff, doing all the odd jobs saved for forced indoor isolation: unpacking spices from the kitchen cupboards before lining them up again neatly; airing out and refolding the winter duvets; alphabetising the DVDs. The sounds of their movements are a comfort against the steady drumbeat blowing in from outside.

Lying there on the sofa, I think of when our friendships were fresh. In late winter 2002, the girls and I were laying around like Grecian goddesses, sprawled around in the living room, robed in layers of white quilting: nighties, hand towels holding our hair from our faces, and dressing gowns. Each item was gleaned from a reconnaissance trip into Belfast city centre to the big Primark. Town held a certain glamour to us then. Usually, we had to buy our clothes with our mas, though none of us would let on without a fight. We'd be trailed down to the shopping centre near our houses. It's as if when you become a ma you instantly become interested only in the places with 'good parking outside'. Inside those shops, Ma would pull me between the rails, hold a top to my chest, and tell me to 'try that'. Pulling my top over my head, I'd pray for the ground to swallow me up. But on our own downtown, we could believe our own fantasies. We were there *after work*; meeting *the girls*; or shopping for a *big night out*. We all bought into a kind of shared imagination.

There in front of us Primark loomed large, colonnades holding up the sign above the doors. We peeled off our sunglasses as we went in, though lord knows that we could have done with them on in the floodlights inside. Clothes lay everywhere, thrown about like a bombsite. We rolled up our sleeves, hunting the perfect *girls night* pyjama sets. Each matching set held close to our chests to hide our sizing from the others: there were some things you could write to a news editor in London about in the Agony Aunt section but *never* was it appropriate to ask your friends if they too had aching tits exploding from their skin.

Later that night, I wrapped the towelling gown tighter over myself. The material scratched my nipples raw. I swallowed back the need to itch them. Christ, I'd never hear the end of it. *Ould Fiadh itchy nips,* they'd never stop.

*Pop Idol* was on the television. Danielle's hand throttled the cordless phone. She was repeatedly dialling the number to vote for Will. I was more of a fan of Gareth, though I didn't want to divide the room. Like a motor failing to start, the lid screeched under Aisling's grip as she tried to crack open a Body Shop face mask. The edges of the pot were crusted shut. Once open the green gloop shone with the promise of clear skin. Of romances with boys with glossy spiked hair; their voices would be silky, and undoubtedly with an American accent. It smelled eye-wateringly minty. We slathered the masks on to our faces. Neon green flaked from the edges. Nobody was willing to admit regretting how close we'd applied it to our eyes. I didn't want to be the first to remove it, subtly wiping away the tears that streamed from my eyes.

—Here, hold that one second, Danielle said as she thrust the phone into Aisling's hand. —Keep dialling!

Digging around in her bag, she lifted out a bottle, bright orange, nearly neon. She held it up like the priest does with the body of Christ.

—Here we go, girls!

Aisling and I jumped up off the sofa, grasping at the bottle.

—Giz a look!

The lid opened with a hiss. We inhaled deeply. We were a coven, gathering around the bottle, the orange liquid reflecting off our shiny green faces. I was willing either of them to be the first to take a sip. What if it was fucking rotten? I had to steel myself to hide any possible need to spew it. I'd had a sip of beer at the caravan park a couple of years before, and it tasted both acidic and too bubbly. A strange sensation. Danielle was the first to go in.

—Fucking bores, she said under her breath.

Her eyes stared off into the distance like a veteran. She'd never mentioned drinking before, but I always felt that she kept some parts of herself hidden. There was constantly an air of mystery. I watched as the television studio lights reflected in her eyes.

—Go on then, she said without moving her eyes, passing the glass bottle to her left.

It wasn't clear who she was asking to go next, but I assumed me. It being my house and all, it only seemed fair.

Right enough, it was fuckin' stinking. I couldn't for the life of me let the girls know. Even at that stage, they thought I was a bit of a frigid for having Andy as a pal without so much as a kiss. Danielle said she was fingered in the Abbey Centre toilets a few months before then, but I don't believe her. The fella was a friend of a friend's brother. She's such a spoofer.

We passed the bottle, bouncing it between us until there is only dregs left swirling around the glass. Not long after: the spins arrived. My head felt like the inside of a salad strainer, wet almost.

I couldn't quite explain it to the girls. They were both sat there so normal. Like it was all not a bother to them, sure they were still watching the TV. Every time I tried to focus on Gareth's face on the screen, he smeared off to the side, then back around into my vision. The music was turned down as the tension mounted. Why was there so much scaffolding on the stage? It was like the builders were in already, preparing to take it all down piece by piece. Gareth was bouncing on to the stage, down the metal stairs. He was in his white suit; Christ, he was such an angel. I tried to tell the girls this, though they don't react at all. I'm not even sure whether I made a noise. My eyebrows itched my face as I thought about the final. Those spikes, too. Shouldn't be legal. It was all too much for me to bear in this moment. He kept singing 'Unchained Melody'. The other two looked bored to tears, being Will girls and all. Danielle still had the cordless phone in her fist ready to redial. Just say the word, Ant and Dec, and she'll do it. My ma's phone bill be damned when there's bigger issues at stake right now. This wasn't some joke.

Either Ant or Dec said down the camera lens and straight into my soul: *This competition is on a knife-edge.* That was my cue. *Every single vote is important.* I couldn't stand idly by while my ma unknowingly paid for votes for the wrong winner.

—Phone, I slurred.

—I'm already on it, Aisling responded, already hitting the redial button on the phone.

—Give me it.

My hand was outstretched, a slight jerk of it signals for her to put it in my palm. Fuck, I had turned into my ma.

Ant or Dec had just said the results would be at five past ten. Two more hours. I couldn't take it. I didn't even know if I'd be awake for the results.

—You. Swear to God, I said at Danielle.

—Who put a penny in her?

Danielle's back was to me, but she told me to take myself off to the toilet. As it happens, I didn't, when I really should have. Less than half an hour later, I was curled around the big baking bowl, snow drifts of tea tree and mint face mask floating into an orangey bile soup.

The town is always closed for what feels like a lifetime during the fortnight around the Twelfth. So, when the shops and bars begin to come out of hibernation, we jump at the chance to socialise again. Danielle is the first to suggest going into the city centre for a dander around the shops.

I'm fucking skint, so I'm there for moral support only. Danielle and Aisling have been topping their balance up with temp work: getting people to go to whichever nightclub is the deadest that night, sneaking into the halls to leave flyers on literally every flat surface. Aisling scoops out a fiver from her purse and offers to split a pot of tea with me. She's a good egg. She walks like Bambi on ice as she brings the tray down to our table by the window. We watch the people emerging from their forced isolation, like newborn chicks venturing out of the nest, unsure of what the world holds, what will be melted and burnt. The roads are gummy from the bonfires. Fallen election posters lie around the streets, a glimpse of half-charred static smiles peering out from where the flames didn't reach.

When Danielle asked what me and Aisling did the week before, during the Twelfth, I give her a quick rundown of the absolute inertia of the last fortnight. I return the question to her.

—Ah, you know, this and that.

—Same, babe, same.

We both laugh it off, as if for an audience. Aisling pours the tea, stoney-baked. She would prefer it to be the elephant in the room. The great unacknowledged.

# 6

The Garritys' gaff is swish, not like any of the rest of our places. The kitchen is permanently being redone, the worktops marbled, the curtains hung in perfect folds. We're sat around the large oak table, quiet while we wait for his parents to vacate the premises. They are off out for the night into the town, to see one of those touring London West End shows. We've been tasked with looking after some cousin or other. The only instruction is to ensure he's 'good'. I'm not sure that Andy and I are the right pair to be guiding the Good Ship; we're not exactly a shining example for the wee one. Andy's da is taking a pan of Ovaltine off the hob. Carefully decanting the paler-than-expected liquid into three mugs.

—That should do yous, he says.

Andy and I make eye contact for a second, then there's a mutual understanding that for the sake of our evening we should avoid doing that again until the place is ours. His ma Deirdre appears at the bottom of the stairs. Pressing up close to the hall mirror, her nose almost touches the glass as she pops her earrings in. Every sequin on her dress beams as if making a case for being pulled out of the back of the wardrobe more often. Andy hurries the pair of them out to the beeping taxi waiting outside. Soon as the door clicks shut, he is herding his cousin Ryan up the stairs. His hands splayed out on Ryan's back, readying himself in case he changes his mind and takes a tear back downstairs to freedom. I'm following behind, mugs in hand.

Walking into Andy's room is like stepping onto another planet: the smell is thick with Lynx Africa and sweaty socks. His ma's careful curation of the rest of the house has no mandate here. A blow-up mattress is on the floor: a thin duvet is peeled back;

flattened pillows lay on top. Ryan's thrown himself onto Andy's bed, telling him he's not sleeping on the floor. I stand off to the side of the room, while the pair of them wrestle. Boxes of dusty toys are stuffed up on top of the wardrobe, an Action Man's arm stretches out towards the bare bulb on the ceiling. Posters are plastered across the walls, hiding most of the Mickey Mouse wallpaper underneath. In the inches between the World Cup 2006 and Playboy posters, Mickey's swollen gloved hand waves. On the desk, piles of plates and revision cards; both look ancient. Andy lifts him down onto the floor.

—Where's your night light?

Ryan's wee face has broken into a smile. He's all hyped up on pre-bedtime adrenaline, squeals that he's scundered for Andy being afraid of the dark. Me being there spurs him on. His eyes darting across between Andy and I, seeing how far he can push it before he gets a hiding.

—My ma says—

He doesn't get to finish his sentence before Andy knocks him onto the mattress. A chokehold subdues him. I take myself back to the kitchen.

Once the kid's tucked up in bed with his Ovaltine, we head out into the back garden. The ground has that type of cold that soaks up your trousers and into your bones. But we pay it no mind, instead lighting up the joint which appears like treasure from inside Andy's jacket. The world appears anew as we pass it between us. The stars shine a little brighter and a comforting fog descends on me. I'm feeling cosy on the concrete ground, settling my back into the pebble dash wall.

We talk shite, about this and that. Mostly we debate whether *Mean Girls* is a classic twenty-first century film. Up there with *Donnie Darko* and *Spirited Away*, I argue while flailing my arms out. Andy is enacting a theatrical yawn, when Dee shows up, bursting in the door with a slam.

—You been through my things, son?

Andy giggles. It's infectious. I try to stem it, but it erupts. David's fucking fuming at us. Splotches of rage speckle across his cheeks. He's right into Andy's face. They are so close that their shoulders touch. In slow-motion Andy's laughter ripples, pulling his face into a smile. His eyes creased. The crack arrives before I know what's happening. Dee's hit him.

—You'll be paying for that.

I can't stop laughing. It's just flowing out of me. The whole time I'm staring at the leaves moving on the hedgerow, waving to me.

—Oi. What are you playin' at? You think something's hilarious?

At first, I'm not even aware it's me he's talking to. He appears directly between me and the hedge.

—You know what's funny? Your wee mate. The fucking slag. Sucks off anybody for a bottle. She's a joke. Laugh at that.

I hear him, but it doesn't fully settle. He goes again.

—Suck-n-Fuck Danielle. Sure, half the estate's got videos of her.

He's reaching into his pocket. Pulling out his phone.

—My directorial and leading man debut, he says, smirking to Andy.

He turns the screen to Andy first. I can hear the squeals. Then it's in front of me. I see her. The lighting is golden, and her skin appears endless. She's outdoors, but her top has been pulled around her waist. Her bra straps are moved from her shoulders and pulled down, the back-clasp still attached.

—Fuck. Stop. Give me that, she says, stretching her hand out to the camera, out towards me.

—Delete it.

Time stretches. I grab at the phone but he snatches it back. He's laughing now, leaning into Andy. I hear the audio start again from the beginning.

—Fuck's sake, Dee. Delete that.

—Love, a picture says a thousand words. How many for a video?

Andy has a fit of giggles at this.

—Andy, come on. You serious?

The laughter shakes his whole body. He can't stop. Dee begins mimicking her squeals, then in a high-pitched voice he says, —Stop. Give me that. Cupping his hands on his chest, pretending to lick imaginary tits. Quick as it started, his mouth turns, showing his bottom teeth. His nose scrunched as if sniffing shit. —Fucking slag still texts me.

My legs feel like jelly beneath me as I make my way through their house. I grab my bag from the counter. Their house appears as if drawn from memory: the fundamentals are there – the table, the stove – but each detail feels wrong somehow. The Ovaltine pot now dried rests on the draining board. I steady myself at the kitchen sick, concentrating hard on not spewing. A vision of myself ricochets off the kitchen window. I cannot see them out there. Seconds later, I'm out the door and heading towards the gate. I stop to look back. Neither have followed me.

# 7

All summer, results feel forever away, but when it arrives it's like no time at all since the exams. The future has snuck up on me. We were sat around the kitchen table. Ma was mid pouring the tea into our mugs when the thud stopped us all dead in our tracks. Weighed down with possibility, the envelope lands on the mat.

Ma, Da, and I all stare at each other, as if expecting the envelope to dander in and announce the results: *Aye, you are for big things, love. Cambridge! Oxford! That PPE course only Tories do, well you're the exception, baby! Pack your bags!*

The three of us move towards the door. I lift it up. Rip the top of it off.

Ma is doing her *big relaxing breaths.* Sure, that will do it to really soothe me. Would she ever fuck up?

—Careful you don't tear the letter!

—I know.

The page sticks to the wee plastic address window on the envelope, so I take another tear at it. Ma just watches on. She knows better this time.

Then, it's in my hands. The future feels heavy held there in my fists. My eyes scan the page up and down, checking that the text beneath is actually addressed to me. Sure, enough it is. They're both shifting awkwardly, waiting for me to say anything. Here goes. I read:

Fiadh Donnelly
English Literature: B
Geography: C
History: D

You could hear a pin drop in that hallway. All Ma says is, —Oh. OK.

And that's it. Next thing I know, we are bundled into the car to head down to the school. The teachers are waiting to comfort any students who didn't get into their first choice university and help with a last minute university place. The dregs of university courses, the ones about toes and teeth, that nobody *really* wants to do. My heart drops. I didn't get the grades even with the after-school History tutoring over in Holywood, with that creepy man in his sunroom, laden with *Day of the Triffids* plants. His ears growing hairs as long as the aerial roots splayed around the room.

Ma checks in with the receptionist, who directs us to the maths block to queue to speak to a teacher. The wait is long and silent. Pure torture. Every second feels like a lifetime. The windows are still fogged with memories of the darkness. The corridor has a sharp nip to it. It reminds me of mornings spent here; we approached each day as if this was purgatory. There was the rare occasion where I was first in, right after the substitute teacher. She was one of those ones who had a distinct air of vulnerability, like blood in the water; the class just knew she was dripping in inexperience. We never even took the time to call her proper name, Ms Harris. She was young enough that she could be one of our older cousins, in fact, she was the cousin of a girl in the other class, Julie. Julie'd let slip one day that Ms Harris was actually Eileen. So, naturally, we all never uttered the words Ms Harris again. The lads had taken a liking to calling her 'Eels'. So, Eels it was forever.

Eels sat up front at the big desk. She's methodically unpacking her satchel: dry markers, a big red flask, a new travel pack of Kleenex. Fuck she wasn't making it easy on herself.

—Alright, Eels.

—Fiadh, please.

By the time she stood to scold me, I was already halfway down the classroom, beelining for the back row. Getting the seats right at the back was like gold dust. I took my blazer off and put it on the chair in front and my folder on the one to my right. Staking my claim so the girls could sit next to me. Who could be holed having one of the teacher's pets beside you for the triple lesson. You'd die off.

The girls were taking their time. They were holed up in the loos twenty minutes ago, swapping craic from the days before. It was usually the same old recycled stories. Once a story goes round about you in school, it'll haunt you for the rest of your days. That morning we were talking about how Claire McGill's ma buys her clothes in a charity shop. Danielle was fixing her eyeliner in the mirror when she caught sight of Claire coming in. It was bound to be a bad day from that omen alone. Aisling was staring at her hands, scared to notice Claire's presence for fear it would set Danielle off. She needn't have given it much thought though, Claire bounced right over to Danielle, and turned on the tap. Water splashed up on Danielle's shirt, turning the white cotton translucent. I took myself off as soon as I heard the blood-curdling shriek from Danielle.

I was there watching the classroom door open and close as people drifted in bit by bit, but there was nobody worth shaking myself out of my half-asleep state for. Then Danielle and Aisling slumped in. Danielle looked like she'd run a marathon, knackered but pleased with herself. Only then do I notice that Aisling's hair is on the top of her head, like a hairy tennis ball, held in place with bright bobbles. She'd not even done her make-up that morning. She looked atrocious.

—Love.

—What?

—Oh, love. You want a mirror?

—Fuck up, would ye.

—Nah, I can't let you be out like that.

Aisling rolled her eyes and threw her head onto the tabletop. She screamed loud enough for Eels to jump from her chair and make her way down the aisle, heading towards us at top speed. Her shoes made a zipping noise as her feet rubbed against the lino.

—Girls. What is going on down here?

Neither of us responded. I became *very* interested in a poster on the noticeboard.

—Fiadh. Now! I want to know what this is about.

—Aye, you and me both, Eels.

—Don't.

Aisling screamed again then left the room. In her wake was a damp pressing of blood on the plastic chair. Eels gave me the nod to follow her. A rare enough move, usually only reserved for when somebody's boking their ring in the bogs. When I got into the toilets, Aisling was sobbing. Her heaving breath echoed against the tiles. Her hand gripping her middle tight.

A ripping sound brings me back to myself, into the corridor where I sit now with my parents. The force of the door opening makes us all jump. He stands there, looking puzzled at a piece of card in his hand, as if trying to decipher some ancient hieroglyphs. A moment later, 'Ms Donnelly' is called. Ma and I look at each other. The teacher changes tack, and invites the three of us in.

When we get in, the teacher gives me a long spiel about *things working out in the long run.* I haven't even had a full cup of tea this day. Give me strength.

He asks a series of questions printed on a sheet in front of him. They could have at least found a teacher who fucking knew me from Adam.

—And what would I like to study?

—Well, I'd like to go to Queen's to do History, but sure lookit, see if you can make that work in the long run will ye?

A slow smile stretches over his face. I bet he can't believe he's ended up here advising me on career opportunities.

—And is there a second choice in mind? A different course? There are no openings for the rest of your subjects at Queen's, so how about a different university?

Ma interrupts, —What about Film at Queen's, hmm? You always liked that. Or something like . . .

Ma stumbles fanning open the Queen's University brochure. The shiny pages are slippy in her hands. She thumbs through a few pages before humming in satisfaction. Bingo, her face says she's figured it out.

—Or how about International Relations. That sounds fun!

Her eyes tell me that she does not in fact think that sounds fun.

—Ma, thanks, but no. Probably not.

—Well, you have to pick something love, so hurry up. The man's not got all day.

She shoots him that smile she reserves for men in their thirties who look like they know their way around their own laundry pile. Christ the night, as if she's flirting with him, on today of all days. I barely conceal the scream bubbling up in me. The sheer power of it ensures that I'm up on my feet and leaving the room. I can't be dealing with this shite right now. I push my way into the toilets, locking the cubicle door behind me. Out of nowhere, I'm crying, mopping up the eyeliner stains with single ply bog roll. The depth of my indignity knows no end today.

The cold water splashed on my face takes the redness down a notch, but I'm still puffy eyed. This whole day is fucking desperate. For the first time in my life, I've not checked my messages on my phone all day. I've fourteen texts and two missed calls from Aisling. She is not held back by the constrictions of text message limits on her phone; she's on contract, unlimited texts, so she sends a message per word for the effect. Fucking show off. She is such a melter. I steel my nerves before opening the stream of texts: she's got into her first choice at Queen's. Of course, she did. My mouth tastes sour. I text back All **good here**. I splash more water on my face. I leave the toilets dripping water from the ends of my hair.

Eels is there as I leave the bogs. She looks at me, with something like a smirk. That fucking bitch, I swear. I mirror her face back at her. The sentiment *have that you crabbid ould bitch* is implied in the slow squint I pair with it. The hallway is quiet. The soles of my feet slap on the lino as I approach the classroom. Through the window panel, I can see that the room is empty except for the teacher. He's looking at his phone, which lights the underside of his face a pale blue. It reminds me of when Andy and I would pick buttercups and put it under the other's chin. A glowing prediction of whether the other had wet the bed. Giggles or rage would always ensue, and possibly a chase if the predictor stood their ground that the buttercup never lies. *Sure, it's only a plant! Why would a plant lie!* Other times, the girls and I would be huddled around the green in the playground. We would conjure up through the stem whether one of us had a boyfriend, which somehow was hidden from the other two. We lived in a fantasy that we were able to contain multitudes of mysteries. It allowed us the freedom to imagine worlds for each of us, ones where we were anything we wanted: high-flying businesswomen in stilettoed heels and taking important calls on the go; doctors about to perform high-risk surgery on a gorgeous billionaire; or, in Danielle's case, being a gorgeous billionaire, preferably not on the operating table. The range of our existences knew no bounds when the buttercup floated just beyond our chins. The buttercup knew it all. We just had to ask. But once the flower was removed, our fantasies faded, bringing reality back into view. Around our way, everybody seemed to know everything about everyone. One small transgression and the whole area would be rife with whispers. A bill unpaid or being caught kissing behind the row of shops would do it. Shame knows no limits. It was all strangely predictable, lives tumbling from one thing to the next, with no room for excitement, as if it were foreseen. Flowing from GCSEs to first jobs to marriage to babies. I'm tired already.

I knock on the door, bringing the teacher back into the room. He waves me in and tells me that Ma and Da have gone to wait in the car for me. They've recommended me for Film Studies at Queen's. He had taken the liberty of ringing through to reserve the spot for me in case it fills up while I was away. That's when I tell him what I want to do.

# 8

Later that the night, the sounds of the kitchen sing through the house, followed by the much less melodic call for dinner which comes seconds later. I put on my slippers, the foam soles flattened by time, before making my way down the stairs. Pasta bubbles like a volcano on the stove, while pans cascade into the sink.

—Need any help, Ma? I ask when coming through the door.

—Sure, it's done, isn't it? Ma says as she's setting down the wooden spoon and landing the tea towel over her shoulder.

I serve up the food, heaping great big spoonfuls of spaghetti onto the plates. The cushion of pasta accepts the ladles of Bolognese, creating a sea of sauce that the Parmesan will float on.

Da enters the room, dusting down his hands on his jeans in anticipation of a good feed. He lifts the legs of his trousers between thumb and forefinger before settling down into his seat at the head of the dinner table.

—Love, pass us a glass of milk, will ya? he asks as I lean down to the fridge for the orange juice. I decide to reach just for the milk instead.

Throwing open the windows and propping the back door open with a bag, Ma lets the August air seep into the kitchen. Singed with the smell of freshly lit barbeques, the meat sizzling on the grills in nearby gardens, the breeze hot with the sprawling possibility of bright evenings. In the final act in our pre-dinner ritual, I bring the cutlery to the table, then pass around ripped kitchen roll from the spool.

—Are you going to say grace? Da jokes as he shovels the pasta into his mouth. The first bite washes over him quickly, while the second simmers his hunger. At this stage, he reaches for a slice of buttered bread. Everything at our dinner table can be made into a sandwich.

Ma asks in what seems to be one breath, —What have you planned for the evening? Anything nice? Are you for going out? Sure, what are Danielle and Aisling's plans for the next term? And what will their mothers think of that? Them moving out when they could be tucked up in their own beds at home. Think of the money they could save! Those student grants are hardly enough to run a house on, is it?

The butterflies settle in my stomach. I haven't told them that I've not accepted the Queen's University Film Studies place, and I didn't even want to do Film anyway. They were so pleased with themselves in the car home from the school after the results. In the front seat, they'd agreed that Film was just like History, if not better. You could get through more films in the time it takes to read a history book, they said. All pleased with themselves, they agreed that sure wasn't mulling over the past awful boring?

—Ma, I interrupt her monologue on the economics of good housekeeping, —I have something to tell you both.

Da drops his fork onto the plate, his eyes fearful of what's to come.

—Don't worry, it's not bad or anything, I offer to the silence. —On the online portal, I didn't accept the place for Film at Queen's.

—What? But, love, you said . . .

—It's not a big deal. I didn't know whether I was going to do it.

Earlier, the teacher had rang through to the university in Liverpool and secured me a last-minute place. The offer letter would arrive in a few days. Truth be told, it hadn't really settled on me yet.

—Do what, Fiadh, love? Ma asks, concern knotted in her brows.

—I've accepted English in Liverpool instead. You know how much I love books. It'd be great. And I did well in Mr Hill's class! I got a B!

Quietness settles in the room.

—Books? Da says. —What're you going to do with that? And how're you planning this supposed move to Liverpool?

I tell him that a letter from the student guidance centre should be dropping through the letterbox in the next day or two.

The chair scrapes across the tiled floor forcefully enough to make me wince. I stare straight ahead until my mother disappears out of sight, then out of the house.

—For God's sake, Fiadh, why did you have to go and do that? he says, before following her.

That went better than expected, I think, as I stack the cutlery onto plates then the plates on top of each other.

Books are double-parked on the shelves across my teenage bedroom. The classics are lined up in front of the Goosebumps series, a shock of green peering out from the back row in the gaps. Open drawers, close drawers, repeat. A feeling settles in my stomach, like waking from a nightmare where you've gone to school without your clothes on. I scribble on an old Hello Kitty notepad: underwear, clothes, pens, DVDs, books, photographs. Picking up the items, I struggle to decide what is worth holding onto for my new life across the water. Every single thing in this box room makes my skin crawl with a pre-emptive embarrassment: the ticket stubs for Girls Aloud; the festival wristband embedded with fossilised dirt. I tip these artefacts along with the piles of DVDs, books, and photographs into a bin liner. Not even worthy of the charity shop.

I unpack the suitcase, again. This time folding the items which will represent the new me: blue jeans, black boots, slogan T-shirts, sparkly top, and a jumper. For nights out with new friends I am yet to meet, I pack my purple Fujifilm camera wrapped in a pair of woollen socks for safekeeping.

I pull on a baggy grey jumper, complete with holes at the wrists as make-shift homes for my thumbs. Assessing myself in the mirror, I roll the sleeves up to the elbow to try and conceal the previous iterations of myself told through knit. The jeans, too, are frayed at the ankle from hours upon hours of walking around Belfast city centre in the rain. A heavy vodka buzz in tow to stave off the chill from the sea air blowing in. We would sit on the wet ground at the Waterfront, holding our stomachs tight with our arms to battle the Baltic air. It is always so cold here, I think, while considering a summer scarf to bring on nights out. All my best things are now packed, wrapped like treasure in the little grey suitcase.

Leaving my room, I psych myself up for the results night celebrations in the pub. I bounce down the stairs two steps at a time. Stuffing a fistful of change and my keys into my bag, I step out of the house and towards the car waiting in the street. I slam the taxi door shut, always with a force which frightens the life out of me.

—Where you for, love? the taxi driver asks without moving an inch.

That night like many that went before it, we gather in a bar surrounded with dark wooden panels, deep booths, and a black stone floor. In the corner, the fire is burning in August. I arrive early to pull over enough seats around the bar table. I want everybody to be sitting for my news. The rest of the group arrive in dribs and drabs. First, Aisling, with her over-stretched, over-washed grey jeans. We hug, and I go to buy myself a pint of cheap cider.

—You alright, babes? she says.

I say that I'm fine, but she hears something else.

The others arrive in a pair: Danielle and Andy. The noise comes in with them, filling the room with laughter.

—Glad yous are here. Grumpy hole here won't tell me what's up with her. We're meant to be celebrating!

—Would you ever give over? I'm getting to it! I guess I have some news.

—You pregnant, love? Aisling jokes.

—So, lads, I'll be moving to Liverpool. I've got a place through clearing, it was all very sudden, I'm still not sure where I can live,

I'll be back before you know it, sure it's close enough to be back in time for dinner.

The words tumble out. My breath is heaving in and out of my chest. Sweating, I remove my jacket.

Aisling is first to speak, —Oh, love, England? I'm sorry for your troubles.

The sincerity hits my chest and I gasp. On the inward suction of air, I say, —Pints?

—Yeah, go on then, seeing as you'll be gone long enough it's your round, Andy says.

I slip past the bar, out the door and onto the main road. There's a small park out the front. I sit there for a moment on the wall, fumbling through my bag, lipstick and tissues flowing out over my hands. I'm not sure what I'm looking for until I put my hand on a single cigarette loose from the box. The stem is broken; I snap it in my fingers like a branch and light what remains of the filtered side.

When I return to the bar, I order and pay for drinks. My hands create a web of fingers to balance three pints on, before returning for the last. As I set down the glasses, Andy says, —Ah we thought you'd done a runner across the water already! You were gone long enough, love.

His hand reaches over and lifts a pint, taking a long gulp. Over the top of his glass, his eyes lock with mine.

With a sharp inhale, I say, —So, what're your plans for the next year then?

Andy catches the words on his breath, —Ah sure, I don't even know where I'm for tomorrow never mind the next year.

As soon as the words are pulled inside him, he exhales, creating room for a sup of beer.

—You know what I mean, how did it go for you?

—Ah, sure you know, I'm for Queen's.

Andy is doing Medicine, and Danielle and Aisling are for Politics and English. The conversation turns to where in the city they will be living next year. Halls are a write-off as they all live too close to the university. The three of them discuss renting a house in the Holylands area of Belfast, where they will unfurl into their future selves.

I lean back over the edge of the bar stool, stretching my back taut as mooring lines. I watch my friends through new eyes and want to hold this moment in my mind. Just as suddenly I shake it off, feeling my body blush with mortification for this indulgence.

Later, Danielle and I huddle close under a heat lamp. Between us, we share a menthol cigarette and discuss 'The Future' as if it's ours to hold. I take longer drags than my throat can handle as if to dissolve the tension.

—I think I'll miss this place, you know.

—I know.

I half smile and ask what she will do here without me.

—Will you visit?

I mumble, —Yeah, of course! Will you come over to see me too?

—Ah, sure you'll be busy with your new-fangled life.

Instinctively, my mouth twitches into a downward smile. Drink splashes my top lip; a coat of sugary cider is left as my tongue mops up the residue. Without the prop of a glass to my face, I feel naked under my friend's furrowed gaze.

We stand quietly, taking big puffs of smoke. It clouds out our noses like dragons' breath. The embers melt into the filter before being crushed underfoot. Danielle kicks it off her sole and extends her hand out to my arm. Wordlessly, we walk back into the bar, and resume where we left off.

It's now a ritual that after every night out in the taxi on the way home, we have a set routine for dropping each other off, ensuring each other's safe return. Living the furthest stretch from town, I'm always last to be dropped off. Hugging in the back of the car, we say what will be our last goodbyes before my move to Liverpool. With me telling each, —I'll see you in the next week or so before I go. Let's do coffee.

Yeah, they say, one by one as they leave the taxi, slamming the doors to walk up darkened driveways and into their houses. Eventually, it's just me and the driver. I give him the address, and some rudimentary directions which he doesn't need, then slump into silence in the back seat. Opening my bag, I check that the keys are still in the zipped pocket. I remove my phone and text Ma, home in a minute, knowing that she will have sat up in bed pretending to read while she waited on my safe return. I check my keys again, the drink making me doubt myself. I open my texts, not knowing what to send to the girls, now that my days are few here. I know I'll not have a chance to see them before I go. The driver stops the meter outside my house. I hand him some shrapnel, cobbled together amongst the girls. As I close the door, the whole house is in darkness save for the glow coming from Ma and Da's room. It clicks off as soon as I reach my bedroom door.

# Part Two

# 9

The duvet is wrapped up around my neck, material concertinaed like a sixteenth-century ruff. Each layer working in tandem to prop my head up. My room feels like a gallery, with the trinkets for living now all packed up. The shelf is overflowing, teddies and old mugs lined in front of a row of books. An old photo of the girls, our arms stretched to the sky as we run into the sea, in Donegal or possibly Newcastle. The room now feels as cold as on that shore. It's a struggle to peel myself from my comfort and head downstairs.

The suitcase sits lonely at the bottom of the stairs, left out last night in preparation for my early departure. The 7 a.m. flight was the only one out of Belfast that I could afford on such short notice. Lifting my bag with my right arm, then my left, I try to assess if I've gone over the maximum weight. I'll have to discard some knitwear at the terminal if it is. I wonder if Liverpool will be as cold as they say it is. Best not to risk it, I think, and unzip my case to remove Sylvia Plath's *The Bell Jar* along with an unread copy of *Ulysses*. Ma appears around the kitchen door.

—You ready, sweetheart?

I do the obligatory pat down of my pockets for passport, phone, purse. Good to go. Once we're buckled in, Ma's shoulders sink down into herself. Nobody speaks during the drive. It's like Sunday Mass after a particularly heavy Saturday night on the cans. Tranquility soured by contemplation. Out the window, there is only the rear-view of rows of terraced houses, lined up like people turning away in protest. I blink my eyes tight, trying to imprint the image. Scouring the cascade of homes, I can't find my own from this angle, each becomes a replica of the previous.

As I see the billboard for the International Airport appear, my body feels like it is at the top of a free fall at a childhood indoor play-area. Rumour had it in 1995 that a kid jumped off the top of the free fall slide too close to the edge in Jungle Jim's near the Abbey Centre. They misjudged the jump and caught their arm in the safety nets on the side. Disjointed shoulder, the pop of a socket, held only in place by skin pulled down by gravity and up into its netted trap. I think I remember blood, too. That may have come later, though. Everybody had their birthdays there. Scoops of vanilla ice cream were dropped on cubes of jelly, before slowly melting around the pink goo. Ma would pick me up after these parties. I'd smell of sweat and other people's socks, the stench clinging to me from the ball pit. In the car on the way home, we would stop at a chip shop. Vinegar and salt wafted around the car, as she peeled open the soggy paper. From inside the car, we watched the walkers along the towpath. Our hands dipping in and out of the chip bag. Raindrop baubles glittering in the window.

Suddenly, the car jolts forward: the handbrake is thrown on. We're here. Crowds gather around backpacked students. Families waving as they begin to drive away. When I step out of the car, time is accelerated in a flurry of needing to run inside to the toilet.

—I'm sorry, I'll be back, I say, rushing to the entrance, looking left and right to find the way. There's a queue of people for the ladies' toilets, so I go into the disabled one, feeling relief at the large, enclosed room which cocoons me. My stomach falls out of me, hissing, or so it seems, as I sit on the porcelain. The tissue paper hurts and is so thin in my hands that it dissolves with every wipe. My hands are damp with piss. I wash them red raw, but the sensation doesn't dissipate. When I come back out into the fresh air, it feels like an eternity later; my parents are flustered at going over the allotted fifteen minutes for drop-off. Da is sweating that he should really have parked in the long stay car park. He's turning the ticket over in his hands, staring off across all the stationary cars in the distance. It leaves us with only a moment to say our goodbyes. Ma can barely make eye contact. She fumbles around in her bag for a pound coin or two for the gate on the way out.

—Thanks for the lift. I'll text you when I land.

—Be safe, they both say, before stepping back into their sides of the car.

As their car pulls off, I watch them turn their heads away, in an act of love designed to shield me from their sorrow. Once I'm moving, I don't look back as I step over the zebra crossing to the doorway. Mr Tayto, a national mascot for lack of any other, stands in front of the words 'Welcome home!'

The flight is punctuated with clapping and blaring horns announcing raffle tickets, fundraisers, and cheaper-on-this-flight perfumes. I jump out of my skin every time. After the plane settles above the clouds, the engine goes from screaming to a soft hum. It bounces over potholes in the air, dipping up and down like a car going over the roads in Donegal. The fear settles in my fingertips, prickling the skin. Closing my eyes, I think of the dips in the road at Milford which sent my stomach to rest up near my heart. I imagine the rest of the journey to Donegal. The twisting road was faithful to the contours of the sea. The car would spring along, seemingly powered by each downward thrust after every bump. We would eventually reach Downings Bay, where we had a caravan to stay during the summer. Our car was packed to the rafters with everything of importance to us. My suitcase was packed with teddies, northern crisps, and books. We took everything we loved from Belfast for safekeeping.

As we entered the town, the Beach Hotel would appear on the left, only then we would know at last that we'd made it to safety. The tree-lined drive into the caravan site welcomed us into our temporary shelter. Once the car doors opened, it was as if our shoulders unknotted for the first time in a year. Da rushed to unpack his TV with built in VHS, dodging the raindrops as he ran inside. Ma held open the door for him as he dived inside. Here there was a kind of playfulness which didn't exist across the border for them. It was as if they could forget themselves.

Paying no mind to ourselves, the days sprawled into infinity. From sunrise to sunset, we were always in the water. Our bodies floated in and out with the tide. Surfboards were carried between two of us, me, and some other kids on the site, as we descended into the sea. Sandwiches would be carefully concealed within our clothes on the soft sand, far enough away from the sea to remain dry. Our days were spent in this servitude to the water.

A voice crackles over the intercom. —Can all passengers please fasten their seatbelts.

It's as if the tarmac jumps up to the plane as it lands. The ground and wheels clap together, rippling out to the passengers. Flight attendants zip up and down the aisle, then just as quick we're shooed off, ready for their next departure. The airport from the tarmac looks like a bunker: grey, boxy, squat. Inside, the labyrinthine corridors lead me to the arrivals hall. Heaving my luggage, I feel every ridge on the floor tiles. My arm strains as I drag my suitcase behind me.

Outside, a queue of black taxis parked up in a curved U tight to the kerb. A giant yellow submarine stands on an island between the two lanes of traffic. In the shadow, the drivers are huddled together deep in conversation, putting the world's wrongs to right. Coats bunch around throats, necks are bowed, as if in preparation for genuflection. They commune, cigarettes or coffee cups balanced between forefingers and thumbs. I would not interrupt their vigil even if finances allowed.

Buses line the road, winding up to the right. I fish a piece of paper from the depths of my pocket. It's folded in on itself, an unsuccessful origami. I peel the leaves of the note apart from themselves. '86A, 80A' is scrawled in blue biro pen. 'Don't get off until the end,' the advice ominously reads. I see the bus parked up at the last of the shelters outside the terminal. Fearful of it leaving as I arrive, I speed up. The bus doors open like curtains, soft and with a slight hitch as if caught on a rail. Ovened air puffs out from inside. It's sickly. The driver asks where I am going but does not state the ticket price. Instead, he pops his hand out as if I should know what he's owed already. I hand over a scrunched-up fiver, hoping the sweat has not turned the currency into mush in my fist.

—Anything smaller, love?

I shake my head. He sighs and gives over the change.

It's rammed. Groups of subdued hen dos returning as if from war. Staff clocking off from their shifts. Sullen faces watch out the windows, no care for who might get on. The only seat available on the bus is at the back. I opt to stand with my bag in the aisle, for fear of losing my life's possessions *en route*. Leaning against my case, I watch Liverpool pass by outside the window.

The city stands vast around me. Winding roads appear to the right, curving down towards the docks. In the distance, a building holds what looks like a spaceship, a circular disk overlooking the city. Glamorous women totter across cobbled streets in heel boots. I make my way to the arranged meeting spot, a chain coffee shop on Bold Street. I take a coffee which is much too strong for me to stomach. With each over-caffeinated sip, I'm testing the limits of the anti-scoots medication taken earlier. This whole adventure was so last minute that I couldn't secure student housing, so a friend of a friend who studied here recommended their landlady.

An older woman comes in, walking with a slight stoop like she is carrying the weight of the world, or at least that of the Irish diaspora, on her shoulders. Her eyes squint around the overpriced coffee shop clientele, before she hones in.

—Are you Fiadh?

She pronounces the 'd' with an emphasis which sounds like phlegm rattling in her throat.

—Hi, yeah. Is it Mrs Cooper?

She doesn't sit down; instead she places both her arms on the back of the chair opposite me. The wood groans under her weight.

—Are you ready to go, or are you just lounging here? I don't have all day, you know.

My purse and phone slip out of my hands, as I fumble to stuff them into the zip pocket on my suitcase. Coffee spills onto the table. *Fuck*.

—Are you going to be like this the whole time?

We make our way out to the street. Fumes from smoked meat wave out from a Caribbean restaurant. It's like nothing I've encountered before. Spicy. Delicious. Shops point their speakers out into the street. Up at the top of the street stands the remains of a sandstone church; the exterior looks like matchsticks bent from charring. The steps to this building raise it on a pedestal, a monument to destruction. I want to stop and get a proper look at it, maybe take a photo on my phone to send home to Ma and Da to show that I've made it in one piece, but Mrs Cooper hurries me along. Her head's been buried in her phone since we met. She hasn't looked up once.

As if noticing me for the first time, she scoffs as I walk past her car, unaware that this red car out of all the red cars on this street is hers. She pops the boot on an old car which blends at the edges to a deep rust. I gently put my case in for fear it will crack the metal. Further up the road, the streets we take are wide, with a walkway between the lanes. Benches line the middle of this vast space of possibility. There are people sitting, talking, and relaxing in these public spaces. I think of home and the spaces which I've inhabited: I felt constantly seen, even if against my will. I wonder do people feel this way here too. Belfast City Hall on a summer's day, the grass freshly cut and so soft to sit on. But taking up the offer feels like a statement. Sitting yourself on the ground in one spot opens you up to heckles from passers-by: the old 'smile it might never happen' from the older men who glance a split second frown on your face as you try to read a text message on a sun-glared screen; the smick who wolf-whistles then asks will you see his mate; the cries from the preacher at the gates, predicting an eternity of burning in hell for one previously unknown misdeed or another. It's not for the faint hearted.

The car veers left. The houses stand as if leaning over the road. It all zips past, until a sharp left brings us into the driveway. The car crunches over the gravel slowly, like twigs breaking in an open fire. The sound makes the base of my spine tingle, hairs standing on end.

Lugging the suitcase from the boot, it feels bulkier now, as if it gathered weight on the way here. I throw my shoulder up to gain enough momentum to pull the case from the car. Mrs Cooper looks on as if I'm growing another head.

It's a huge, red-brick house, with gravel paths leading around both sides of the building. Plants in brightly coloured pots flank the doorway. Stained glass segments held together with solder create an ornamental design on the panelling. It is like nothing I have seen before, so beautiful in its intricacy. It's a wonder that a football has never accidentally bounced through it. When we were little, Andy and I were forever knocking a ball through the neighbour's window. In the summertime, before we were old enough to drink in the park, we would gather on the street outside my ma's to kick a ball around. He, especially, never learnt the strength of his own kick. The white paint box daubed on brick was faded, marked by blasters kicked at the two-dimensional goal for what I could only imagine was generations of kids. I remember this: the first time he whacked it through Mrs Kearney's window. The sun was draping over his face, his hand offered a shaded salute. He couldn't have seen shit in that light, but still, he took a step back and ran towards the mark. His leg cranked and released, sending the ball over the wall. A small thud followed by tinkling glass. Mrs Kearney was out in a shot. She'd only seen Andy stood there in the sunshine, staring towards her door, as I ran for cover.

—You wee bastard! Away on around your own door.

It wasn't long until she reported back to my ma. I heard all about it that night over dinner. I can still feel the steam of the boiled potatoes on my face, as I stared down into my untouched meal. Ma said Mrs Kearney has been beyond the pale for years now. Her mind slipped beyond her after her husband was caught up in a bomb in town. Her nerves were never right after and now she was telling anybody who would listen that she had been the victim of a sectarian attack. We had to be careful with people, Ma warned me then. The cracks are never far from the surface. People are awful fragile.

Stood behind Mrs Cooper, I watch as her shoulder assists her housekeys to release the lock. The door is a wonder. Every pane of glass a fingerprint with its own unique dappling on the surface. Inside the hallway, Mrs Cooper barges ahead into the kitchen. My footsteps echo on the tile as I follow behind her. She fusses with the kettle and peers into the fridge, paying me no mind. For want of anything else to do, I stand and watch her. She twists her body to grab the kettle, which has just made a satisfying click.

—Oh! Your room, will I show you it?

The stairs creak under Mrs Cooper's footsteps. I trace each step as if crossing a frozen lake, scared to fall through thin ice. The woodwork's sigh under my weight is committed to memory, for use later when sneaking back into the house, alone or otherwise. She opens the door then hands over the key to my new room. Everything should be in order, she tells me, as she trundles down the stairs again. In the bedroom, the sheets are floral and brown. I wonder, do brown coloured flowers exist only in seventies textiles? I kneel on the dark brown carpet which chafes the skin into feeling burnt upon contact. Unpacking my things, I remove my knitwear, dresses, and tights: only the essential clothing; a capsule wardrobe.

Time is no object here, as nobody will be calling me down for my tea. So, I take ease in moving the clothing from the suitcase to the wardrobe one by one. There is a faint thud followed by a symphony on the floor as I lift a cream-coloured jumper. A whole collection of Sylvanian Families tumbles to the carpet, many losing ears in the fall-out. My ma must have snuck them in to ease me into my new life. I remember Ma taking me down to the big toy shop in the town. For all the size of me, I felt like my eyes were big enough to swallow everything in sight. It was a cathedral stacked high with toys to the rafters. My neck could barely support my head, swivelling around the store. My heart stopped when I saw them: the villages of Sylvanian Families. A group of rabbits dressed in pinafores were hanging clothes on a washing line atop a houseboat. Ducks making their beds in a three-storey townhouse. I coveted them all, bouncing between each of the houses. Ma hunched down to my level, pointing out the intricacies: the little jumpers; a tiny plastic milkshake; watering cans for the potted flowers lining the houses. I drank it all in. There were no words for how much I wanted to hold one, just one, in my hands. We walked away that day, leaving the villagers behind. Months later, a family of Sylvanian rabbits appeared under the Christmas tree. They look so tired in my hand now. The once-flocked skin of each rubbed raw from loving. They sing as they drop from my hand down into the bin.

The next morning, I wake early to light spilling in through the paper-thin curtains. Rays refracted through thread create shadowy whispers on the wall. It's like I am inside a tent, with the sun streaming in and the air coming through the zip. As the wind rattles through the single-glazed window, I imagine the sound of the trees whistling the breeze through their branches. The smell of the salt-air wafting into a café which sells toffee sundaes from the top of a cliff, gazing down over the sprawling beach. People running fast into the water and faster out. Shrieking. Somewhere between horror and ecstasy. The window frame shakes like a cop banging the door on a morning raid. It rattles me back. I remember where I am.

Despite the sunshine, the room feels stagnant and cold like the inside of a cave; dampness hugs the air and I myself. Wrapping up in an oversized jumper, I fix myself a slice of toast and a cup of tea. I bring it back to my room and lift my notebook to write about this first day in Liverpool. The page is glaring in its blankness. There is nothing beautiful in this moment, there is nothing to say. I give up after a minute or two, get dressed and leave behind a half mug of cooling tea.

This new city smells unpleasant: of newly laid tarmac; of coffee shops wafting nauseatingly strong brews; and dust blowing in the wind from the rotating cement trucks. I walk down Mount Pleasant, which to my disappointment is anything other than the name suggests. It mostly consists of an enormous car park and church.

When I reach it, the high street is vast and various. Topshop. Urban Outfitters. A Thornton's café. Melted chocolate drips from a metal stand. Down the road there's a shop just for hiking. My head's swimming. I could barely choose from the few shops in North Belfast's local shopping centre never mind this. We had mini-Topshop or Dunnes. That was it, really. At the junction of Bold Street and Church Street, I take it all in, an ant out of the colony ready to be squished underfoot. I take sanctuary in a Tudor building repurposed as a chain bookstore. Inside, dark oak stairs twist high into the rafters. The smell of coffee entices me further into the attic. A woman is thumping the coffee handle beneath the counter. Three sharp whacks does it, before she squishes coffee down and attaches it to the machine. Burlap bags overflowing with beans line the shelves behind her. Arabica. Robusta. House blend. When I get there, I panic and ask for a cup of tea.

—What kind?

My heart picks up a beat. What kind of question is that?

—Barry's? Lyons?

The barista responds, breakfast? Yeah, I say, not really sure what flavour breakfast is.

I'm killing time before I have to enrol to receive my student card. Taking each slow sip is torture. Blistering hot and tasting of dishwater. Little flavourless leaves have escaped the bag, gritting my teeth.

A row of armchairs line up next to the windows. I sit on a hard armchair with my mug watching the people in the street below. Posters protesting council cuts and nightclubs are papered onto the walls of an old, disused bank. What was once the grand entrance now houses the city's poor. Makeshift homes are laid out with draped blankets. A man sits inside his fort, book in hand and dog at his feet. A little cup collects coins from passers-by. I watch him turn the pages. Breath-blown on the surface, the tea has cooled enough now. I set up the table: removing from my handbag a notebook, some blue biros, and *Wuthering Heights*. I crack the spine on my first text of the term, and let the pages furl out like bird's wings.

A honeycomb of glass and metal domes over the library. By the time I arrive, it's late afternoon and the city is cloaked in half-light. I step in through sliding doors. A pair of 'Welcome!' T-shirted stewards stand in the entrance, leaflets cradled in their arms. They point me to a man perched behind a tall desk, his face knitted tight as a button. Piles of blank student cards lie in wait, ready to meet their matches. Possibly a mop haired teenager from Sheffield or Manchester, a mature student nipping out on their lunch break, or me. He points towards the chair pressed against a white wall. As soon as my arse hits the plastic, the camera flash goes off. No warning.

—Like Kate Moss, he says, not looking up.

He waves me on. Out pops my new student card to the right of the desk. Without looking away from his monitor, he points for me to retrieve it from the printer. The silence lets me know I should leave.

I come dressed the part, with new socks, bag, bobble pinning my hair back. Golden leaves lie all over the footpath. It would be hard to miss the School of English: it's a bricked Pringles tube with windows on all sides right next to the Anglican cathedral. From the reception windows I can see the whole city. Straight ahead, the window shows me the city unrolling itself down to the docks. Back towards the entrance, the view cannot hold the sight of the Anglican cathedral. Mid-morning light bounces off the walls. Stripes fade across the grey carpet.

Map in hand I make my way through the labyrinth. The floorboards shake as I walk along the corridor to the seminar room. I've scribbled the room number on my wrist, taking sly glances every few seconds to test my memory. The voices reach me before I've turned the corner. A clatter of new accents, lilting, unlike anything I recognise. I haven't the balls to walk right up to them, so I stand at the periphery, waiting for an opening into a conversation I can barely understand a word of. As one, the crowd moves at the behest of some unseen signal. We file in one after another, blindly choosing who to sit with. The lecturer stands in front of the classroom, shuffling notes scribbled diagonally on lined notepaper. When they begin, the pages are abandoned.

We are divided into groups to 'stimulate conversation and intellectual debate,' as The Icebreaker. All in the name of getting to know each other, we say our names, where we're from, and what our favourite book is. These ones have so much to say. I have just got my answers out when their heads swivel onto the next person. They are chatting so fast I can barely keep up. Like a nightmare, the whole table turns and stares at me again. *Fuck, what did I miss.* My smile tugs up my face, the two corners pulled into position by invisible riggers. I tell them my name again. What else am I meant to say?

A girl with a thick accent that I'm yet to decipher the origins of, says, —What, babe?

I try again. Their eyes glaze. Nobody understands. A silence falls over the group. Awkward fidgeting on their chairs. Downturned eyes, flickering up to make eye contact with one another. Before carrying on talking with each other about what Shakespeare they studied at secondary school.

At the end of the seminar, I pack my bag slowly, hoping to keep my mouth shut for a little while longer. My feet keep a pace slow enough to allow the luxury of empty corridors. Outside, freedom. I walk across the road, sitting on the steps at the base of the Anglican cathedral. The closer I get to this building, the bigger it gets, enveloping not only the skyline, but the earth, sinking deeper and deeper into the excavated land. Gravestones line the path down to the lower ground. Above the entrance stands a statue of a man rendered in oxidised copper. With palms faced outwards, he faces out from the church, as if ready to dive into the earth. The sun appears from behind the clouds. I turn my face up to the sky and soak in the sunshine. Red, yellow, and then purple veins fill up my vision. I imagine the light filling my skull, refracting around my brain and back out my eyes.

I text Danielle and then Aisling, filling them in on all I've been up to. Mining for information on every single thing they've seen, done, talked about. I'm craving it all. Danielle texts back immediately, telling me her head is opening from too much of everything the night before.

From inside my bag, I pull out an apple. Bruised, the peel is loose under my teeth. I bite the flesh, breaking the skin with a crunch. The liquid feels sticky under the hot September sun. For a brief moment, I forget that I have to return to class. Juice streams down my chin, curving the corner to make a river down my neck. I tilt my head back to assist. I take another bite, neck still arched, the trickle runs fast this time. A sugar-sticky trail goes from my mouth to my throat. I wipe the sweet residue with my sleeve, before heading back inside.

Back in the classroom, I make a conscious decision to 'start afresh.' Striding across the room, confidence exudes out of me, or so I think.

—Hi! How was your break?!

It sounds like a squeal leaving my body. Sharp. Startling. Like nails on a chalkboard. They look up at me from their seats, their eyes diagonally gazing without moving their heads. A spokesperson says, —Yeah. Good.

They say no more. Nothing.

—Ah, great! Sounds lovely!

One of them laughs nervously, holding her chin down, failing to stifle the giggles. It sets them all off. I join in and they stare at me like I've got two heads growing from my neck.

The spokesperson speaks as if for them all, —What're you laughing at?

My face feels hot. The spokesperson tells me, in a tone drenched in mockery, that the whole class had been to the pub during the break. On the way back, they spotted me dribbling apple juice, dripping down from my chin, looking at the sun's rays coming through my eyelids. I laugh, so quietly that I look like a ventriloquist dummy without a puppeteer.

I shift my chair around to face the front of the classroom, sitting that way until the end of the seminar. Not a word is said by or to me. All I can think about is looking normal. I don't want to look like I give a shit. The lecturer is droning on about the wonders of literature. Jane Austen. Shakespeare. Toni Morrison. I can hear the words, but my head won't focus on it. Sweat patches are hot under my arms. My breathing sounds too deep. Slow. One breath in. Long one out. Is this normal? When it's over, I stuff my book in my bag, and leave first. My legs don't know what's hit them with the speed that I descend towards Chinatown. I pass the bus stop, afraid to stop in case anybody catches up on me. I don't stop until I reach Mrs Cooper's house an hour or so later. The plastic sole of my shoes has rubbed at the heel, revealing a material centre, fraying threads chalked with dust from the city.

# 10

Sitting in my room, I wonder when 'Freshers' will begin. A wet glob of glitter eyeliner dries on my eyelids. Blue sparkles hardening into place for the night. Fearful of smudging, I sit with my eyes closed. Mentally I retrace my steps up Bold Street, then across to Hardman Street; each of these vast roads are wallpapered with adverts of women in bikinis advertising how 'up for it' they are through a colour coded stamp received upon entry to the club for the bargain price of £5. Others show indistinct crowds with their arms up. The room curiously bright, showing the revellers' smiling faces. There's an air of despair, like hostages in glow-sticks and neon net skirts. I pull on a pair of tight Primark jeans, black boots, and a metallic top which hangs low at the waist. It was Aisling's and I hope no photographs end up on Facebook of me in it. I inhale a laugh, thinking I was probably jumping the gun. The only people I had met so far were in my seminar classes. Still, I grab my bag, and pull the heavy wooden door behind me, clicking the latch. I push once on the panel to check it's closed. The landlady had threatened earlier that I would be liable for loss and damages, if the occasion ever arose.

When I arrive outside the Brutalist building, it looks like the set of a BBC crime drama. Somewhere dimly lit, the lighting obscured by trees. The front entrance could be mistaken for a council-run community centre, where bodies could be found under the basketball court. There is a reception desk which would not look out of place at the Valley Leisure Centre on the outskirts of North Belfast. I imagine the woman behind the desk asking what I'm for today. Swimming, I would say, comforted in the knowledge that she will sell me a tea and individually wrapped fingers of sugary shortbread after. My hair would still be dripping with eye-wateringly potent chlorine, my eyes stung pink from attempts to catch a glimpse of the world beneath the water-level. The teal blue reflecting pale images of bodies wading through the pool. Goggles then dropped from a height, followed by the white explosion of air meeting water, bubbling downward like an inverted geyser, a minute later, arms and legs kicking out. Though, in Liverpool, there is nobody behind this desk. In fact, there is nobody in sight at all.

I follow the vague pulsing sound down the corridor. Molly's Tavern, the student bar, is on the left of the building. It's decked out in painted pictures of orange pint glasses topped with white cloud foam, resembling the tops of ice-creams. My new Primark shoes stick to the tiles, making it a feat to walk across the floor. When I reach the bar, I finally turn and take it all in. Only three of the booths are occupied: two girls deep in conversation; a group of lads knocking back shots lined up on a wood panel; and a table of three people I recognise from class. They had been sat on another table in that first seminar.

I order a bottle of cider and walk to the group from the course.

I slide into their booth, —Hi, I think I know you from class? Introduction to Literary Studies?

The two lads, Gary and Lee, are debating their favourite football moments of the last century or so. Myself and the other girl try to interject and change the subject, to no avail. The two fellas are caught up in the all-time greatest United goals and whether Matt Busby was the best manager. I sip my pint, every so often raising my eyebrows, —Is that right, yeah?

For fear of going mad, I excuse myself to go to the bogs. Mid-pish I text Aisling to ask how she is getting on at Queen's. When I return to the bar, the three of them have gone. Their half empty pints remained behind. Fucking arseholes. I left my bag with them in the booth. I run across the room to check whether it's been pilfered, sighing with relief when I see it knocked on the floor, contents all still inside. My heart is beating out of my chest. The sweetness of the cider is repeating on me. I can't get out of there quick enough. The shame sticks to me, weighing my bag down heavy on my shoulder. I try to walk calmly from the bar, aware of the two occupied tables watching me as I leave. Their gaze burns into the back of my head as I push through the swinging doors.

Later that evening, I settle into bed with Carrie and the girls from *Sex and the City*. My phone vibrates on the bedside unit, drilling its way closer to the edge. Stretching over, I flip up my phone to answer the call.

—Awk, hiya, love. I'm not disturbing you, am I?

Shifting the weight from my back on to my side, I move the phone to my other ear and prop myself against the pillow.

—Yeah, now's good. Everything OK?

My ma wants to hear about the new cosmopolitan life I'm meant to be living. I tell her I had been to a Greek restaurant with some friends the night before. I embellish the truth to soften the inevitable mother's worry that she will feel. In reality, I had bought the three for two side salads in the local supermarket which I specifically chose to give a Mediterranean I'm-anywhere-but-here feel.

—That sounds great, love, she says.

She does not ask any questions about these friends. Instead, she goes on a rambling monologue about seeing Aisling's ma down the shops, out picking up tea towels and bits for the girls' new flat. The things no teenager thinks about buying, Ma reports. She barely stops for breath between words, pouring out how much fun the girls are having over at Queen's. How Da has signed up to one of those subscription services that posts out DVDs. How everything has gone on without me.

—When are you home next? she asks, finally pausing to fill her lungs.

I don't know the answer but I tell her I'll look at flights, knowing well that my bank balance won't allow such a luxury.

My chest has felt tight since the phone call from Ma. I can't shake the feeling of failure; I left them behind, for what? I have been in England for three weeks now and I very rarely use my voice to speak to anybody who hasn't received money to be in my company: my landlady, the shop assistant in Tesco, the librarian. The odd time I'll make a passing comment in class but usually it falls on deaf ears. With each of these interactions I have only spoken to test the limits of my existence. Sometimes when I approach the sensor barriers at shop doors, they do not move: I might have disappeared completely, floating around this northern English city like a ghost. Nobody makes eye contact in the street like at home. In Belfast, I would bump into a friend of a friend and be stopped for a yarn to hear the latest story. Here, I smile at people I pass in the university corridor and am met with a blank stare. Am I even really here?

Days before in the library, I google 'How to make friends at university'. The top hit informs me to be 'available, approachable, and friendly'. I read the article and take notes in the back of my Pukka notepad.

1 – *Body Language matters: unfold your arms! Don't create an obstruction between you and new friends.*
2 – *Don't be shy! Everybody is as nervous as you!*
3 – *Be proactive! Go out there and make life-long friends.*

For a minute or two, I try to decipher these hieroglyphics I have scrawled on the page. Do I not have friends because I have folded arms? I expect when I unravel my arms that a hoard of people will emerge from behind the bookshelves in the library: like a zombie apocalypse with coffee dates. I hug myself tighter.

It's the end of September. Leaves are shrinking dry into their branches, readying for the fall. The bus takes me out of the city along the backs of the old docklands. Bumper to bumper in traffic, we crawl behind the red-bricked warehouses. Tall five-storey buildings, their shoulders standing broad into the sky. Ships sailed from this dock around the world, spreading the reach of Empire. It's fucking massive when you see it up close. Terraced houses lie opposite housing the workers, labouring for so little in return.

An old woman in the row of seats opposite catches me looking around for any sign of the beach. Sand dunes or brightly coloured plastic buckets hung outside shopfronts. There's none of that.

—Where you for, love? The beach?

I check the folded-up directions scribbled on notepaper. She begins to shuffle into the aisle, pulling a wheelie bag behind her. Fixing a knitted hat to her head, she pats the perimeters. Forehead then her ears. She makes her way to the front, and gestures for me to follow. I help her with her bag as we get off the bus. She tells me that this is the quickest route, pointing down a road. It's like any other high street, with stores that nobody ever seems to go into or come out of. Shops niche and bizarre: one only sells carpets while another specialises in doll's houses.

Air as sharp as knives lets me know I'm in the right place. A moment later, the shore appears, unrolling from behind a grassy bank. My cheeks are beginning to pinken, my nose loses feeling. A scarf blankets my neck and shoulders, keeping whatever heat I have close to me. I'm walking diagonal in the wind, searching the sands for them. I'd read online that they were here. A hundred of them are scattered along the beach. Iron statues stand prone, staring out to the sea. The tide washing sand and seaweed around their ankles. In the distance, I can see some of their heads jutting out from the water. The sea breeze blasts all thoughts from my head, apart from: where can I get a tea around here? I retrace my steps, back along the promenade towards the line of shops.

It appears as if I'd conjured it up from the horizon. A little café, the only open shop in a row of shuttered units. Inside, the waitress takes my order. She's old enough to be my ma. Eyes knitted up in the middle as she asks if I'd like to order some cake. I take my purse out, shake the coins out of the concertinaed receipts. There is about four quid in there: enough for a tea and my bus fare back into the city.

I text Aisling and then Danielle, to see how they're getting on. With Andy, I send a series of observations from around the city. They let me know they're together, in a bar near the Students' Union. We'd been there together before. After our GCSEs, we had drawn scribbles on our inside wrists, careful to smudge them past recognition, to fool the bouncers on the door to the upstairs club. Danielle had mastered the art of nonchalance even then, swaying her way past them, as if she owned the place. Aisling, Andy, and I would be skulking in behind, wearing our fear all over our faces.

Danielle texts: Are you home for Halloween? I'm not, I tell her. The following message comes from Aisling, who tells me the three of them are booking flights that night to come visit over Halloween. It's Andy who replies next: so, what're we wearing then?

The waitress is wiping up behind me, closing the café for the day. As I hand over my change to pay, she gives me a box. It'd only go to waste otherwise, she tells me. It's filled with carrot cake and scones. A mini jar of jam, a wrapper of butter. Her face is so kind it nearly breaks my heart. The thanks slip out, as my face holds back tears.

# 11

Derek the lecturer has stopped speaking, and the class falls silent. I sit in the lowermost seat in the 'U' of tables. That week we're studying Eva Hoffman's *Lost in Translation*. He asks us to think of trauma, what that means to us, what being at home means. A guy at the front says home is where my mum does the laundry. A ripple of laughter. I go next. I'm hearing sounds come out of my mouth. Tumbled together knotting into words I cannot control. I find myself verbally unravelling. I speak of experiences passed down like worn heirlooms: checkpoints in the city centre; armed patrols in the streets; death, hurt, pain, fear. A vivid memory, not my own, appears to me, and I voice it: a department store in Belfast city centre exploded, people dazed walking the streets, fire-engines dousing the flames of the building. Then my mother, years after these events, fearing for me going to the city centre alone with friends. I was thirteen-years-old at the time.

At some point while I was talking, Derek has moved from his chair to perch on the edge of his desk. He's leaning forward, out towards me, listening intently. When I stop, his head swivels around the room. Any responses, he asks. A lad from Milton Keynes tells the room that it wouldn't have happened that way if it weren't for 'the terrorists'. Derek nods along, before bouncing back to me, waiting for a response which doesn't arrive.

After class, I make a run for the library. Puddles gather like tar bubbling; the water landing hard and slow on the ground. I forgot my umbrella, so I use my tote bag filled with books as a barrier from the weather. When I step inside the doors, I shake myself off like a dog coming in from the garden, splattering droplets from my body and hair. My coat is freezing cold with water. It peels from my body slowly like a layer of skin being shed. The clear barriers are swallowed into the gates, letting me enter the library. A puff of cold air blasts down my back. It's early October in the north of England.

I find a seat at a computer, sign on, and plug my earphones in. While waiting for the virtual desktop to load my essay, I select 'Clubland Classics' to drown out the chattering of the other people surrounding me. A steady drip makes its way down my forehead and then nose, to finally meet its end on the desk. At intervals, I mop up the puddle with my sleeve. The movement of people in my peripheral vision distracts me. I log on to Facebook. A message icon flashes on screen. It's Gary from the other night:

Asked to share this around. Are you coming?

followed by an event invite to a screening of Daphne Du Maurier's *Rebecca* in the School of English. It's in less than an hour. The message icon brightens again. A little red number appears above the speech bubbles. I open it:

Send on to others too.

Who would I be sending it on to? My ma? Sure, we've only just started. How do others have a network already? Still, I check my calendar on my phone, though I know I have no plans.

Fuck it, I think, sure I'm already on campus. I log off and take myself to the toilets to assess the damage the weather has caused to my appearance. Times have changed as I'd not even stopped in to the bogs to get a gawp at myself before rushing to get going on my work. The floors are white with sparkles reflecting from the strip lighting. Eye to eye with myself in the mirror, I take a step back to get a good look. Black lines drip down my face, like coal tear drops. Fucking hell, this is bad. Unspooled one-ply toilet roll acts as a make-shift make-up remover. With each scrub, the make-up dries and fades to a grey stain on my skin.

Dust lines the porcelain sink. Speckles of grey and black dot the white. I wonder if they are flakes of dead skin, mould spores, or the debris from my impromptu abrasive facial. I swill the water in the sink, then splash my face with the too-hot water. My face flushes red as the traces of grey fade from around my eyes. For good measure, I splash again, and again, and again. Each time holding my hands to my face a moment longer, pressing the heat in. Condensation from the tap and my breath steam the mirror. Waves of breath ripple from my body; settling with less force than the one before. The toilet floor is a small lake now. For a moment, I consider holding my head under the hand drier. But it will still be raining by the time I leave the building. In the mirror, I see myself as if born anew.

At night, the university takes on a new persona. Shadows wrap around the buildings, every brick a phantom carved out by the darkness. The corridors of the School of English are lit by motion sensor lighting. For a few steps I walk into a void with each turn of the corner. I take out a scrap of paper from the back of my jeans: '2-01b' scrawled in smudged pencil on the back of a receipt. The building is a maze: I retrace my steps following the numbers on the doors as they descend.

Up ahead light escapes from an oblong window cut into the door. I stand still, heart beating out of my chest. Wiping my hands on my top doesn't shift the clamminess on my palms. My mouth feels like sand, as if my tongue is stuck to my teeth. I wish my body would get it together to balance my hydration out.

The light clicks off overhead. I remain still so as not to draw attention to myself.

Fucking hell. How can I turn back now?

*Tink, tink, tink*: light flashes in the corridor. Someone's just stepped in through the double swing doors, and sees me, stood there in the flashing lights which then settle to fill the corridor. She looks like a Florence and the Machine tribute act with her floral headband and an ethereal shirt, billowing as she moves towards me. I'm fucking scundered. Stood here in the darkness.

She laughs, —Are you OK?

I tell her I'm looking for the film screening, and she points over my shoulder to the room. I follow her in. A crowd has gathered. More faces than I can recognise. Gary gives a little wave from up the front. He's pushing the DVD in as the projector rumbles into life.

By instinct, I sit down next to the girl from the corridor. The lights are dimmed for the viewing. I sip slowly on a bottle of Coke throughout as I did not get the memo that drinking on university property was acceptable. She leans over and whispers do I want a can of Carlsberg.

Afterwards, I thank her for the beer and offer to return the favour, though I know I only have a tenner in my purse. She tells me she knows a place not far from here. I take my chance and go.

Each side of the bar is lined with small booths. At a squish, each could hold no more than four people. I hadn't noticed this place on the way past during the day, but it is a beacon now. Music plays loud over the speakers. Stevie Wonder. Toots and the Maytals. Candles are on all the tables, dripping wax on to wine bottles. The room is dark and homely. We take a booth right at the back.

Her name is Chloë, I find out, and she's from Bristol. We talk ravenously about the process of moving our lives to this new city. She's living in halls, sharing with four other people. Total melters. One is near nocturnal, haunting the kitchen at night. It's a lot to adjust to, she says. Up north is a big change for her. 'The north' means something very different here. The beer buzz runs through my veins, instilling me with a confidence that I have not known before. I slip myself out of the booth and say —same again?

On returning, I push the beer across the table. I bought pints for us to linger over. I did not want to return to Mrs Cooper's just yet. The days in that house meld into one long blurry stint of staring out the window. Chloë reaches for her phone. Her face beams as if she is staring into sunshine reflecting on snow.

—Do you mind if my friend from the flat above me in halls joins us?

I don't mind, though butterflies settle in my stomach. We sit and wait, the camaraderie between us now changed with the pending addition of the unknown, for me at least. Hannah walks in with a force bordering on manic. She sees us and throws her arms in the air several feet before she reaches the booth. Her arms flung around Chloë, she kisses her head. I awkwardly wait for the moment to introduce myself. Hannah rotates on her heel and gives me the same intensity that she greeted Chloë with. She speaks to me as if we have known each other a lifetime, holding my elbows with her hands as she asks me how I am.

As suddenly as she began this interaction, she's gone. She returns with three bottles of cheap beer and begins to tell us about her evening. Hannah discusses the intricacies of her life with such ferocity it is as if she has known both Chloë and I forever. Her personality is expansive, absorbing those in her radius. Drawing people in to whatever she is doing. As the night progresses, Hannah asks about where I am from. Belfast, but it's not as rough as you might think, I say, surprising myself. Hannah doesn't know it. The time zips past quicker than I'd realised. It's after midnight and I've now missed my last bus back to Mrs Cooper's, rendering my day pass ticket useless. Hannah's already sliding herself out of the booth as she knocks back the dregs of her beer, —Come on then, let's go on.

She shrugs on her coat while barrelling out towards the street. Chloë and I follow behind her. We take a left down Bold Street, looking at Liverpool sprawling and unfolding during the dark-hours. It's like a different city at night: the street is lit from the bars and restaurants lining the length of the cobbles. People move in and out of groups huddled together to gossip and smoke. We walk past, ourselves huddled close together, nearly touching. Hannah declares that she had been to 'the greatest place' near here. Chloë and I make eye contact for a second, wondering how we are already playing catch up after so short a time in this new city.

Weaving through backstreets, we arrive on Seel Street. Crowds of people queue outside clubs, lining each side of the road. I soak in the names of these newly discovered treasures: Bar Fly, Heebies, The Peacock. We walk to the bottom of the street to get cash out from the machine, and then retrace our steps. Hannah veers us left down an alley. It looks like one of those 'get home safe' adverts. Stupidity or bravery has me follow her though. The cobbles have me wobbling in the darkness, then a red neon sign appears: Mojo. The music blasts so loud from the inside of this bar that the cobbles vibrate. We have a cigarette before approaching to queue up along the wall outside. Chloë asks, —How much is it in? while poking through her purse. Hannah tells us not to worry about it.

Inside, the DJ plays deafening indie music. The boys in here have come dressed the part. Skinny jeans. Mopped hair. T-shirts, aged or designer, covered in holes. It's glorious. Along exposed brick walls are the tables long and wide. People jump up on them. Dancing and singing at top volume. Their mouths mime unheard. The three of us throw ourselves into it. Going from dancing to knocking back beer and tequila. Outside in the smoking area, we share a pack of menthols. We wax lyrical about gossip, verbally introducing the workings of our lives. I tell them about the girls at home. About sleepovers at Aisling's. Danielle and the guy at the shop. They tell me about their versions of Aisling and Danielle. There's a moment of contemplation. Quiet only punctuated by the sound of the bass from the bar. Cigarettes are inhaled down to stubs. We box off our pasts before we carry on.

In the toilets, I barely keep my balance in the cubicle. The room is wavy. My bag spills out the contents on the damp floor. I stuff everything back in and pat down my skirt. It's not until I'm out of the cubicle and staring at my own reflection that I realise how blocked I am. I grip the sink hard. My hands try to keep the room from spinning around me: then steadying myself by holding one hand on the sink, I use the other to tidy up my eyeliner. I step back into the club. Hannah and Chloë are dancing in the corner. They greet me by throwing their hands up and embracing me. Our bodies entangled as we dance, holding waists, spinning around like that scene in *Titanic*. Once the room spins of its own accord, we tear off towards home. Linking arms to buy the necessary chips and cheese on the way. I drench mine in garlic mayonnaise and vinegar. We sit on the church steps as I phone a taxi. Chloë waves her phone at me, the screen blindingly bright. They are going the other direction, so she's getting a taxi for her and Hannah.

—Here, type my number in and prank me so I have yours?

When my taxi arrives, we hug goodbye like we've known each other forever. Text me when you're in the door, I tell them. On the way home, I text both Aisling and Danielle the same message: I miss you. I copy the text to the thread with Andy. Through drink-thick vision, I watch the text dance around my screen, before I delete it.

The taxi pulls up outside Mrs Cooper's house. One lonely fiver in my purse remains from the night. It just about pays my fare. I shut the front door slowly and then creep up the stairs. Once I'm in my room, I strip off and let the night-fresh air in the room begin to sober me. When I open my phone, Hannah's text: I'm home.

## 12

Mrs Cooper's in a rage about something. From my bed, I can hear the sound of her echoing up through the floorboards. I sink lower into my duvet and hope for peace. The kitchen door slams like a leather whip cracking. Next comes footsteps thudding up the stairs. Her feet have crashed down on every floorboard on the way up. Throwing the duvet back, I stand out of bed, waiting for the bang on the door. A brief moment passes before it comes.

—Good morning, love.

She has a smile plastered on her face. Her eyes look manic, flickering around all my facial features, but never settling on my eyes.

—Can you come with me to the kitchen?

Fuck, what now? I pop my slippers on and walk down. She's already waiting, her head tilted forward and eyebrows raised to the top of her forehead, as if to say 'See?' Though I do not see what she is insinuating. There are tea towels folded neatly and hung on the oven door. A dusty cafetière on top of the microwave. Letters yet unopened on the table. I follow her eyes. I see it. A bottle sat on the countertop, the condensation glistening on the exterior, pooling like steam gathered on a window on a rainy day. Mrs Cooper goes to it, placing her hand on the glass as if it might burn her.

—Well?

Her voice sounds like a knife scraping a plate. It puts my nerves on edge, rippling across my face.

—Ah, I must have left that out earlier. I'll pop it back in the fridge now.

—No, love. That is not the point. Where were you raised? Don't leave anything out on the counter here. Do you think I like to come in here to smell food going off?

My head is throbbing from the night before. I can feel the sweat prickle on my skin. I can't squeeze the words out of my throat. I fear I'll spew the contents of my stomach on to her tiles. Sorry, sorry, I say, walking out of the room. The sighing reverberates from the kitchen as I stumble up the stairs. I just make it back into my bedroom when the convulsions start. Everything is heaved from me into the bin. Acidic fur gathers on my tongue. When I stop, tears are streaming down my cheeks.

Swaddled in layers, I head out the door. There's a soft click as the latch closes behind me. It's one of those evenings which makes your heart beg to be home, under a heat lamp in a beer garden, or any garden in fact, surrounded by friends who don't require reeling out a backstory. They already know me through and through. No explanations needed. No need to slow my voice, to give better attention to my vowels.

The doors whoosh open in front of me. Blasts of hot air blow my hair down into my face as I step inside. Shined cement leads up towards the ticket box. A fella with floppy hair sits behind the counter. He doesn't look up from his screen when I ask how it's going. The speed of his fingers seems to pick up. A long sigh before he finally looks up at me. One fella dressed to the nines is checking his watch.

—One of those days, is it?
—Sorry?

His head tilts forward as if being released from a rope holding it up. Part-man, part-mechanical puppet. A queue of couples gathers behind me, impatiently shuffling while they wait for whatever this is to end.

—It's a day, yes, he says with a tone as flat as train tracks.
—Ah, great. Glad we're all experiencing the same. It's a day for me too. And probably half the queue.
—You're meant to tell me what you want to see.
—*Audition*. I'd like one ticket to *Audition*.

Receipts spool out from the little printer, one swipe tears them off. He tells me it's Screen 3, and before I can ask where that is, he's already looking over my shoulder at the people next in line.

By my watch I've still got twenty minutes to kill before the screening. I drag my feet over to the coffee shop, then set up at a table next to three guys. In a line-up, it'd be hard to tell them apart. They're dressed as if in compulsory uniform: checked shirts; constricting jeans; high-tops; wispy over-conditioned hair. They're having a conversation about the works of Takashi Miike. The first one is red in the face that *Audition* is the greatest film, not even just Miike's greatest film, maybe even the greatest film ever made. The second chortles, tips his head to him while looking at the third, a nonchalant 'what is he like?' motion. The final bloke tells them both they're wrong, and in fact he is the possessor of the only right opinion: it's all overrated. He's beginning to wax on about *The Dark Knight*, when the first throws his hands to his head, screaming.

—Have you not seen *Nicky the Killer*? Christopher Nolan has nothing on Miike!

I speak, not to them, but to the rafters. Correcting their mistakes.

—Ichi.

The three of them look at me at once, as if I've sneezed or screamed bloody murder.

—It's *Ichi the Killer*.

Now they're looking between each other. A little laugh bursts in one of their chests. I'm told in no uncertain terms that I am mistaken, first, and when I disagree, they say I'm wrong. They carry on discussing Ichi, as if trying to summon the conversation from before this Irish mad woman interrupted them. Christ, I can't wait for Andy and the girls to be over for Halloween.

After the film, it takes a minute for my eyes to adjust to the unexpected darkness in the street. Hannah and Chloë are meeting for drinks in a bar nearby. Hannah told me I was going to love it, and she was right: as I descended the stairs, with each step it got darker and noisier. The door swings open as a couple burst out. Inside, statues of Mary are all over the place, dripping in neon paint. Pews line the walls, where people sit holding pints never quite full from the knocks they take to move through the crowds. It takes a few laps of the bar to find them, tucked into a booth hidden behind a confession box. Hannah looks like she's presented me with a bar of gold, which, in fairness, she might as well have. I stay for as long as my bank balance will allow, before slipping out without the ceremony of goodbyes.

A parcel waits for me when I turn the key in the front door. A care package bursting with proper chocolate from home, crisps with flavouring so strong it'll linger on your tongue for days, and a note from Ma telling me how proud she is. I go to send a text to say thanks but decide to ring tomorrow. With the aftermath of music ringing in my ears, I open my laptop on my bed. The heat from it warms my knees as I open Wikipedia, checking my workings from the cinema earlier. I know I am right about *Ichi*.

# 13

The arrivals hall at Liverpool airport is a torrent of stag dos coming and going from the city. I lean up against the metal railing, watching the Flight Status board change from 'Arriving Soon' to 'Landed' for each of the flights. Malaga. Amsterdam. Berlin. Then finally Belfast. I'm kicking myself that I didn't pack a pen to write their names on a piece of paper. They would eat that shit up. Streams of people come out the double doors: couples reuniting; the newly arrived looking around like they've landed on another planet, and to be fair, they wouldn't be far off once they clock the giant yellow submarine just beyond the exit. The three of them come trundling out together, slowly, as if approaching a predator. A scream bellows from my chest and out my mouth. Unconsciously, I'm holding my hands like a megaphone around my face. There was no need for the sign.

Danielle screeches, —Awk, love!

Aisling is behind her pulling along a wheelie case. Just beyond her, there's Andy.

Outside the terminal, we board the bus. I pay on for all four of us with a tenner. The bus driver doesn't seem to give a shit, given that there's not much change to be dropped into my hand. The rain pelts the bus, as if trying to break through the glass to get into the warmth of inside. Andy and I are turned around in our seats to face the other two. Danielle is ripping into Aisling about her near boking with the turbulence. The roads here are just as rocky, bouncing over pot holes until we turn into streets I begin to recognise.

I lead them off the bus. Head down in the rain, they follow me with blind trust. We pile into Mrs Cooper's house, sneaking up the stairs as quickly as we can. Bundling into the room like sardines, holding down our laughter so that cretin doesn't come knocking on the door. Mrs Cooper is forever sticking her oar in.

We're playing house as Andy unrolls his sleeping bag, laying it beside the bed. Aisling's brought a travel pillow, while Danielle throws her jacket theatrically on the floor. One arm bows out, presenting her coat-bed.

—Fit for a Queen! So, where's these cheap bars you were talking about then, Fee?

All will be revealed, I tell her, before pulling a twelve-glass of store-brand vodka from under my bed. The smell would knock your head clean off. The bottles of coke in the shop were extortionate, so I whip out some shot glasses and cordial. That'll do. Andy heads to the bog to get a glass of water. He's waxing lyrical that it hydrates as you drink, so there's 'virtually no hangover'. Us three girls respond nearly in unison, —Away on.

The four of us are getting ready together. It's a novelty. Aisling has Andy cross-legged on the floor, as she sweeps make-up on him. Thick layers of eyeliner looped around our eyes, then smeared into messy grey smudges. We're meant to look like the undead, but it's giving the appearance of bit part roles in a school production of Oliver Twist. A quick slice of red lipstick across the neck and other creative, yet seductive, places on the body: a shock of red across a tit; across a cheekbone. With each layer of make-up, we move towards our ultimate goal: being the Biggest Rides in Liverpool. Packed in tight in front of the mirror, we admire our handiwork. Danielle whips out a digital camera, points it at our reflections. Knees bent. The camera flashes.

We stumble in heels far too high for us, first into the street and then onto the bus. The bus makes its way into the city like it's sailing the seven seas. Passengers stand in the aisle holding on for dear life. Our hands shake as we pass a bottle of vodka around. Every drop is drained within a few stops. We bounce off the bus, and barrel down towards the club with the longest queue. Everybody has gone all out with their fancy dress. It's cracker. There's Mario and Luigi, any number of superheroes, and the Spice Girls up the line from us. Our outfits are paling in comparison.

Inside, the smoke machine is on full blast, puffing out fog onto the dance floor. Wading through it, my feet knock over discarded bottles. Andy goes in search of the bar, before returning with four beer bottles weaved through his fingers. The bass shakes through my chest. Strobe lights disorientate me as I try to lean into Aisling's ear. I overshoot the mark, ending up with a face full of hair. She doesn't seem to notice, pulling me in tight under her arm as some song from the nineties blasts out the speakers. It pulls long forgotten dance moves out from our memories. Hands on hips, pointed fingers. Not just us, but all the girls are in sync. Andy, God love him, is doing a two-step. Before the next song gets going, I pull him to the smoking area, gurgling through my beer-fog about how great it is for him to be here. For all of them to be here. He makes me feel calm as he takes me under his arm. The pressure of him on my shoulder reminds me of home, of complete security.

But there's no time for being sentimental, the dance floor awaits. Aisling is hovering on the edges, eyes wide, when she sees Andy coming. It only takes two songs before they're wrapped around each other. It's 'Sexy Back' that does it. Giving Aisling enough of a push to go for it. Drink loosening them up. Danielle thumbs towards them, then shouts in my ear that they've been at this for weeks.

Outside the takeaway, my ears throb, as if my head is ringing. Danielle and I share a huge sprawling pizza. The box is draped across both of our knees. Rubbery cheese slops onto our chins, and we laugh while wiping it off one another. Across the street, Aisling and Andy are pressed against a betting shop window. A giant cardboard cut-out of a football pundit's head hovers behind them. Eyes peaking over the tops of their heads.

Danielle screams across the road. —Oi, love birds, you two staying there or coming with us?

About six people turn to see if they are the intended recipient of 'love birds.' The pair untangle from each other, before making their way over to us. We all slide into the back of a black taxi, barrelling off towards Mrs Cooper's. Aisling keeps the conversation going for all of us, now her mouth is freed from Andy's.

Back at the gaff, we stage-whisper to each other. Pint glasses of water are ferried into my bedroom. We each glug, hoping that it will keep any hangovers at bay. Danielle puts any doubts to rest, letting the two sweethearts know that there'll be absolutely none of whatever they had planned, not while she's in the room. She lies on her coat, pushes her bag under her head, and settles between the pair.

—You two better not get any big ideas while I'm in the room. I'll be fucking sick. Stop it.

Aisling and Danielle are bickering in whispers on the floor, as Andy begins to snore. His breath vibrating around the room. I drift off to sleep, their sounds easing me into my own dreams.

The sound of rain battering the window wakes us up. Aisling rolls herself into the wall, hiding from the night before. Crusty mascara sews my eyelashes together. I unpick it with my fingers, dusting it lightly onto the floor beside me. Tepid water keeps us all from shrivelling into prunes. For an hour or so, we each lie there, silently looking on our phones. Danielle is the first to crack. She's ready to see the city, she announces more to herself than anybody else. Her ma told her to go on the Beatles tour for her, see where Paul McCartney grew up. Apparently, he is always hanging around the city.

—Who knows, maybe he'll be my rich older man who keeps me living a life of luxury.

Andy's shoulders begin to shake. —Keeps in luxury? You're joking.

—You'll be turfed out, love. This is my palace!

Unsurprisingly, we don't meet any millionaires. The tour bus is shaped like a yellow submarine and finishes by driving into the water at the docks. Shortly after, Aisling is boking outside the Tate Modern. Between retches, she tells Danielle that she's a melter for making her get out of bed for this.

That night, we huddle around my laptop watching *Sex and the City* DVDs. We drink more tea than Mrs Cooper's kettle has ever made. We refuel on chips and pizza, cokes, and chocolate biscuits. They buoy themselves for the flight home tomorrow, as I cherish having them close for one more night.

# 14

It is nearing three months since I left home. Exams are just around the corner now. The nights seem longer here than they ever did in Belfast. I walk back from the library and the air is frosty, stinging my fingers and nose as I wait on the number eighty-two bus. My handbag is stuffed to the brim with books taken out from the library. The weight pulls on my bra strap, the plastic buckle piercing my skin. I shift the bag from one shoulder to the other. It leaves red welts pressed into my flesh.

The bus pulls around the corner of Renshaw Street. A folded-up day ticket is pulled from my jeans pocket. As my hand brushes it, my phone beeps just as I step on. Hot air from the breath of so many passengers steams my glasses up, blinding me for a moment. The aisle is packed with Christmas shopping bags. Gifts stacked high upon knees. Once I've set my handbag between my ankles on the floor, I reach for my phone. It's Hannah asking Chloë and me to meet her for a drink in town later. I put my phone back in my pocket. I'm foundered, properly chilled to the bone and all I can concentrate on is getting into the warmth of my own bed, or at least the bed which is mine for the remainder of my tenancy.

The streets in this area are lined with leafy trees usually, but now in winter they are skeletons of their former selves. The view between the branches up towards the sky make them seem like lung capillaries, lit up in black and grey. The wind blowing the branches like breath inflating and deflating the boundaries holding them in one coherent shape; always moving as one ripple across the sky. There's crispy foliage hardened by the low temperatures. Ice must be due. The birds will be unable to get their food from the ground if this weather holds up. I wonder if they are holed up in their nests in the trees, weathering the wind.

Inside the house, the wind echoes around the room, shaking the sash windows in their frames. The curtains blow inwards, flapping into the house like a plastic bag opened quickly. I put on a cheap pair of matching fleece pyjamas like I'm a child on Christmas Eve; the material coats my body in a security I haven't known in my adulthood. I think about going to the kitchen to make myself a hot water bottle to complete the feeling, but the thought of bumping into Mrs Cooper makes me sit tight. I make a note to buy myself a kettle in Tesco for my room.

My phone beeps and vibrates on the bedside unit. Chloë wants to know if I want to join her and Hannah for a 'few swift pints' in the pub. She texts the address, before I have even responded. For a moment, I remain in the bed, leaning the phone against my chest. I really can't afford another night out, never mind the amount I would have to spend in ensuring enough was drank to keep me feeling warm in this weather. I pretend not to have seen the message, roll over and turn the bedside lamp off.

When I open my eyes again, the room is dark, save for the yellow streetlights streaming in the window, reflecting its beams around the brown interior. My phone vibrates on the bedside table next to my head. I pull the duvet over me and ignore it. The buzz eventually subsides, and I slip into sleep again.

Classes have finished for the term, so I have no real reason to get out of bed anyway. I eventually stumble downstairs at 3 p.m. and make myself a coffee in the kitchen. I hold the mug to my nose and inhale. I imagine the smell of freshly roasted beans, carefully ground, and served with frothy milky foam. The leather couch sighs as it accepts my body while I lower into its cushions. I can nearly hear the rain hitting the window. Condensation steaming up the glass, hiding the outside world from view. A person on the next table would ask if they could borrow the sugar from my table. But I'm here. The kitchen in South Liverpool is as

I left it. The lights are off to save on the electricity bill, which Mrs Cooper has become increasingly obsessed with. The Post-it note remains stuck to the tiles behind the kettle: 'One boil of a kettle equals an hour of lighting!' She clearly did not get the memo about the Irish and their tea consumption.

I pop the kettle on again. Water bubbles dance inside. Da has an ear for when the eruptions are just about to hit their peak, he'd lift it off the boil seconds before it would click off. Over the years, this became a game we would play, guessing when the right moment to strike would be, hands hovering over the handle, ready. Ma didn't have the same patience as us, instead she'd be off into another room, tidying up. She'd often return long after it had reached the boil, the water tepid as she poured it. I'm brought back to myself, as the kettle click drops like a guillotine.

Decorations have covered the city centre for what feels like weeks now. Draped string bulbs hang up and down the roads. The days become soggier and darker as it gets closer to my going home date. I booked the flight as a return to my arrival back in September. Da told me it was cheaper to book it then to get ahead of the crowds. Now it's too expensive to book another. So, I've been spending every moment thinking about how long there is to go until I'm on that plane again. Loneliness veins through the city now that Chloë and Hannah have left for home. Skeleton staff in the library are all I talk to now, as I make a pilgrimage to print my boarding pass, kept safe inside a poly-pocket.

When it comes to it, I can't decide what to bring with me, so I lay out more than I would need for a lifetime. T-shirts, journals, and big chunky Topshop necklaces are lined up on my bed, ready to be packed. The bag is bursting at the seams as I stuff in my books, bending them at the sides to pull the zip taut. I rummage around in my bag for one last check: passport, boarding pass, phone, purse. I push the handle on the door downward and slowly edge the door closed to make no noise, not wanting to alert Mrs Cooper. Still, she hears.

—That you, love?

She booms from the front room. *Fuck*. Like an apparition, she appears at the bottom of the stairway, blocking the corridor to the front door. Adjusting the bag on my shoulder, I say, —That's me away now. I'll be back after the break.

—How long's the break again?

—Ah, it's only for a few weeks. I'll be back before I know it.

I laugh, but there is no joy in this thought.

—And I assume you will be paying your share of the heating bills while you're away? If you could leave the money owed on the side before you go it'd mean the world. I'm not able to heat this place myself. I'd be much better off taking proper lodgers and not students.

Mrs Cooper does not move from where she stands. She watches for what I will do next. Dropping my bag, I unzip it and fish around for my purse in the depths. My hand finds everything else first: tissues, receipts, and pens. Then I feel it. Grabbing the tenner from the purse I approach Mrs Cooper, her hand is outstretched waiting for the offering.

I step out the door and onto the pavement, hoping I see nobody on the way to the bus. My hair is thrown up in a bun on top of my head and I'm head to toe in sports gear. I don't want to be caught dead looking like this, God forbid if Hannah or Chloë were to see me now. The rain pours, but far too many people are packed under the bus shelter, so I stand in an alcove to avoid the biggest drops. While there, I check my phone for any messages or missed calls: nothing. I click through the screen to open my messages and text the girls' group on Blackberry Messenger, —See you all after the holidays! Hope Santa's good to ye.

The chatter in the group chat bounces on without an acknowledgement. Chloë and Hannah message about the unfurling of holiday plans before them: Christmas Eve pints in village pubs; Boxing Night night out in Liverpool; and surely the biggest of them all, New Year's Eve. Only the glitziest and most glam dresses will do. They ricochet outfit choices, venue ideas, and if they should invite that wee ride from the Modernism module. He has a girlfriend, they think. This doesn't matter to Chloë though. She's undeterred.

—Sure, just because there's a goalie doesn't mean you can't score.

Aye, that's enough of that for the year, I think, before turning my phone on silent, burying it in my pocket. Homewards.

# 15

Andy and I sit in a greasy spoon, both pawing at the Christmas temporary staff application forms he printed at his ma's house. The high-street café chain had just opened in a brand-spanking new shopping complex in the city. We both agreed how much fun it would be to work together; it'd be cracker to be paid to hang out. We're sipping on tea brewed in a big metal pot, dividing it out between us. Him filling my cup as I read over the application forms. There's a moment of sheer bliss right when we see the waitress bring our sausage sodas towards our table. We dig in, mouths half-filled with carbs as we natter about our Christmas plan to get work for a few weeks, to tide us over until we're back in university. We scrawl our names on the page, passing the pen between ourselves. A huge blank text box sits under the word: Experience?

—Does being a full-time legend count? he says.

A few days later, we both interview, one after the other, the interviewer sliding over the bench to interview Andy after me. We start the next day, stacking cans of San Pellegrino, which neither of us had ever heard of never mind tasted. The metal seal on the cans was enough to portray the grandeur held within. The manager explicitly told us these were beyond our employee complimentary drinks. We spend most of our days playing 'who would you rather' and listing the most repulsive options for the other. Who would you rather: Santa or the Pope? Disciplinaries came when customers overheard these debates. Our manager sneers to us that Santa isn't even *real,* as if the penalty of the game was to ride the one you picked. A kind of riding Russian roulette.

We skipped off shift at the end of the day, bunching our aprons and T-shirts in our lockers. Stripping off our milk-stained clothing from our skin in the windowless staff room. I spritz the air with perfume between us and run through it. I throw a dress over my head and him a shirt over his. Stowed away in his satchel, there's a bottle of rosé for us to drink before heading out. The benches in the middle of the locker-room become our makeshift bar. In lieu of glasses, we pass the bottle between us, taking generous swigs.

The music on the shop floor is ominously lacking in the staff room, a fact which is celebrated in the run up to the Christmas holidays. Filling the silence, I jump to my feet and begin singing, like a choir of cats. For encouragement, I take another long gulp of the bottle, spin round on my heel and sing at the top of my lungs. The wine sloshes around in my otherwise empty stomach. I pass the wine-bottle-microphone to Andy, who, between gulps, continues the chorus. We only quieten when the 9.30 p.m. shift workers begin to trickle into the room, one by one, taking the craic out the door with them.

—Ah, fuck this, Andy says.

He offers me his crooked arm, singing as we descend the staircase to exit the building. I hastily text Danielle and Aisling: **You for going out tonight?** Neither respond before I'm sober enough to reply in any sensible way. One thing leads to another and suddenly we are in a glitter-walled club at 2 a.m., shouting so loud that we can simultaneously hear so much it hurts while also hearing nothing at all that was said.

Andy shouts in my ear, —Real gold! Cuts your throat a little! Drunk quicker!

I think he's gone mad. At the bar, he orders four of the Goldschläger for good measure. One to pop the cherry then one to really experience it without the thrill of the new. The first burns down with an intense festive taste. Andy lifts the second, clinks my shot glass, and knocks it back.

I say, —See you tomorrow!

I throw my head back to receive the burning liquid. The night passes with strobe lights and shot glasses. It blurs until there is no memory there at all. A total void where I should be.

Morning light filters through the curtains, peeling my eyelids from my dried-out head. I remember the outline of mouths moving on the dance floor. No audible words, only the static sound pulsing from inside my own head. The music feels like it's within my head, like a dentist's drill breaking through my eardrums. Lifting one hand to my face, I feel the tender squishiness of bruising on my cheek. The front of my dress is mottled with sick, and, thankfully, only Andy in the bed beside me.

Fucking hell, everything hurts, I mumble to myself as I shunt up onto my forearms, scanning the room for a pint of water. There's no such luck to be found amongst the chaos. My phone is tucked under the pillow. Three missed calls from the café manager, and one text explaining we'd been seen drinking in work, so they won't be needing us in again. I roll back over and go to sleep for a couple of hours.

The sound of the buzzer in the flat wakes me. It is so shrill it scrapes my nerve-endings. Andy pops his head around the corner of the doorway. He has a mug of tea in his hand. There's one on for me in the kitchen, he tells me.

—Jesus wept. My head is banging. Have you any painkillers in your bag?

I shake my head. I don't remember where my bag is never mind the contents.

—What the fuck happened? I say as I assess my body, covered in deep cuts, red raw bruises around my legs and thighs, and a dull ache around my middle. I move with the blankets draped over my shoulders into the living room.

—Goldschläger, mate. Drinks in, wits out. Fun though! he says.

I'm not entirely sure what that means. The buzzer on the flat continues.

—For fuck's sake, I'm dying here, can't they fuck off?

He jumps up so quickly it makes me jolt. He thunders to the intercom, —What?!

Apologetic, Andy opens the door to let Danielle into the flat.

—Good night then, lads? she says, raising her eyebrows to me while Andy has his back turned at the fridge.

He milks the teas, offering his own mug to Danielle as he fixes himself another. I sip my tea slowly, hoping the heat from the mug will ease my aches.

I ask Andy, —Did I take a tumble or something?

—Must have.

When I slowly peel the covers away, Danielle catches a glimpse of my legs and, for seemingly the first time, the bruise on my cheek.

—What happened to you, love? Did you get into a fight?

Andy laughs, —Aye a fight with the pavement!

—I can't really remember, to be honest. All a bit of a mad one last night. Never again though!

—Aye, love, that's what they all say.

A cold sweat slicks over me as my ears begin to ring. It's hard to keep up with the conversation but I see Andy becoming more animated. Cheshire cat grin spreading over his face, his head nodding towards me. His arms are wide now, leaning over to nudge Danielle, bringing her in on a joke. The ringing is getting louder in my head. I can barely concentrate. A whisper of a smile forces its way across my face. I don't want to let on how close to boking I am. This hangover is a killer. Never again will another shot pass my lips, I promise.

Andy sticks *Come Dine with Me* on the TV and we settle into silence. My body aches. I ask Andy if I can borrow a tracksuit so I can get a taxi with whatever dignity I have left. Inside the sanctuary of the locked toilet, I phone a taxi while applying a soft layer of concealer to my eye. I must have hit the deck pretty hard. All the numbers I try are engaged while one rings out. The battery on my phone is holding on for dear life. Sure, I was meant to be home in my own bed, charger plugged in to the wall, bottle of coke – full fat – on the bedside table prepared from yesterday afternoon. I was meant to be managing this much better. Instead, I'm gripping the cold porcelain sink, staring straight down the plug hole. The smell of mould in this bathroom feels like its own climate: humid, colder that the rest of the flat. There are two furry bulbs growing from the wall around the shower, fungi protruding like limbs from the dark fuzz on the brick. In the sink, two braids of hair clog the plug. Water floods around it, washing up grime from the strands, sticking to the sides of the bowl. I'm sick. It brings no relief, seeing it swimming there with old hair.

In an attempt to salvage myself from the wreck, I pat on some cheap concealer under my eyes. The combination somehow creates a grey illusion on my face, highlighting each of the hours I haven't slept. My arms and legs are blooming with fresh bruises. I lightly touch each to test whether there's anything more concerning beneath the flesh, broken bones, sprains. The tights I was wearing are cut to ribbons, held to my body with the hardened stickiness of blood. I need my bed. Desperately.

My legs kiss the cold ceramic seat. There's fresh pink on the toilet paper. Then a sharp sting between my thighs. As I wipe again, the dryness of the tissue adds to the pain. My calves are bruising, the early stages of pink and red splotches speckling my legs. It's all too tender to the touch. I feel suddenly lightheaded. It's as if the inside of my head is pulsing, the world feels like it's collapsing in. My bones feel like they're rattling in my hands as I type the taxi numbers again. Perched on the edge of the bath, I pray one of them sends a car to take me back to my bed. The one receptionist I get through to says —Nothing available in your area, love. Call back in fifteen.

Bitter experience tells me that they always say that, and then stop answering. I throw my tights in the bin, and head towards the city centre. I'll get the fucking bus.

# 16

Pulling myself up from my bed the next day is torture. Lifting the duvet feels like ripping off a plaster from an unhealed wound. To add insult to injury Ma hasn't put the heating on. She did a quiz recently in one of her magazines which gave advice on how to cut costs at home. I can see my own breath in here, more incentive to get the layers on and get out into the town.

Even at this early hour, Royal Avenue is decked out in flickering Christmas lights: Santa's arms light up to give the semblance of waving; stars upon stars hanging from electric bunting; *Nollaig Shona Daoibh*. The Continental Market is in full flow within the gates of City Hall. A herd of people pushing towards the Lavery's beer tent, to get a taste of Bradbury Place on Donegall Square. My hangover is calling out for a caffeine hit to chase the brain fog away. As if by luck or miracle, a coffee shop appears on the horizon, a godsend for my dehydrated soul. As usual, I order a latte with an extra shot, and heap in two sugars: that should go part of the way to reviving me. The music blaring out of the coffee shop radio is nauseating; the chimes from the Christmas music are drilling right into my skull. I just about make it outside with my coffee in hand, and park myself on the steps outside an upmarket department store. The coldness of the flagstones is sharp against me, making the sting in my legs sing.

Once the caffeine hits my bloodstream, I press on past this, past the Ulster Hall and the BBC, up towards a pool hall. I hadn't seen the girls all that much since I came back, with working all the hours going at the coffee shop. Aisling and Danielle arrive shortly after I do, armed with the usual questions about how life is in the 'big city'. We hadn't seen much of it in the daylight while they were over, so there's a lot of ground to cover.

—Do they have a big Topshop there? What shops are there that we don't have?

—And what about the boys? Any rides?

I mumble through some of the names of the vintage shops which dot around the city, though it means nothing to both them and me. I'd never actually bought a thing in any of them. The musky smell of dust lingers on those dresses too long. Rotten. An awkward silence follows. I ask what they've been up to, and if there is anything going on with them. I want them to give me the feeling of how it was before I left. Friendship is like picking up a book, they say, but right now, I cannot speak the language.

We take it in turns to play, though none of us are that invested in the winning. In truth, more effort goes into the joking around the failed shots than the successes. After several games, a man comes over and sets his coin on the side of the table. We finish up and take our pints outside to the alley-long smoking area. We pace until we find a spot under a heat lamp, so we can sustain the winter weather until our beer-jackets come on us.

Aisling, who always feels the drink first, says, —So, what's happening with Andy, then?

I choke on my feg smoke as I inhale. My eyebrows scrunch and wave like a caterpillar moving across the floor. When I exhale, I say, —What d'ya mean?

My heart rate begins to pulse in my neck, I can feel myself clamming up and feeling confused.

Danielle changes the subject, —So, what're the other students like across the water?

Several pints later, Aisling and Danielle are leaning against the wall in the smoking area. I'm sidling my way through the crowd while balancing three pints in a triangle grip. I eventually make it over to them without spilling too much beer on those I passed. They both take their drinks with the care of the moon-landing;

nobody wants to navigate back to the bar to start this process over again. I hand Danielle my pint so I can light a cigarette.

When she passes it back to me, she says, —Oh go on then, tell us.

I exhale smoke and say, —What?

Aisling, now bleutered, is the first to crack. —You and Andy, go on, spill.

She takes a well-timed drag to allow the question to stew. A laugh escapes up my throat in a bubble.

—What're you talking about?

My mind races. Images of vomiting. Gurgling no. Danielle shushes Aisling, telling her not to pry.

—I haven't a clue what's going on?

A feeling swells in me, making my heart feel like it'll come through my neck. With every beat, I feel nausea rise. The hairs on my skin stand on end as my body temperature drops. It's in my ears. My head. The low thump marching into battle. I am not equipped with the words to arm my voice with.

—I don't know what you mean.

Aisling spits out, —Ah, come off it. Thought you told us everything.

The next thing I know I'm standing at the bus shelter outside the main doors to the bar. I've left my coat in the smoking area propped against the wall. I think, fuck it, and leave it behind. I walk to the SOS van. A yellow bus equipped with everything anybody could need when on the rip: biscuits or a lift to get stitches at the hospital. I pour myself a cup of sugary tea from the canister. The man in the yellow jacket asks me if I'm alright. Before I can muster a response, I am further down the street.

—Yeah. Fine, I say to nobody in particular.

Sanctuary is provided by the sugary liquid as it warms my insides, streaming down my throat. The taxi picks me up outside the UGC cinema. I get in, still clutching the empty paper cup which held my tea. The sides of the cardboard buckle under my grip.

—No drinking in the car, love, the driver says.

Scrunching the cup, I stuff it into my handbag. He turns in his seat to check I've not made a mess in his vehicle. He eyes me, checking I'm not too far gone for a taxi. I reach for my phone, and see I have numerous missed calls and texts from Danielle, and one with an incomprehensible series of letters from Aisling. I turn my phone off and stuff it in with the cup.

# 17

There's an ache when I pee.
    Burning.
        Throbbing.

Stinging between by legs.
    Sharp.
        Sudden.

Bruising on my things. In shades of purple and green.
    Speckled with red dots.
        Pinpricks.

Like the tops of each capillary have individually burst.
    A dot to dot on flesh.

## 18

The buildings are dusty with disrepair; the original long eroded, only held together now by its alterations. Lashings of posters and billboards are stuck to the walls, obscuring any brickwork underneath. Graffiti climbs the walls, magenta, florescent, indecipherable. The city unravels like threads, with side entries and cul-de-sacs twisting as they lead me towards the Brook. With every step I can feel the sole of my knock-off baseball shoes falling through, slapping the sodden pavement like a flip-flop. I know vaguely where I'm going; it's somewhere down one of these streets. Discreet, the doorway appears unadorned, hidden in plain sight next to a shuttered-up shop. Like a prayer, my hand meets the frame, before I'm brave enough to take the first step inside.

The doorway isn't much to write home about. A foyer no bigger than a cardboard box, carpeted in a colour that looks like it used to be bright beige, the freshness worn down by feet stamping the cold off their boots, finding shelter inside this building. The stairs start immediately as you go in, ascending to a wide corridor, with lino flooring, curving up the base of the walls. The whole space feels like being inside a Tupperware box, everything is shiny and laminated in the hope of preservation or sterilisation.

Cartoon condoms wave from the walls. *Stay Safe, Play Safe! Come on in!* a speech bubble says, while the tail of a friendly cartoon sperm points 'this way' to the reception. This place, I swear to God.

The woman behind the desk doesn't even notice me come in. She's staring down at the sudoku puzzle from yesterday's paper. Numbers scribbled out and written in the margins. I'm standing at the counter, arms on the glass countertop when she finally takes stock of another person in the room. She jumps. Without speaking she spins on her chair to a paperwork tray on the table behind her. She clips a couple of forms to a board with a ballpoint pen attached to it by a string. Pointing towards the row of chairs against the backwall, she tells me to bring them back when I'm done filling them in.

The first questions are a doddle: name, age, date of birth. I get to 'GP surgery contact details' next and decide that is a risk too far. What if the nurse who went to school with Ma touts? Nah, life wouldn't be worth living. I leave it blank and move onto the more difficult questions: Number of Sexual Partners; Last Period Date; Days Since Sex. My head is melted with all of this.

Before I even get the chance to fill in the answers, time's up, and a nurse steps towards me.

—You done with that?

I hand it to her almost blank. The page has been softened by my sweaty palms. I apologise for it.

Inside the room, the nurse takes my blood pressure, my temperature, and hands me a tube with a little twizzler to get a sample. Covering all bases, she tells me. I'm sure you are. It stings. I can't keep it in for long. When I pull the swab out, it's tinged with pink. I return from behind the blue curtain.

—Everything alright, love? You made a quare gasp in there.

She's wearing blue gloves, as I hand her the tube containing my swab. It drops into a clear plastic envelope. A barcode sticker is attached to the front.

—Letter, text, or telephone for your results?

Absolutely fucking not. I'm sweating now, I can't risk anybody picking up a letter on the doormat. Ma wouldn't be able to contain herself. She'd have to steam it open and reseal. I'd never know. And telephone? What if I don't get to it in time? What if there's voicemail evidence? And I can't even begin to process what sort of person you would have to be to get STD results texted to you. Nah to all of this. I try to say all this in not so many words.

—Yeah.

That's all that comes out. Just the one word.
—Yes to what, love?
—Yeah, no, can you not just tell me now? Or can I come back?
It turns out you can't haggle with healthcare. I accept defeat and hand over my phone number, for nothing but texts only.

The nurse has swivelled round in her chair, sitting square on to the computer. Her nails make a dull noise against the keyboard, a kind of soft clicking noise with each tap as if the machine is alive and responsive to touch. I'm daydreaming about climbing into my bed, the duvet swallowing me up as I descend through the down. Plaid jammies and a hot water bottle. Rain ticking off the window as it bounces from pane to windowsill. I hope the Chinese is open by the time I get home. The cure.

—Love?

The nurse's voice brings me back to the bare-bulb glow of the clinic.

—When was the last time you had sex?

I tell her the truth: I can't remember. She tilts her head forward, urging me on.

*Goldschläger. Dancing. Hurt my knee.* I've my legging pulled up by the time I realise what I'm at. She's put her hand on my shoulder. She's asking the words which turn me inside out, —Are you OK?

Once the tears start, I can't stop, streaming across cheek to nose. The salty drips move past my lips. Underneath me, the legs of the chair tremble with my body.

Soft as butter, the nurse tells me what we're going to do. The questions come quick now, more efficient. She ticks them off a sheet, before telling me she'll be right back. When she returns, she has a plastic container of water and a blister pack containing a single pill. I'm going to take a tablet now, just in case, I'm told. I must take it there and then. The tablet feels dry as it goes down my throat. The nurse is speaking again. She's saying that we're going to do some more swabs, for the police, if that is what I want to do.

I'm up out of my seat. Police? I can't. I don't even know what went on. I'll be more than just a tout; I'll be a liar. I'm on my way out of the room when the sting between my thighs punctures my stride. My body doubles over. With one arm around my shoulder, I'm guided by the nurse back to the hard plastic seat. She's over at the sink, getting another plastic cup of water for me. I'm offered a tea, too. But no words or movements come in response to this kindness.

—Do you have somebody who can come be with you for this?
—No.

The next few minutes happen in a sequence of bulletins that I semi-understand. *City Hospital . . . waiting . . . doctors will take care . . . phone call . . . you will need to . . .* The texture of the words prickle. Waves of nausea wash over my skin. Shivering. *Swab kit . . . name . . . try to . . . very brave . . . you've options . . . copper . . . discomfort . . . can I call . . . risk . . .* I can't do this.

I've bombed out of there without so much as a packet of free NHS condoms. I'm halfway towards the City Hall when it finally dawns on me. Every person I pass has that look on their face like they know where I've been, what I've done. They can read it in my facial expression. I tuck my head into myself and barrel on towards home.

Ma is on the phone to one of her mates from the community centre when I come in the door. She doesn't put the phone away from the space between her chin and shoulder, instead she raises one hand to wave, before pointing her thumb at the phone, just in case I thought she was just pretending. I drop my bag on the kitchen floor, and instinctively check the fridge for anything to eat. There are jars of chutneys, jams, and a full cheeseboard wrapped in cellophane, ready to go. A whole leg of lamb. A clove-studded ham. The vegetable drawer is fit to burst. There's nothing in the fridge I can touch before the big day, for fear of Ma's wrath. Her days of careful preparation, and her sanity, all hinge on every morsel remaining accounted for until the exact moment. I play it safe, pressing crisps between two buttered slabs of plain white loaf.

# 19

When I get up on Christmas Eve, the tree is glittering at the bottom of the stairs, presents wrapped in gold and red wrapping paper neatly tucked in at its foot. Ma must have got up at the crack of dawn; the house smells of roasted ham, cinnamon candles, and the heat of the fairy lights bouncing off our plastic tree. I come down the stairs in my red plaid pyjamas, two sizes too big, paired with slippers with deep grey shadows of past wears.

—Awk love, why aren't you wearing your dressing gown? You'll catch your death.

Even before a word has slipped out of my mouth, she continues, —I'll not hear a word of it. Go on back up those stairs and get it. We'll be inviting no colds in this house.

I turn back up the stairs to grab the dressing gown I've had since I was twelve. It used to be pink; now it would be best described as a shade of dust. Wrapping myself up in it, a cold sweat films my skin. The soft fleecy material is itching my arms. It's as if the room is shrinking, suffocating me.

When I come back downstairs, Ma gets a good look at me. Her eyes tell me that I'm looking worse for wear this morning. The ache is building. Undeniably. My thighs are stippled in purple and scratches. My underwear is stained in streaks of red, which have begun to dry down to rust on the cotton. I feel sick. These cramps are fucking killing me, it feels like a cheese grater on my insides. I try and distort my body into comfort but with every movement the pain persists. Ma's hand stretches out to mine, she asks if I'm OK. She wants to know if it's my 'time of the month'. Yeah, sure, I agree with her. Anything to get her to stop with the questions. She shuffles off to get me some paracetamol from under the kitchen sink. This ache is unlike any I've felt before, a deep stinging burn. Andy was holding me. Vomit on my dress and in my hair. I run to the toilet to spew up the toast I've just eaten. A torrent flowing from me to the bowl.

Two church spires jut out towards the sky. As a child, they reminded me of bunny ears set in stone. Inside, the hall is bigger than I remember, space extending into every crevice and corner, shadows falling everywhere. The crowd begins to trickle in, from home or the pub. Raised eyebrows let me know whether Ma reckons they've had a skinful already. We go to church once a year, for Christmas Eve midnight Mass, which in this part of the world is always held at 9 p.m. It's the one time of year where the whole neighbourhood comes together in complete pageantry. Old Mrs Hannity shuffles in, a plastic bonnet tied around her newly set hair, saving it from any stray raindrops. The Millar boys come in five minutes after the rest of their family, sitting just enough off to the side to have plausible deniability that they were ever in the church. Their heads scan the room, checking out who else has been roped into this. In the final moments before it begins, older men slip into the back pews. The stench of long days spent inside the Landsdowne pub drifts in behind them.

Father Peter welcomes us; his voice sounds as if it's being transmitted from an old radio broadcast: tinny, silken, so boring. Like the rest of the congregation, he's decked out in his Christmas finery. Gold and white draped over him. I wonder if he's wearing a jumper under it, with all the heat this place has. Still, Ma has made both Da and me take our coats off. To make sure that people know we're not looking for a quick exit, she tells us.

The words are hard to forget, like riding a bike or singing an old song, it's always there, dormant. We, the congregation, speak as one, —For we have sinned against you.

The three of us are kneeling, the cushioned rail for our kneecaps offering anything but comfort. Ma's face is scrunched as she moves her weight from one knee to the other. Back on our feet, we shake hands with as many people as possible around us. —Peace be with you, mumbled with every palm touched. Ma is taking a mental note of who she can see, and more importantly, who she can't.

Before we're freed to go back to our Christmases, Father Peter gives a sermon about charity and Christmas cheer, sharing and forgiveness. Ma's head is tilted, her eyes scanning left and right. I can nearly hear the cogs turning in her head, chalking up to-do lists ahead of the big day tomorrow: what time the roast should be in the oven, peeling the spuds, is there enough drink in for us?

Hellos are said to everybody, Ma making sure that we've not missed anybody on our way out. Da and I are hovering by the gate, nodding a hello to anybody we know by name. The walk home takes three times as long, with us stopping for her to chat to so-and-so whose son was in my year in primary school. Her catching up with us, electric with gossip. Back in the house, a domed plate of cold meats is set in front of me. It is more than I've eaten in the previous three months. I'm no longer used to these portions. We sit at the dinner table, sharing a cheese board and bottles of wine. Ma, Da, and me.

We shovel the food into us, mostly in silence. The only sound is Da's chewing. After, he carries the plates into the kitchen and goes to light the fire in the living room. I lift a cushion and sit in front of it, warming my shoulders and back.

Ma says, —When you're that close, you'll overheat; you'll not feel the benefit of it when you move!

I shift diagonally away from the fire and towards the sofa. Together we sit watching *Wallace & Gromit: The Wrong Trousers* on the TV. It's a holiday tradition for us, watching the plasticine duo ignore the emotional cues from one another: we laugh at their obliviousness.

Ma insists on recording the news if she knows she will be out in the evening. It's nearly midnight by the time we are just sticking on the ten o'clock news. The news reader has updated us where Santa was on his journey from the North Pole to Northern

Ireland. Children are then warned to be tucked up in bed, Santa will be arriving soon. The regular headlines carry on: deaths at a steel factory in China; the Sri Lankan Civil War; news from Palestine's Gaza Strip. I take the laptop upstairs to my room. Then I set my tea on the bedside table and open the screen.

When I log on to Facebook, the first image that appears on my screen is of Aisling, Danielle and Andy down in the Landsdowne. The background tells me they are just up the road from where I am now. I mute the television in my bedroom and watch the presenter's mouth, the words fizzing with the future. The wind carries the din of the pub, hushing over the traffic. The time stamp tells me that the photo was uploaded by Aisling just twenty-seven minutes ago. I would have been in the kitchen then, watching for the button on the kettle to pop. The blood on my face flushes cold with embarrassment.

Throwing back the covers from my bed, I hurl across the room to check my phone is on. Surely, I missed the call; the signal can be wild patchy. We've never let anything come between us; that's always been the sanctity of our friendship; we used to always forgive our own trespasses. I soothe myself that maybe the signal went off in the area with a surge of well-wishers texting at once, like what happens on New Year's. The exclusion weighs on my chest. I close the laptop screen over and grab my towel for a shower.

The water pours around my head, flowing straight from my hairline into my eyes and mouth. My breath pumps against my chest. As I crank the temperature hotter, the room begins to steam up. Tender thighs have given way to bruising, a dull ache under my skin. My nails pierce my skin. There is tingling in my arms. Adrenaline. My hands scratch at the skin on my upper thighs first. I am still in control. I know that I can hide it under a mini skirt. The heat in the shower fades my vision. Everything feels like static electricity. Bubbles from the shampoo feel like they are somehow pushing out from within me. My nails are muddied with watered down blood. Crimson sticks to under the nailbed. I take the cap from the bottle of the shampoo, and begin on my chest, my arms, and then my neck. I press the edges into my flesh, twisting. The compulsion doesn't end until the heat forces me to sit on the shower floor. Dizziness as if the room were pulsing. Huffing in air through the droplets.

The next morning, I sit with a coffee at the kitchen table. The cookbooks are stacked high to the left and right of the hob, little paper marker off-shoots appearing from the leaves. The lights are still off on the tree; the house is eerily quiet. I'm up early to stick the leg of lamb in the oven. To busy my hands, I roll the napkins around cutlery. I type out my usual festive text to everyone. It sends. I delete it from my sent box to hide my shame.

It comes to me in waves. I'm thrown about the room. My voice is drowning in my head. Muffled. No. It's always just out of reach. As if I'm not making myself clear. The room is swirling. Photograph edges grow spiky, elongating, like fingers stretching out. The rug is wobbling under my legs, shaking them; my feet no longer trust the ground. My face tingles, flushing cold. A thick skin covers my ears, holding in the sound of screaming inside my head. The TV is flickering coloured lights around the room, but I can't hear it. The bin meets my chin. Vomit curls up the sides, ricocheting off Quality Street wrappers. The plastic hushes me as I gag. As a kid, I wrapped the violet cellophane around my glasses, layering a yellow or blue, creating a kaleidoscope out of the bare bulbs in the living room. Now, they swim in a current of bile and boke.

# 20

Boxing Day sales are never what they're cracked up to be. 'Up to 70% Off' the ads on the TV have been claiming. There's not a chance of finding anything worth having at that knock-down price, though. But I can't be moping about the house forever. I pull on my jeggings with my old Doc Martens layered over the top. A new jumper that Ma knit me for Christmas drapes my hands, doubling as clothing and gloves.

I always mean to go to the local coffee chain, but truth be told, the Seattle fellas know how to do it better. I feel my anxiety begin to leave my body as soon as I have a heavily sugared coffee. The shops have taken on a kind of haunted sadness with the Christmas decorations remaining up, the music slowly beginning to phase back to regular background tunes. It's sad to see the decorations this way, shining as if it will stop them from being bunged up in a warehouse for the next nine months. I slide past all the tat on sale and make my way to the Christmas chocolates in want of a home. Outside I snap the ear off a reindeer shaped chocolate lolly. They never taste as good as they look.

Sunshine comes through the glass walls of the shopping centre, marbling reds and blues on the pavement, like a wave on cement blocks. I'm still fifteen minutes early, so I take the long route through House of Fraser, twisting and turning through the rails, narrowly avoiding sales assistants approaching with their finger on the trigger of the latest Yves Saint Laurent perfume. Out the other side, my face is tilted up to the winter sun – if such a thing can really exist. There he is. Right there. Fuck.

Our eyes catch. He doesn't look away. Instead, he turns to face me square on. He pauses for a moment before walking straight towards me.

He shouts, one hand cupping his mouth, —Oi, Fee!

What feels like an electric shock reverberates out from my stomach, quickening my feet in the opposite direction. I'm walking as fast as I can, without looking like I'm breaking out into a jog through the shopping centre. Andy's following, continuing to shout my name. Would he ever away and fuck off?

The flagstones are unsteady under my feet. Next thing I've gone arse over tit. I'm done for. Accepting my fate, I lie there and stare up at the balconies of shops on the higher levels. And then, there he is. Above me.

—Training for the marathon, are ya?

His hand outstretched, pulling me to my feet. The words dry in my mouth, sticking to the space around my tongue. I'm on my feet, steadying myself. His hand remains on my arm. The grip tightens as I try and pull away. The words won't come. Slowly, he moves his head towards mine. A flicker crosses his face, looking around for a nearly imperceptible moment. He leans in closer, locking his gaze on me.

—Fucking dare you to ignore me again. He spits, before his face shifts to a smile. —I thought we were pals?

People buzz around us on the upper balconies. The sound of them is close and intense; I can hear everything and nothing all at once. My cheeks are cold and sweaty. An electric surge of adrenaline shakes my bones as I push away. As they power me away from him, my leg muscles feel like jelly beneath me. Each step to the exit feels like Everest. I don't dare look back at him, even though I can hear my name echoing through the sound of Saturday shoppers.

Once around the corner, I pick up speed. Taking no chances with him changing his mind. I'm off. I take a right down Pottinger's Entry, the brickwork awning close. A busker stops strumming as I run over his guitar case, splashing coppers over the street. I only slow when I burst out on to High Street. I can see the greasy spoon where I'm meeting the girls.

The café occupies the corner building, facing the derelict district, shells of grand Victorian buildings falling into rack and ruin. Kids with their three leets of cider stumbling through the area, searching for a boarded doorway begging to be pushed through. I open the door into 'the best diner in the city'. The red plastic covered seats in the booths hold decades worth of secret discussions: hangover breakfasts, crisis talks after an affair, lunch-hour sanctuary. It's glorious.

The woman at the front till welcomes me, just as I see Danielle's arm shooting into up from the booth they've grabbed in the far corner. I give the waitress a little wave to let her know that I'm sorted for now. Danielle is pouring a pot of tea as I sit down.

—The day I've had, swear. I inhale, as I lift the mug to my lips. I tell them I've just ran into Andy up in the shops.

Before I can continue, the two girls both gush.

—Ah you two! When will you two just wise the bap and come out and say it!

—Mon out with it! Tell us!

—You two need your heads seeing to. He's awful!

Aisling bristles. Her eyes rolling into the back of her head. She mumbles into her tea, —Nothing here is good enough for you now.

—What was that?

I should have said nothing. Responding at all has given Aisling the green light. Her speech picks up speed, racing from one word to the next as she tells me that Andy is very sought after, actually. She should know, she says, with a look to Danielle with practised ease, barely masking her seething. I can feel the words forming, though unable to find their form on my lips. A cold rush tingles down my body, from my face into my arms. I'm holding the mug of tea tight, letting it burn my hands.

# Part Three

## 21

The ceramic warps the little beacons of light, creating tides on the tiles. This is it though: I can't stop thinking about my legs, never mind the fucking light. In my hand, I'm squeezing the metal prongs tight. The outline leaves a little indent in my flesh. My muscles tense, harder again, as I sew the tips of the tweezers through the skin on my thigh. Dipping the metal in and out, the punctures increase in size. Once the pain settles, I go in again and again, building up the depth of the cut each time. My hand slips on the final pierce, and a pool of blood creates a perfect sphere on my skin. It looks like a lollipop, a bulbous clot shining. I don't wipe it up just yet, but let it slowly trickle down my leg as I stand. A single stripe on my pale thigh.

I hear the phone chime. No doubt it's Chloë. Wondering where I am. I know I'm late. She can wait though. I continue knitting my skin, creating a bleeding ellipsis. I smear it with my fingertips before I clean up. As always, I fold a tissue over and over until it becomes a perfect square. After that, I roll on a pair of tights. The sensation is electric: the threads fusing with the cut as it weeps.

The club is tucked in a cave-like basement underneath Heebie Jeebies. Sweat and breath drip from a ceiling close enough to touch. The three of us huddle together and imagine Seel Street above. Hannah is pressed up against the bar with Chloë and me behind her. She shouts over her shoulder to check our orders. She's buying this one as a 'belated festive gift.' Her arm stretches, offering a shot glass with a lemon slice balanced on top. Tequila, for fuck's sake. Warm tins of Red Stripe wash away the burning taste.

On the dance floor, our feet stick to the ground. Beer stamped down to its sugars. Florence and the Machine's 'Rabbit Heart' blares through the amps. The opening strings send us into euphoria. We jump and twist, knocking our way around in front of the speakers. Screaming the words, twirling circles with our arms outstretched wide, not a care in the world for consequence. I feel invincible with those two beside me. Buzzing. Our limbs are slowed by the pints, but still we dance. I have never felt an affinity with anyone the way I do with these women. We conspire in smoking areas, discussing our planned conquests. Singling out the men in the bar, setting our sights on them. Dancing close, keeping our eyes on each other, then laughing it off as we stumble to the bar again.

The nights zip past in a blur of quad vods, blue alcopops with a carefully placed straws to stop the rush of bubbles into our stomachs. In another bar, Sweet Female Attitude's 'Flowers' plays from the jukebox which looks like a laptop screen stuck to a cigarette machine. Next, some sort of beer mixed with tequila, little lines of coke, or ket, or mcat. It doesn't really matter to be fair. They all leave the same drip down the back of my throat; a faucet burning from my nose. The same metallic taste.

We get talking to some guy who says he's from a *new sonic art gallery that you probably haven't heard of.* Traipsing out of the club, we follow him to a house party on the outskirts of the city. He doesn't introduce us to anybody when we arrive. Instead, he leads me by the hand to the bog, tips the white powder from the bag onto the cistern. He pulls out a bank card.

—Thought you were called Barry or something? I say, pointing to the bank card.

—Ben. It's Ben. And that's my ould fella.

Shameless, he uses his Da's credit card to rack a line on the top of the bog. The English, I swear. I don't even bother to respond. My eyes are fixed as he rolls up a fiver. Tucking the blue Queen into the rolled paper, leaving only her eyes poking out. She can take her face for a shite and all, I think. A little laugh escapes me.

## Exile

Ben's face crumples in on itself, as if his eyebrows were folding into his sockets.

—Colonialism, innit? is all I say.

In my head, I repeat 'innit'. Where'd that come from?

—You what? Colons?

This time with the extra effort of enunciating my words as clearly as I can, —I said, colonialism.

The cogs in his head look like they're trying to find the combination of words that will reduce me to silence. I don't give him the benefit of quietness for long.

—She's an ould bitch, isn't she? Your Queen. Destroyed half the world. Empire, you know? She's even on ours, too. The notes. Everywhere.

A look comes over Ben that tells me he wishes he'd invited any other blonde into the loo with him. He wasn't banking on being trapped in a small space with a walking history lesson, even if I do come with tits.

He gestures to the powdery slug. —That's yours.

My phone buzzes in my pocket. I only lift it out to check it isn't Hannah or Chloë on the hunt for me. It's beyond belief: an automated text from the hospital to say I'm not riddled with STDs. I don't even care how generic it is, as if spurted out by a machine. I'm over the fucking moon. Quick as lightening, the line zips from the porcelain up my nostril. I get an instant headrush before that rotten taste settles at the back of my throat. My jaw tenses. Back in the living room turned dance floor, my neck suddenly feels longer on my shoulders. I'm worried about how I can hold my head up. What does it weigh? Like a stone? I must have some muscly neck on me to keep it up indefinitely.

What feels like a lifetime of contemplation about the strength of my muscles passes by without me saying a word to a soul. I'm staring into Ben's eyes, he's chattering away about something, and all I can think about it the logistics of keeping my head up. Christ, maybe he's an absolute ride, I think, scanning his face for confirmation. I make a conscious decision to *act normal*. Hands bounce from pockets to resting on my stomach to holding each other, back to the pockets. I'm sweating now. I concentrate on not sweating, which brings a fresh glisten on my top lip. My eyes open a little wider as I struggle to keep smiling. When I check back, my mouth is running a mile a second as we are deep in a conversation about knitwear: Jumpers! Scarves! Gloves! There isn't a knitted thing I wouldn't have an opinion on in that moment. I don't even knit. The room is lit up by one of those plug-in disco lights, alternating between blue, purple, yellow. His face is radiant, lit up in rainbow colours. He's actually unbelievably attractive, now that I'm getting a proper look at him. My face is touting on me. A downward pout and jump of the eyebrows give away what's going on in my head. I zone into the room again as he's walking away, disappearing off to the bogs again. He makes sure to go alone this time.

We crawl our way back to Hannah's flat after the party. Inside, everything is Marks & Spencer; so brand-new that the tags remain on pots and pans lined up in her room. Catching me in the process of eyeing up these wares, she snorts like a strangled goose.

—Oh, Mum sends those things for me. I don't even know how to cook!

All Ma sends me is big bags of crisps. The stench would knock your head off. As if to halt any thoughts of domesticity, Hannah squawks as she waves a new bottle of Smirnoff.

—Bitches, who's for shots?!

Her wrist twists violently, unleashing a snap as the metal top is broken. She shares the bottle around without keeping tabs on how much is left for the next night out. All the drink from the night has gone to my head. My skull is balloon-light as if it could float off through the roof. An acidic feeling burns my throat. I suggest mixer, but all she has is a sticky bottle of lime cordial. That'll do to take the edge off, she says, filling our mugs with tap water and a dash of squash.

As the night wears on into the morning, my head spins. We each lie against the wall with our heads propped backwards.

One corner of a *Breakfast at Tiffany's* poster peels away. It's like Audrey is hunched over towards us. The vodka has quickly deteriorated. A bottle of green liquid is passed between us. It tastes like sour apple sweets. Like parties in sixth year. Like the up-close breath of some fella as our heads mash together. The nostalgia dulls the sadness, briefly. I don't remember exactly how I started talking, but I did. When I realised what I was saying it was already out.

—Do you ever, like, not remember something, but you know it's probably there?

Chloë says, —Yeah, no, I don't know? What?

I tell them of the night with Andy. The bruises. The questioning. The void in my memory. I spend a lot of time describing the taste of the gold-laden shots. Cinnamon. Syrupy. I had never drunk it when I was out with the girls. They weren't there, I say. I should have missed them that night. I should have called. Aisling could have kept me right.

—Wow, wow, wow. Hold the fuck up. Go back to the fella.

—I don't think there's anything else to tell?

Hannah's now leaning up on her knees, looking directly at me while gripping the neck of the bottle. The neon liquid sloshes about inside me. Garbled words spill out. The suspicion both Aisling and Danielle had in the days after. Asking me to conjure memory where there was only darkness. A vacancy.

—And have you asked him what the fuck they meant?!

I mumble to myself and when I look up, they are both staring at each other with their mouths hung open. The vulnerability dizzies me. There is a soft hum in my ears, like static on a TV.

—What a bastard.

They want to know if they can 'just have a word' with Aisling or Danielle. I laugh, not entirely sure why.

Hannah asks with an alarming amount of sincerity, —Do you want me to cut his dick off?

The silence hangs between us. Floorboards stretch beneath us, creaking as they find their new positions. In the distance, fire doors slam shut as crowds make their way back home, if this building could be called that.

The headache reaches me before I'm able to open my eyes. A deep stench of sweated out alcohol fills Hannah's room. I've slept on the floor, curled around Chloë. The wiry carpet has left an imprint on my cheeks, arms, thighs. Everywhere hurts. Since Christmas, I've lost trust in my body. The doctors at the Brook told me that the morning after pill can cause my cycle to be irregular. My period seems to have missed the bus completely this month, not showing up for the last three weeks. It was due to arrive on Boxing Day, but nothing ever came. I unfold a leaflet from the clinic from my purse and follow its instructions to take a pregnancy test weeks later for confirmation.

Hannah insists on a trip to the shop for hangover supplies. I sneak to the pharmacy aisle, though there's no subtle way to buy a pregnancy test stowed in a security box. At the till, the shop assistant doesn't make eye contact, but she bangs the plastic casing off the counter to ensure everybody in the queue looks up. Back in the flat, Hannah, Chloë, and I crowd around the toilet; I'm sat while the two of them are crammed into the shower unit, for lack of anywhere else to stand in the vertical coffin sized room. I stretch my arms between my legs, shoulder jutting forward, I try to find the stream falling into the bowl. I overshoot the mark, urine washing over my wrist. I get it eventually, holding every muscle as still as possible to keep the test under the flow of piss. The wait for the result is agonising, each second trickling by with an awkward *how-can-we-pretend-this-is-normal* conversation. Hannah does a heroic job, to be fair. She talks about a book she recently read for her Gender Studies module, which unravels into a diatribe about Freud. Her thoughts spoken aloud switch from how Freud needed therapy after all that thinking of sons wanting the ride off their mas to the freedoms inherent in pornography. Chloë and I make eye contact only fleetingly. I examine each dark grey groove in the grouting around the tiles. I wonder at the things this bog has seen over the years of its service in student halls. How many litres of vodka have been spewed into this shitter. How many tampons accidentally flushed. Pregnancy tests, lines of something white and powdery, anything from talc to coke.

Hannah interrupts, —That should do it.

Like peering down into endless void, we all cautiously lean over the stick, which is balanced on the side of the sink. A deep red slash against the white. One red line: negative. Thank fuck. The relief should wash over my body, but it doesn't. My stomach is knitting itself inside out. Hannah and Chloë, yet to say a word, are looking at me.

—Are you OK, babe?

In my mind, I'm running through the list of things I still must do. There is just so much. What will the girls at home say? Do they already know? Heartbeat thumping as if to break through my flesh. It comes quick and fast, landing all over the wall. A torrent of spew. Hannah screeches, while Chloë tells her to wise up. My body flops on the floor. The tiles cold and tingly on my arms. I feel hot and cold at the same time. Hannah lifts me to the bed. I fall asleep with her cocooned behind me, and Chloë on the floor.

# 22

## AN INVENTORY OF THE SENSES

*Sound: Heavy, close choking. Crying. His name. My own. Nobody hears. No.*

*Touch: Pressed flesh. Skin around my eyes bangs against a shelf. Afterwards, my hands find leaky, gloopy drips.*

*Taste: Metallic acidity. Torrents of it.*

*Smell: Salt. Damp.*

*Sight: Toppled over the whole room is at a right angle. It feels tight around me. Are they there?*

*Are*

                    *you*

                                        *there?*

## 23

We're in one of those bars where the clientele ranges from seventeen through to sixty. Men in business suits huddle around the bar, pints are passed over shoulders back down the line. I can spot the underage ones a mile off as they sit around a table, holding their drinks as if they're treasure. Their eyes hop between each other as they bargain for who will be next to try and get served. Pathetic, really. We never had that bother at home. There was that one barman who would relish pouring out a vodka while staring down at our teenage tits. I knew he knew. Didn't matter though if he wasn't questioning us. These ones here have a lot to learn.

Chloë, Hannah, and I hang back, careful not to be too near the tables to look green, but far enough away from the bar that we don't look desperate for one of the ould blokes to buy us our drinks. I'm just waiting for Hannah to put her hand in her pocket; she's always the first to crumble with the rounds. Chloë and I play conversation tennis, asking each other how our mas are, and what about the assessments, are we prepared? Eventually, Hannah cracks and heads to the bar. She doesn't even ask what we're having, the cheeky bitch. We watch her slide in beside the men, then say something before they all turn around. Fucking typical.

One of the suited men comes bounding over, like if a Labrador was trapped inside a human body. His shirt tail is hanging out and his hair is begging to escape from his neck out over his shirt collar. Oh, fuck, why's he watching me? What's she said?

—The birthday girl!

I'm looking around me, wondering where he's about to land.

—Here she is! he says, helpfully putting a hand on my arm.

Fine, I play along, and pluck a character out of thin air for me to be that night: twenty-five, working in real estate, recently single. He eats this shit up. He loves it. What a fucking loser.

Hannah's making her way back over to us with a tray of glasses and a bottle of prosecco. The other business blokes are following her as if she's the Pied Piper of corporate bros. We each grab a glass as the Labrador takes the bottle in his fist to divvy it out. Chloë and Hannah settle into conversation with men they'd never be caught dead speaking to in the light of day. I'm stuck with the Labrador. He wants to know every detail about my last sale, so I tell him: four bed, Allerton, lovely family moving in, they're expecting a baby in the spring. He nods along. I add more and more details: the ex-boyfriend of three-years, who has recently up-and-left me to pay our bills myself. His face scrunches up, bordering on sadness. I pull it back and tell him that it's been a new lease of life for me. I don't even ask him about himself. I can see the ring on his finger.

The bubbles run through me. Chloë holds my drink as I head to the toilet. Without having to turn around, I know he's following. His eye catches mine in the mirror. He doesn't look away. There's forever a crowd in the ladies' bogs, so I go into the disabled toilet, leaving it open an inch. He stops on the threshold as if considering his next move, but then he's in. The door locks behind him. He asks if he should pee first or me. Soft chuckles tuck his chin into his collar. He takes a key out of his pocket, floating it towards me like a ma trying to feed her toddler.

—Here comes the airplane!

I take a deep sniff of whatever it is he's offering, before thinking I'm going to fuck the life out of him. The key hovers under his nostril. Fresh wipe down on his trousers before it's pocketed. Instigating, I push him back against the door and unbuckle him. In a split second, he's pulled my skirt up over my hips. He didn't even wait for me to pull my tights down; he's ripped a fist-sized hole in the crotch. His hand grips my throat, choking me. I can only concentrate on trying to get my breath. My head feels light as a heaviness settles in my stomach. The force feels like a punch, his body slamming into my hips. It's over as quick as it began. I feel the liquid seeping from me. The Labrador fixes himself, careful to tuck his shirt in, before leaving the toilet with the door lying open.

Looking in the mirror, I smooth the fly-aways on my back-combed hair. I pull a huge smile, testing the waters of my acting skills. The tights had to go. Stuffed in the sanitary bin. Revealing raw thighs like chicken's skin.

When I come out of the toilets, I'm tightsless in ankle boots, his jizz sticking my thighs together as I walk. Both Hannah and Chloë raise their eyes at me. Before anything else, I notice Chloë has drunk my prosecco.

I shout at her, —I hope you're buying me a new one!

We've overstayed our welcome. The circle of suits closes ranks around each other. An impenetrable wall. Backs turned to us. Chloë and Hannah begin to walk away. That's when I see the Labrador loudly telling the corporate bros about me. He has his wrist to his own throat as he mocks me. They're laughing. All of them.

We're not ready to go home yet. There's a stream of people heading down towards the city centre, so we follow them in the hope that there'll be somewhere decent to go on the way. Every few weeks a new cocktail bar pops up in the basement or attic of some old building. Hidden away. The best craic is to be found behind a doorway revealed by shifting a heavy-set curtain. Rumour has it that knocking a closed shutter for signs of life inside will bring bouncers peering through the slats. I'm looking, but all the buildings around here look genuinely residential.

Chloë's the first to ask. —What the fuck was that then?

—Awk, he wasn't so bad.

—Did you even catch his name?

—And why would I need that?

Chloë's whole body twists away from me. She's looking directly at Hannah. Their faces are saying everything for them. I've walked on an extra couple of steps by the time I notice that they've stopped in their tracks. They're speaking to each other, their hair falling over their faces, a privacy screen between me and them. Fuck this. It's a miracle my heels don't snap with the speed I approach them at.

—Go on then. What's wrong?

Their commune is over. Chloë looks at me, her eyebrows threading up at the centre, pulling her mouth into a grimace.

—We're worried about you, that's all.

—Away on with your shite.

I won't let my eyes look up. Keeping my head down to scroll through texts, busying my hands. They're both standing in silence, watching me. I can feel it. Standing there, sobering up against my will, I feel the chill in the air. My teeth chatter, despite myself.

—Well? What're we for then? I ask them both, exaggerating my looks between the pair of them.

Still, silence. Not a peep out of the pair of them. Fucking lappers.

—Right, in that case, I'm off.

I stumble back up the cobbled streets, heels trapping in the grooves as I go. The back of the shoes nip at my feet. Rubbing the skin away. I walk on with blood pooling around my toes. Hobbling on for a few more steps before I peel them off, heading homeward barefoot.

We go a couple of days without contact after the Labrador night. Classic silent treatment. To put the days in, I click through the Topshop website. Adding everything to basket before shutting the laptop lid. It can't go on forever, so the three of us meet before our seminar, under the pretence of grabbing an overpriced coffee. The act of picking up a coffee with the girls makes me feel like I'm living my *Sex and the City* dreams, but instead of New York City I'm on Merseyside. To be fair, the girls here go just as hard with the fashion as they do in NYC. I've no doubt. Rollers and tan. Hair curly blow-dried to perfection. But we're a pack of blow ins, sticking out like sore thumbs for our lack of aesthetic finesse. As we arrive, we swap half-embraces, faces turned away. We set up camp on the surprisingly uncomfortable armchairs beside the window. Surrounded by bags overflowing with unread books from the library.

My phone keeps beeping in my coat pocket. I really can't be holed dealing with it right now, so I decide to ignore it. Hannah is telling us about the trials of train travel home, with hours wasted changing at boring townlands. There's nothing to do there but wait to leave. The beeping continues. Another notification coming through before the last text tone has finished. Chloë asks have I gone deaf, with me not checking what's going on with my phone. This bitch, I swear, she's always at me about some shite.

—Would you ever fuck up? I say it with a laugh, knowing that Chloë won't know how to respond.

The conversation labours on, punctuated by buzzing. It's mostly held afloat by Hannah's noble efforts in giving us blow by blow accounts of her daily dramas. She's venting about her housemates: the one who blasts through the bog roll without replacing it, the phantom milk drinker; saint Hannah is the only one capable of taking the bins out. It's all so fucking tedious that I barely muster a grunt in recognition.

The lecturer is mid-sentence when we walk in with hands clawed around takeaway coffees. She's mid-flow, eyes cast up to the ceiling as if reading her presentation off the roof tiles. When I sneak off to the toilet in the first of our seminar breaks, I check my phone. Mostly just to make sure that nobody has croaked it. The BBM group message with the Belfast girls is going off. Aisling and Danielle are messaging as if they couldn't lean out their bedroom window and just talk it out. The crux of it is this: Aisling fucked Andy. And he is *hung*, she says. My stomach feels like it's dropping out my arse. Beige walls feel like they are closing in on me. Lungs bunged with air, not letting a breath in or out. I can't think of anything worse than being in the cubicle in this horrible prefab building. I pull my knickers back up quick, then I shove my phone back in my bag. Aisling has always fancied him. Everybody within a three-mile radius would know. She'd have done anything to sit next to him on the bus to school. It was so embarrassing to witness him ignore her day after day as she stared into the side of his head, hoping he would say something, anything, to her. Well, now he has. And good for her, if only he wasn't such an utter bastard.

I head back into the class to a round table surrounded by Chloë, Hannah and some other English students. I never bothered to learn most of their names. Chances are they're always called Helen or Liz or something. With my accent I could pluck any name out of thin air, call them it directly to their faces and they would be none the wiser. I lean into hamming it up. Making my pronunciations stick to my tongue. Not letting go of the vowels. But today, I've lost my appetite for winding these people up. All I can think about is Aisling. I'm going to have to congratulate her – is that even the right word to say after somebody's got the buck? I text the word 'great!' instead. Once it's sent, the walls shut in on me. Crushing my chest. Prickling up my arms. I can't think.

Hannah asks, —You alright, queen? You're a little pale.

—I'm always fucking pale.

Everybody at the table stares at me like I've grown an extra head. I lift my coat and leave the seminar early. Ignoring the lecturer as he asks where I think I'm going. The power has gone to his head if he thinks he can talk to me like I'm in school. I've paid to be here. He can get fucked if he thinks I'll ask permission to leave.

## 24

A few weeks later, we're sat in a non-descript all-day breakfast joint on Hardman Street. Every surface is wood panelled in here: tables, walls, even the roof. The eggs are floating in a little pool of grease on my plate. It doesn't mix with the ocean of beans. It's a kind of gross fry-up soup. I push my food around before dropping my napkin on top, hiding my poor attempt at eating. Chloë and Hannah are shifting on their seats. They've barely touched theirs either.

—You two need a shite or what?

Neither of them laugh.

—Oh, that was a joke.

Chloë says, —Babe. We've been thinking.

—Oh, that's a start!

—I mean, we've been thinking – that what you said about that fella . . . you know the one. Maybe we should talk to somebody about it?

—We?

It's as if my breathing echos. It's all I can hear. The man behind the counter tries to avoid eye contact, though I catch his theatrical non-interest. He can't be *that* into cleaning the worktop, his arm scrubbing the same spot over and over, and once more for luck.

After what feels like a hundred years, they both take it in turns to try and begin saying whatever they had planned to. False starts as they begin and give up. Chloë manages it first. I should speak to the cops, she says. I'm told they'll help me. I can't even begin to entertain the thought of saying it out loud. The room feels like it's swimming, pulsing around me. I can't. No. In stereo, they both ask why.

Outside, a rush of fresh air hits me. An oppressive stench makes me gag. What little I ate of the eggs meets the pavement. Hannah is suddenly behind me, her hand on the small of my back. I see Chloë through the window, paying for our three lunchtime breakfasts.

Cashflow is beginning to dry up as my wardrobe fills with vintage dresses hoked from bargain bins in charity shops. My student loan has been frittered away on rent and cocaine, life's two necessities. Chloë has hooked me up with a trial shift at her work. She's working part-time in a café near her student halls off Smithdown Road. It's dirty and dingy, specialising in food for the chronically hungover. But still, I feel lucky to have it. Chloë pleaded my case to her boss to give me a shift. She says he is nice and easy to work for. When she told me all of this earlier in the week, the relief on my face was telling. Swaying between tears and elation. I can't bring myself to say how much it means.

Scrubbing up for my first day on the job, I notice how my collarbones collect shower water like little ponds. The joy this gives me keeps me going. Lathered in the cheapest shower gel I could find, I imagine myself in glamorous jobs: fashion journalist; model; possibly, if autotune is to be trusted, an internationally acclaimed singer. Reality hits as I open my eyes. Dark mould crawling out from the bathroom corners. Towels clung with the stench of damp. My clothes weren't fully dry to begin with, but I put them on, feeling the cloth stick to my skin. I leave my hair wet as I head out.

The door makes a satisfying *ding* as I arrive. Frying oil drifts out hot and thick from the kitchen. Almost sticky. Instinctively, I put my hair up into a ponytail to stop myself from poking at it. I haven't touched a thing yet, but I feel dirty already, like I have a layer of oil on my hands, my face.

A thin man comes from the kitchen, swatting his hands on his apron. Skin hangs off him like old leather. Whiskers mottle his face, with little tufts on his cheeks.

## Exile

—Are you the new girl? Whiskers says.

After hearing my voice, he tilts his chin upward in an arc that mimics his eyeroll. He tells me the Irish are lazy workers and are likely to take their money straight over the road to hand to the barkeeper. Would it make sense to hand my wage over the road, instead? I smile, despite myself. It would be just like an English man to take what's not his, I think, though I have sense enough not to speak.

Chloë winces before guiding me away. She gives me the grand tour: the till; the toilets; the coffee machine. She shows me how to cash up at the end of the day. Printing a long receipt. Counting the coins. How to leave the register open for Whiskers to double check. At the end of the day, she said that I'll receive my wages, cash in hand. But not to leave without a dinner being boxed up by the chef. Pay and a feed. I've landed on my feet here. I get to work, donning an apron covered in translucent globules splattered all over the front. A modernist masterpiece in mayonnaise.

I'm like a child playing at running a café. I hold the pen and paper and approach the group who have just walked in and sat in the window booth. They each order a full English breakfast with a whole host of changes: no mushrooms, two sausages instead of bacon, extra egg. I write this on the docket and walk to the hatch to deliver the order. —What the fuck is this? the chef shouts out, loud enough for the customers to hear. I skulk back.

—No fucking swaps, it's on the menu. Can your type not read?

I slowly turn around and approach the group. I open my mouth to begin explaining, though they've heard already.

The girl closest to the window whispers, —It's fine, don't worry.

They slip out of the booth and out the door.

When the boss sees that I didn't allure them into staying, he says that if this were a 'real shift' and not a 'trial' he would dock my wages for losing him business. Tail between my legs, I wipe down the now vacant table. Picking up pawed at cutlery. I'm scundered. Eyes flooding, prickling with embarrassment. Chloë's hand appears on my shoulder. It's OK, she tells me, it gets easier.

Gary enters the café and orders a tea. I clean the coffee machine while having idle chit-chat with him. I haven't seen him since the film screening. We shoot the shit. I ask him if he's going to disappear while my back is turned. He didn't expect to be called out. His hands cover his eyes. Scundered for him. He sits at the counter and asks after Hannah. Is she single? The thin chef bursts from the kitchen, shouting, —I'm not paying you to plan dates to the pub.

That evening, I wash the smell of old milk and coffee beans off my body. Skin scrubbed raw. I pat myself dry with the towel Mrs Cooper rents me for the price of the shift I've just completed. I lie on my bed, with the towel underneath me for long enough that my body feels dry. I feel at the indents along my thighs, like little craters on the surface of the moon. I roll over and strain my neck to look at the landscape of my skin. Dark hair growing in tufts like gorse. I never understood the compulsion to strip away. It's my natural insulation against these northern freezing rains.

I stretch my arm far above me, creating a vacuum-suction against my ear. I slow my breathing to hear the blood pumping through my body. Still, I listen. The *thud, lub* of the blood waves rippling in my veins, echoing in my ears. I think of dried rust crusted underneath my body. How it comes to stain the sheets. A physical education teacher told us in first year of secondary school that if us girls were ever to find our bodies leaky and exposed that we should soak the clothing in a sink filled with hot water and a tub of salt. Osmosis would deal with the rest. The first boyfriend I had insisted that the sight of menstrual blood was worthy of fainting. Though one topic was beyond even language to him: girls and shitting. When I visited his house, if I didn't rush, I would return from the toilet to a look of disgust. I wonder if my body enacted these bouts as a form of defence.

It's April now and the weather is trying its best to break into sunshine. On Hannah's suggestion, the three of us meet for drinks in the park. The clouds in the sky can be damned. In the off-licence the aisles are lined with bottles of everything. My new friends browse the shelves and talk about varieties in details which I do not understand. Merlot. Shiraz. Pinot Noir. It's all wine to me. I stand with my back to them, looking at the labels for interesting patterns that catch my eye. Where is the Buckfast? Andy would have spotted the deep green bottle a mile off, as if he had an internal radar set to hunt out the syrupiest wine in the shop. In lieu, I reach for a coral-coloured wine. It shines bright like rubellite.

The girls have already made their purchases. I hand over my tenner to the shopkeeper, feeling guilt as if I am buying this drink illegally. I should not be doing this. Throughout the week I have been nicking bog roll from the university toilets. Conserving cash. An economic decision, I tell myself, as if it were a choice I could refuse. I really shouldn't be splurging on wine.

We go to Sefton Park with its sprawling greenery, trees, and lake. Sitting on the damp benches we smoke and talk about things we have no idea about: moving to cities in tropical climates; jobs where we might actually matter; the possibility of boyfriends. I fasten my cardigan and tilt back to look up at the sky. My head looking over to the tower blocks in Toxteth, my feet towards the divided mansion houses surrounding the park.

—Are we up for the pub later? Hannah asks.

I have just spent my last tenner on this bottle but it's as if Hannah has read this on my face. She loops her arm around me, leans in and tells me it's on her tonight. In the pub, she disappears to the bar before I finish a drink. Quick to ensure I'm never without a drink in hand. An unsaid understanding that she wouldn't see me excluded.

# 25

*My vision is drink blurry. Everything is wrapped up in cotton swaddling holding it all tight.*

*The soft blood sea whispers to me. Giving way to flowing rivers in my head.*

*A shift as I try to stand but everything beneath me is made of sand.*

*Gasping for air the waves swallow me.*

# 26

Needless to say, I didn't pass my trial shift at Chloë's café job, so I'm back on the job hunt. It's swift and painless, mostly, as I hand in my CV to a few shops and wait. One emails back to say that a popular titty bar is opening in the city and can I send a *portfolio of previous work*. Nah, mate. The internet offers up lots of lucrative gigs for selling pictures of my feet, so if I wanted to make quick cash there were always websites like Soles for Souls.

The job that I interview for is on the outskirts of the city, waitressing at a restaurant, specialising in *aspirational dining on a budget*. At the interview, I am told to take a seat like I am a paying customer. The inside is dark, with surfaces covered in cement. They're going for this post-industrial chic look, but it's more like a prison with comfortable chairs. It feels more like a dungeon that an 'eatery'. I study the menu on the table, as if sitting for a final exam. Steak with choice of pepper, blue-cheese or Diane sauce, with a side of chips or salad. Lasagne, with a side of chips or salad. Bangers and mash, with no options of sides. It doesn't say what the cut of the steak is.

Time drags on for what feels like a lifetime. Nerves are playing on me and showing my fear through sweat stains on my top. I stand up to ask the waitress where the toilets are, so I can freshen up. —Only be another few minutes, love, she says before I've even completely raised myself to standing. I shuffle the chair back underneath me.

Other young women trickle in through the door, and a waitress on duty points them to join me at the long table. After another half an hour, another more senior waitress comes to stand at the end of the table, like a mafia boss. A suit jacket thrown on over her shirt and apron lets us know that this woman is a cut above the other waitresses here. We're thanked for our presence at this event. Fucking hell, what have I got myself in for.

—Hi! I'm Sharon, Head of Customer Dining Experience. You've all been invited here as you've shown *true potential* to exceed in the fast-paced world of hospitality. This job requires commitment, so please leave now if you are not ready to work hard for our customers.

I shift my eyes around the other waitressing-hopefuls; not one other person seems disturbed by this.

Whisked away to an empty private dining room, Sharon shows us how to hold multiple plates using a clawed version of our hands while balancing the rims of the plates on our wrists. After a swift demonstration, she loads up our arms with plates piled with carb-heavy meals recently reheated in the kitchen. Before this, I had never thought about my wrist muscles. Never considered their merits, their strength, flexibility, weakness. It's apparent now that they are rigid and weak. Other girls glide around the room, holding three plates per arm. Sharon is readjusting the two plates that I'm holding. Ceramic burns into my fingertips. Flinty knuckles keep me from moving a muscle to relieve myself. I'm sweating.

We are watched as if we are performing life-saving surgery. Sharon is taking notes on each of us in her waitressing notepad. Her wrist flicking violently across the page when she sees something she disproves of. Side salad fallen from a plate of lasagne. Spilled gravy dripping over the floor. Operating without a smile.

After the kitchen is closed and the dishes are washed, we are told to return to our seats at the banquet style table. Sharon strides over, her last step landing hard, dragging her left foot into position with the other. She claps her hands together in front of her chest.

—How was that then, girls?

A ripple of tired enthusiasm waves down the table.

—Great! The final stage of the interview will commence in, say, ten minutes? I'll call you through one by one and then you're free to go after that. We'll contact you in the coming week to let you know whether you've been successful.

I'm dying to reach into my bag and text Hannah and Chloë, to let them know I haven't been held hostage at this interview. Though it feels pretty close to that right now. None of the other hopefuls move a muscle; they sit there with hands folded on their laps, gazing out the window-front to the darkened rainy street. I wonder whether they think our captors will not allow us to speak, or whether they feel like this quietude is relaxing like the inside of a library. I wish I'd packed my book.

When I am eventually summoned, night has descended beyond the windows. Sharon quizzes me on my knowledge of the restaurant: did I know when they first opened? And what about my credentials? And what about my career ambitions? Where did I see myself in five years' time? I stumbled through with responses so lacking that I immediately forget the words as they tumble from me. Finally, she asked, —Any questions for me?

—What are the kinds of steak you offer? She looks at me like I have grown another head, her eyes gazing off beyond my shoulder to make eye contact with the second invisible Fiadh.

—It's cow, babe.

I'm in need of a drink after the prison-like 'eatery' trial. Not to be left hanging, the girls come through for a last-minute night out. At the cash machine, in an act of self-torture, I check my balance. The minus symbol appears. I use my back to shield the screen from my new friends, embarrassed at how I live, if it can really be called that. They reckon I'm staying in a private room to avoid the squalor of student halls. The word 'private' does a lot of heavy lifting, masquerading as a fancy alternative to a single bed in a rented coffin. One night, I sat with my back against the door to ensure privacy from a wandering landlady with no sense of tenants' rights. Hunkered down, I rubbed my hand back and forth over the carpet. Subterranean layers of skin became exposed with the friction. Red raw. A small pile of fur and flesh building into a little tube under my palm. My nose and eyes streamed.

The girls wouldn't get it. I don't have the heart to tell them that I could not afford the university accommodation. The grant and student loan covered less than half of the rent for it. The room at Mrs Coopers' is a deal for new Irish to the city, usually taken up by those travelling here for work. It's cheaper. At night, I lie there in my rented bed, the surface craggy from age. Hollows where springs once were. In one crater towards the feet, a rogue spring has begun to poke its way to freedom.

—Luxury, Mrs Cooper says.

Aye, maybe when you fucking bought it in the eighties, love.

On my way out to the trial shift earlier that day, I passed the living room, the TV softly murmuring. I popped my head in the door to see her curled up into herself on the sofa, holding the remote under folded arms. I backed out in the hallway, where the sideboard holds vases and a letter holder. Coins splashed into a bowl, a tenner tucked underneath.

The opening of 'Proud Mary' is beginning to blare into the dank room filled with body-conned girls and floppy haired boys. They don't know what to be doing with themselves, swaying from leg to leg. For the more extravagant, a shoulder pops out of time to the music.

—Drinks are on me! I shout to the girls as I arrive at the bar.

My heart hurts when the strumming begins to pick up pace, thinking of Danielle and nights in Lavery's upstairs bar. The night we were kicked out for clambering on top of a table, arms flung forward, glasses shattered in our wake. Sure, it was only a bit of craic we pleaded in our defence as we were turfed into the back alley. The door slammed as we shuffled off, arms and legs flailing in an approximation of dancing.

In Liverpool, the music whips into its apex. Not a fucking soul is doing Tina Turner's dance routine. What the fuck is going on. This can't be allowed to happen. I abandon the girls at the bar, scrunching the tenner into Chloë's hand.

—Get three Carlsberg! I scream, before running off towards the static two-steppers. I break out what I consider to be The Moves. People push away from me while I flick my arms, throw my head down, and bounce about. A mop-haired lanky boy approaches; He's wearing clothes which aren't totally repulsive. They look recently laundered. Still got it, I think. He leans into me, pushes my hair behind my ear and whispers, —You got any gear?

Limbs tangle as we both fall into the back of a black taxi. I tell the cabbie my address through the security glass. The car speeds off into the darkness, our arms and heads plait with each other. The taxi feels like it's zipping through space, the streetlights swim past in amber streaks. I can barely see where we are, but in no time the handbrake slams on and we're tumbling out onto the street.

Getting into the house is filled with the intensity of watching the moon landing. *One small step for Fiadh, one giant leap for Fiadh getting her hole again from an English fella.* I close one of my eyes, which in drunk logic, helps me steady my hand, moving ever slower to the keyhole.

— Fucking hell, girl he says, as he takes the key from my hand.

We're finally in. He looks around the hallway as if he's inadvertently pulled a millionaire student in a basement dive bar on Seel Street.

I splutter, waving one arm into the hallway. —Welcome to my palace. My maid will take your coat.

His face looks unable to read me. It could be the accent or it could be the drink slurring my words. Frankly, who cares? I take his hand and lead him up the stairs. There are some things which do not require language. In my room, time speeds up, or at least it's over before I know it.

The next morning, he's not as I remember. His hair is flaming red for a start, not unattractive. What was his name? Gareth? No, it was something more British than that. I'm sure I remember thinking, wait until Danielle gets wind of this, fucking WILLIAM.

As if reading my mind, he rolls over in the bed. His face is a jump-scare. I am sure I've never seen this man before in my life. Each singular feature is so unmemorable that the moment my eye moves to the next, I forget what I was looking at instantly. His eye colour? Blue or brown. Who knows. I do know he had eyes though, so that is something.

—Tea? I say, before slithering out of the bottom of the bed with the skill of a girl who does not want to be seen in her kecks. Thank fuck I'm wearing them.

Downstairs Mrs Cooper is standing at the kitchen counter. Placed in front of her is her change bowl. She's counting each single penny aloud. When I enter, she's on four pounds sixteen. I'm far too hungover for this carry on, she needs to catch a grip of herself.

—Did you and your visitor have a good night? The neighbours, God love them, have been concerned a pack of wild dogs broke into the house and killed us all.

Fuck this for a game of soldiers. I turn on my heel and head back up the stairs.

—We're out of milk. Mon we go to the café around the corner.

Huge trees line the roads, sheltering us from the drizzle. We dander on in silence until we find a greasy spoon. Bacon baps drenched in tomato sauce come served on chipped plates. Once the last drop of coffee is drained from the cup, I put my coat on.

—Well, I'll be seeing ya.

Which is a very polite way of saying, this never happened.

# 27

*You're a slut.*

# 28

It's one of those bars that hasn't been done up since it opened in the seventies. The chairs creak under the punters. Tiles in the toilets that have years of dried piss calcified in the grouting. Around the table, we have books open under the pretence of studying together. There's *The Tempest*, *The Turn of the Screw*, and *Wuthering Heights* all splayed open amongst the wine glasses. A pack of cigarettes lies with the lid open, as if beckoning us into a smoke break. Chloë and Hannah are writing away in their notebooks. The covers smooth and shiny, more for decoration than their imagination.

In between scribbling handwritten notes, Hannah is texting away on her phone. She's amusing herself as she bounces between the two, a smile cracking over her face. The look on Chloë's face says it all as Derek, our tutor, bounds in the door, confident as you like. Hannah is never done putting her hand up in his class, speaking up into the silence. It's not exactly the Ritz in here, as much as Hannah wishes it was, but Derek's hardly a lavish man. This bar would be the sort of dive he'd haunt. It's no coincidence though; he catches Hannah's eye, and both of their faces break into open grins. Nauseating. Her notebook is slammed shut and all pretension for study goes out the window.

Chloë mumbles for fuck's sake under her breath but audible enough to be heard.

Derek is the sort of man who was probably cool when he was in his twenties: able to keep up with the latest fashions; out in the coolest clubs; necking a tonne of girls. I say probably, but he tells us all of this. In no uncertain terms are we to think that he wasn't *it*. Problem is, he's now in his fifties, married with kids at home, and still hasn't changed his chat. He asks us if we've been to Nation. Rave nights were invented there, we're told. When he was a young thing, he says, he would be out popping pills, dancing, and fucking anybody he wanted. Aye, right.

He's an unholy bore, holding court at the end of the table, asking what we're up to, before launching into a speech about how terrible the books are that we're studying. In his words, he can't believe he's being forced to teach this tripe. In good time, we'll all be able to study the course he designed, in which a white English man will enlighten us on civil rights movements. He tells us about Malcolm X, Martin Luther King, and Rosa Parks. About the leaps and bounds the world has made to where we are now. About how lucky we have it. I bite: I ask what he reckons about the north of Ireland? What about how Catholics were treated? All that death at our doors. Nothing to be done but to box it up inside. Justice was not for us. Could we talk about that equality? He doesn't see the connection, shaking off the query as if I've asked about the Bananas in Pyjamas.

He gets a round in. Four glasses and a bottle of wine for the table. Some shots lined up on a serving tray. The shots he brings are quaint. Deep gold, possibly whiskey. It fucking stinks.

Hannah keeps placing her hand on his arm. Just for a second at a time, but it's long enough for us to notice. He can't take his eyes off her, darting from eyes to tits over and over, signalling to her – and anybody within eyeshot – his intentions. My stomach shrivels. I can see this all coming a mile off.

The next thing, we're standing in the middle of Heebie's with Derek. He's doing a two-step around Hannah. Marking his territory against any bloke who comes within sniffing distance of us. While he has been careful not to be seen touching her, he is getting more adventurous as the drink hits: a hand around her waist, any excuse to touch her lips, and placing a straw from his drink into her mouth. It's like catnip to Hannah.

In the toilets, Chloë and I ask Hannah what's going on.

—Nothing. Derek's sound. Don't you like him? Don't be prudes.

— Isn't he a bit of a rotter? Bit crusty?

She's swiping on a deep red lipstick. It leaves a halfmoon kiss on her pint.

—I mean, maybe it's not the best idea for us to be getting blocked with him, you know?

Hannah rolls her eyes at me. —Oh, and your moral compass is sound. Give it a rest, Fiadh.

—Excuse me?

Chloë hisses at Hannah. —Stop it.

—No, go on, go on, say what you have to. The Patron Saint of Riding has something to get off her chest.

—Fiadh, we love you, *because* you're a slag.

Her words arrive a moment after I've felt the blow. When I look up, Hannah is smiling, trying to soften whatever damage has been caused. I muster a small laugh and walk away.

They follow me back to the dance floor. It only takes a minute before Derek and Hannah begin what I think is meant to be grinding. Although the movement looks like a vertical worm. The man is a walking contraceptive, in my eyes: nothing would keep your pants on more firmly on than witnessing his foray into seduction. Hannah's eating it up though. Making a big show of it, he whispers into her ear. I could spew. She bounds over to us, asking us if we want to join her. They're heading back to Derek's for a 'nightcap'. I tell her I'd rather chew glass. Chloë doesn't quite say it in those terms, but the sentiment is the same. We let Hannah make her own mistakes and take our cue to end the night. Outside, the streets are crammed with people spilling into the road looking for a taxi. We merge with them, pressed up against the throngs of sweaty bodies as we make our way towards the main road.

Chloë dials and redials a taxi company while I dip into a chippy to sort us out with something to soak up all the wine sloshing around our stomachs. My head bobs back on itself as I wait on our chips. I catch a look at myself in the warped mirrors on the walls. The skin on my face feels heavy, as if it's pulling my eyes, my cheeks towards the floor. I raise my eyebrows up to test that my muscles are working. The man behind the counter has appeared in front of me just as I attempt this. A pitying look comes over him, before he gazes over my shoulder to the next customer.

# 29

*Swear to fuck. You're the worst.*

                                                              *Everybody hates you.*

*So embarrassing.*

                                                             *You know that don't you?*

                                                                    *You should.*

## 30

The trees are bursting with spring freshness; it's as if every bud is beginning to bloom in tandem. Around Sefton Park Lake, a sea of daffodils has sprung up. Cherry blossoms shed pink confetti that drifts past my window. The breeze through the single glazing is fresh against my skin. It's a tonic, blowing away the cobwebs. I know when I open the messenger app on my phone what will be waiting for me: birthday texts and questions of what the wide beyond holds for me today.

I'd woken up to a text from Da. As if time was infinite, I waited to reply. Until I had a cup of tea. Until I left the house. Until I was sat in the park. My nails tap the buttons below the screen, a satisfying click with each press. I type **thank you**. I want to add the words 'I love you' or tell him how much I miss him. I cannot. The silence between us has always been a comfort. The long hours passed in quiet harmony in the kitchen. Wordlessly Da would hover around the house, tidying away the dishes and sticking on an endless supply of tea. —You for a brew, love? That's what he would ask, breaking the comfortable quiet. The apple doesn't fall too far from the tree, as they say, so unsurprisingly, I find myself also lacking the vocabulary to express the fondness I have for these memories.

True to form, Ma rings later in the day to ask what the plans are to celebrate the beginning of my final teenage year. At home turning eighteen is *the* landmark birthday, one which shepherds in the possibility of gambling and legal drinking. But, to me, turning nineteen signals a more momentous change: here begins the beginning of the end of life as I know it, the end of my childhood, the training years. This time next year, when I turn twenty, I will be eye-to-eye with the vast cavern of opportunity coming in the next decade, one which includes – if I'm lucky – a career not yet decided. Despite the need to leave the last few months behind, the future menaces like a monster under the bed. I don't say a word of this to Ma. I've not lost the plot. Instead, I tell her I plan to go to a friend's house for pizza, tactfully neglecting to mention the several bottles of wine, too. The call is rounded off with a bulletin of who has recently croaked it at home, separated into two categories: 'Before Their Time' and 'Lived to a Brave Ould Age'. Mrs O'Doherty. Ninety-three. Stroke got her when she was watching television. Only discovered days later by her nephew. Brave ould age. Shane Maguire. Knocked down at only ten-years-old. Awful. Saoirse O'Neill. Found in a pool of her own sick. Not even at home. She'd been staying with her dealer. Needle still in the arm. —God love her mother, Ma says, she wasn't to know.

Unwrapping myself from the comfort of the duvet, I plan how to spend my first birthday away from my family. The freedom of it all is exhausting. In our house, it was tradition to have a hot breakfast, an Irish fry: soda bread, potato bread, toast, sausages, eggs, bacon. All piled high onto one plate with a pot of tea to keep the throat lubricated. I would open my presents from family; Ma and Da always gave me a book voucher for No Alibis bookstore on Botanic Avenue. Our birthday traditions centred around going to this haven. Da forever delighted in the annual telling of the fact that it began the year before the Good Friday Agreement. He always liked to joke that we can all agree on good books, even though he and I could never. In Liverpool, though, I sit on the edge of my sepia-toned room, alone, and think of how to build new traditions for myself in this new city. Pancakes are too American. Too stodgy, even for my palette. A long walk would be straying too far from anything resembling a birthday treat. I don't know what to be at.

I decide to begin with what I know and head to Waterstones on Bold Street. I walk up and down the fiction section and recognise none of the names that Da had cultivated me to love. All the usual characters line the shelves though, a staggering number of them with the first name James: Patterson, Joyce, Baldwin. It's a pile of wank. I wonder how many Fiadhs are writing out there. My mind craves company to discuss this with. To be sat having pints with Andy and the girls chatting is a kind of heaven. I can only dream of it now. The loneliness comes up on me fast and thick. Under my skin, I have a tingling sensation, cold and prickly. A buzzing in my ears; I mentally note to myself that I should look up 'tinnitus' on the internet later. I probably should write that down. My breathing becomes sharp and my heart a drum. I sit on the floor next to the Literary Criticism shelf, tucked away in the back of the bookstore. The ground beneath me feels like it's made of jelly. I open my bag to drain the last of a bottle of Fanta.

Whispering from the other side of the bookcase brings me out of myself. When my eyes focus on the room, I see a bookseller, closer than I'd realised.

—You alright, queen?

—Tinnitus.

That is all I can say. I'm making no fucking sense and I know it. The sweat is glistening over my skin, patches appearing on my T-shirt. The bookseller looks like Morticia Adams. Hair to her waist. Paler than me. Nearly blue. Kneeling next to me, her voice is velvet soft. She'll be back with water. Wait there. I do as I'm told. Morticia returns with some tepid water. Her hands hover between us, in case I drop the cup. Powered by pure mortification, I thank her, scoop my bag from the floor and leave. I don't dare take a look back.

# 31

The days have smudged into one, each undiscernible from the last. Most of the time I'm alone, walking around supermarkets and pound shops. Desperately searching for anything – a teapot, some cushions – that will pull me from this despair. I can't get it right. I never feel like I'm here. Even with Chloë and Hannah. Today's worse than the others. A haze of solitude shadows everywhere I go. Loneliness gives off a high-pitched frequency; it's a sound that blisters the ears of anybody too close to me. Intermittently I check the signal on my phone throughout the day. It's been suspiciously quiet since the call with Ma earlier. I turn it off and on. Still, no messages from any of my friends at home. I chance my arm sneaking down to use Mrs Cooper's landline to prank myself, to be sure that the line hasn't been cut off for an unpaid bill. The bank has tried every medium except carrier pigeon to get hold of me. Bounced cheques. Unarranged overdraft fines. The buttons click as I dial. *0-7-9* . . . My phone shakes into life in my hand. Case closed. Billy No-Mates: Confirmed.

They're bound to text tonight, no point worrying about it now. So, I do the only thing I can: put on a very short black shift dress from a vintage shop on Hardman Street; pair it with black platform heels; slick my eyes with cat winged eyeliner; head out with a half-bottle of Glen's vodka tucked into my handbag. It is my birthday night out after all. They've come armed with a balloon, destined for the sky. We're for that creepy bar in town, the one where the owner gives all the student girls free prosecco. You know he thinks you are a complete ride if the sparklers come out. Hannah, Chloë, and I have pulled out all the stops to ensure that we get the full works, tequila, and all. It'll help us on our way. It's an economical choice more than anything. Not to mention the confidence boost it gives us knowing we're hot as fuck before we head on somewhere with lads our own age.

As sure as night follows day, the owner strides over, holding the bottle high above his head. There are a few minutes of clapping while we wait for the industrial sized sparkler to fizzle out. Sidling in, he stretches his arm around me. Kisses soak my cheek. Better not streak my make-up, I swear to fuck. He reeks of sweat doused in a spicy cologne. It'd make you hurl. Glasses emptied as quick as they were poured. We make an escape when he nips to the loo. We head out towards Seel Street. Dipping into a dive bar down some rickety entry. Leaning over the bar, I shout for a cosmopolitan. A twirly-tached barman tells me they only do 'Five Dollar Shakes'. Christ the night. Insufferable. Comes in a milk bottle and all. A glorified boozy milkshake. A recipe to curdle with the prosecco from earlier. Disaster.

Chloë literally bumps into a lanky fella, shirt buttoned up to his neck. Harrington jacket exposing plaid inside. She apologises, all hands on his chest, checking if she's drenched him. It was invitation enough for us to get chatting to his mates. A group of lads dressed to the nines. Could have walked right off the set of This is England. They have a recording studio in the centre of the city. We head there with them. Following them up to the top floor of an office building. They put on music. Bands literally nobody has ever heard of before, because it was recorded right there in that room. People begin flowing in around 3 a.m. From the centre of a crowd, Gary appears. Cans in a bag, he parks up on a windowsill. The glass behind him sodden with condensation. I go to say hello just to pass myself. He is obnoxious and insulting as ever. Opening with a little jibe at me. Schoolboy tactics.

—Seriously, look at those tree trunks, he says about my legs.

Clearly he hasn't updated his flirting techniques since primary school, I tell him. Somehow, he takes the hump at that, skulking off.

Lord knows what time it is, but I'm heavy enough in the drink that I begin to lose the thread of conversations. I try to listen from the start, but my eyes drift off to stare at an object – a chair, a used cup – at the other side of the room. Once I return my focus to the chat again, it's like I was never even listening in the first place. All I can hear is my own breathing, a comfort close to soothing me off to sleep while I'd stood up. I take a bump of coke and attempt to perk myself up. Resting is for the dead. I'm not sure if I spoke this aloud to myself. My eyes are half-closed as I intimate a seductive gaze at a boy across the room. Words become slippery in my mouth; a delicious greasiness my tongue cannot shake free from.

The sofa swallows me, hugging my shoulders as I slump back into it. Head bowing into my chest, I think of him. What it was like, before he destroyed everything. The nights at his gaff, where we'd talk movies. The hot chocolates and joints. Taking turns building forts, despite being far too old and far too high to be at it. His hair is similar to mine: mousy blonde, thin. People used to say we could be related. A girl on the other end of the sofa turns to me as I laugh to myself. I mumble, I think.

—Spirited Away.

Later, more lines rack up on the toilet lid. Gary and I are hunched over, our heads almost touching. Somehow, it's always him and I, finding each other amongst the faff out there. In this moment, I think he's perfection. His eyelashes look like they're growing heavy, as he's scanning down my face. I stroke his cheek a little too hard. Stubble scratches my hand. Repulsive as rubbing sandpaper. It's in motion now though. One thing leads to another before an unmemorable attempt at a ride. The curve of my back is pressed up against the sink, and my head knocks on the mirror. He's trying desperately to fulfil his end of the bargain, but the coke is refusing to play ball. He gives up.

—One for the road?

He clears his throat of phlegm and humiliation. Swallowing it back. The ever-reliable baggy is pulled out of his jeans.

## 32

The fluorescent library lights sting my eyes. In this building, the aircon is set to Baltic, which is some feat of engineering to have inside colder when outside is an Arctic tundra. Cans of extremely caffeinated fizzy drinks keep me going through the night while I write any old tripe to reach the word count. Adding in flourishes of words like Jackson Pollock taking the lid off paint and fucking it right there onto the canvas. Unlike him, for me there's not a fucking plan in sight, but sure, it all counts. I've developed a slight shake in my hand, my eye twitches. I don't even look at the screen when I type. Language jazz. Who knows what word or point will come next.

I pace along the bookcases, scanning the spines for inspiration for where this essay should be headed. I stand in front of the books labelled 'Modernism and . . .', hoping that something jumps out to me. I'm still not sure what primary texts I'm going to go with at this stage. Woolf? Joyce? Who fucking knows. I should have gone to the lectures, instead of lying in that springy single bed wishing for an early release to death.

Gary saunters past the end of the shelves. He doesn't appear to clock me at first but takes a few steps back to do a double take.

—Fancy seeing you here.

—I'm a right Studious Sally, really, I say, not taking my eyes off the textbooks I'm conjuring into my essay. As if taking my eyes off the books will allow the ideas to run away. Jumping out the book, down the aisle. Forever gone.

—Don't take this the wrong way, but you look . . . rough, girl.

—No make-up, love, but cheers. You're looking well yourself.

His hands go up in a motion as if trying to hold back an attack. Backing away between the bookshelves, he tells me he'll be back soon. I carry on rifling amongst the books, before cradling more than I can carry in the crook of my arm. I'm back at my desk, desperately searching through the index for a name of an author I recognise. Just one, that's all I need, and I'll be able to run with this essay. I've only twelve hours on the clock before the deadline.

Gary pops his head over the top of my monitor. —Got a surprise for you.

I tell him I can't, I've got shit to do. A lucky dip brings 'Modernism, Joyce, and the City' into my hands.

—Come on, it'll help. It'll cheer you up.

I don't need to be asked twice. I'm up stuffing my things in my bags, leaving behind stacks of useless books.

He leads the way, holding out his hand behind him, just far enough away from my own to make me hurry. Like a prince opening a door to a horse-drawn carriage, he opens the door to the disabled toilet. I step right in, taking a curtsey on the way past.

—The medics do it to get them in the zone.

A tiny zip-lock of white powder is taken from his jeans. Keeps the medics awake before their exams, he tells me. And we need all the help we get. A little mountain of it snorts up from his key. Dunked back into the baggie, he holds out an offering over to me. The medics can't be wrong, I think. He begins to laugh to himself.

—You're alright, you know.

—Thanks?

Gary suddenly has the most magnetic energy. I can't stop looking at his arms, his hands, as he spins the bag around. The toilet seat bangs shut as he sits down. He asks if I'm feeling it. I am. Alert beyond belief. Noticing the patterns on the tiles. The sound of water dripping in the cistern.

The next morning, I wake up beside Gary in his student accommodation. Head on a pillow bulldozed flat. Stinks of cheap microwave noodles. Crusting over in bowls around the joint. A single

*Trainspotting* poster reminds me to Choose Life. We're top and tailing, while being wrapped up in blankets.

My first thought is one of pure panic, —Fuck, fuck, fuck. I didn't send Derek my essay.

—Just hit send now, lad, Gary says as he's rubbing the sleep from his eyes. His socked feet are emerging from the corner of the bed. The vulnerability of it makes me sick.

—I haven't even started it!

—Fuck. Well, good luck with that.

The bed crunches as he rolls over back to sleep. I stand into my jeans then throw on my jumper. Drafts of emailed excuses are crafted in my head. Been in a coma! Kidnapped! I strike gold. A chest infection will do it. The internet is taking an age to load up on my phone browser. Bit by bit assembling into a picture my inbox. Soon as the message is sent, Professor McAlister replies. A doctor's note is needed. Fuck. I ignore it.

Weeks flow past, between job interviews and nights out, it all just passes me by. Everything is ticking along until an email lands in my inbox. It's the head of the department. They want to meet for a chat. I've not been to class in a very long time, and it's even longer since I submitted anything. When I get to the university building, my feet echo on the stone flooring in the hallways, as if announcing my arrival. Staff are crammed into offices, four to a room. Nearly as bad as halls. I knock quietly on the door, and hear an even quieter *come in* in response. Inside, the room is warm and cosy. There are two armchairs and books lining every surface, from walls to floor. I couldn't even name that many authors. An electric heater warms my feet as I settle into a chair.

Professor McAlister asks me to call her Liz. She's a newly appointed Head of Department. She looks like an aunt. Her kind face is open and pitying as she leans over.

—Is everything alright?

I tell her it is. Everything is more than alright. I'm doing really well. Independence has done wonders for me, I say. Liverpool is magic.

—OK. Well, can we talk about how you feel about the course? How do you think it's going?

—Things are great. I'm really enjoying it here.

Her tone changes quick as the wind. She tells me I'm failing. I try to explain that my head has been up the wall, but I'm not sure that's what actually comes out of my mouth. It's all been too much. The move. Being alone. My breath catches. Whispered, I tell her I am so overwhelmed.

—Aren't we all that way?

Another couple of weeks pass; I hear nothing from Liz. I try to catch up on all the reading I've missed. *Wide Sargasso Sea*. *Mrs Dalloway*. Fuck I've even got a copy of *Lolita*. I send emails to the girls in class who I know haven't missed a session. The swotty types with the colour coded notes. I even try Chloë, who I know spends her free waking hours in the library now. I beg for all of their notes. Nobody replies. I'm shouting for help into the abyss. It is not long until I receive a curt email from Professor McAlister telling me I will be unenrolled.

# 33

Darkness slips into the room. Curtains billow like a body breaking out of a sleeping bag. I expect arms to burst from near the rail, then a leg to kick out. The head would be the last to appear, gazing around the room through slowly blinking eyes. It's fucking freezing. Wind bites at my cheeks. Bitingly cold. I can feel the pain of it, but my skin is a foreign country. As if watching from afar, the sensations are dulled. A buzzing current flows through my arms. Restless. Muscles are iron-heavy. The weight of me is sinking through layers of consciousness. Thoughts pile on top of each other. Fighting for primacy. I am broke. Lonely. Terribly unlovable. Awful. I am worthless. Dreams of throwing myself away without event or ceremony. Balled up and chucked in the bin. Or off a bridge. Wade into a lake. Just disappear into obscurity. The curtain falls limp.

The edge of the toilet is cold on the back of my thighs. I'm weighing up a whole box of paracetamol in my hand. Each pop of the blister pack is a rush, like getting that first draw on a feg. The release comes on quick. I wash back the tablets with cheap rosé, one of those brands that lists the 'flavour' as strawberry or cherry. Not a mention of a grape on the whole label. The vomit comes in torrents after pill number four. I overdid it on the wine. A rookie error, I think to myself, as I see the little undissolved capsules landing on the bathroom tiles. I can't fucking do *anything* right.

I pop all of the tablets out of their foil casing. Each one landing into the palm of my hand like tic-tacs. I pour the wine into a pint glass. Smacking palm to mouth, I shovel the tablets into my gob. I don't stop for breath.

*Gulp.*
*Slap.*
*Gulp.*
*Slap.*

What happens next is a sequence of blurry images: Chloë ringing. I threw my phone down the toilet, with such force the bog water splashes over the floor. I don't remember waking, but Mrs Cooper reports she found me in a pool of spew and toilet slew. I'm surprised I woke up.

Through a cracked water-logged screen, I see I have fourteen missed calls and twenty texts. Ah, fuck. Scrolling through my phone is worse than I could have imagined. I had text Chloë and Hannah a series of messages.

**Goodbye, love. Don't worry. Remember me.**

Fucking hell, I thought I was being ambiguous and mysterious. Reads more like a scream. I should ring them right away and let them know I'm OK, but I don't. I head back to bed.

They arrive shortly after. Mrs Cooper must have let them in the front door. Hannah's screaming, slapping her hands off my bedroom door. Her ma had jumped in the car with her, bombing it down from Manchester. Emotional support. I can't fucking do this with this hangover.

When I open the door to them, the concern pushes me to anger. This is fucking mortifying. Hannah's ma, Kate, insists that I call my ma. I won't. Is she fucking mad? Get the fuck. Ma would make everything worse. Kate keeps pawing at me. Pushing hair out of my face. Subtly checking my temperate with the back of her hand.

—Pack a bag. You're coming to ours. I'm not leaving you here. Hannah is searching the wardrobe for an overnight bag.

—Stop, fucking stop. I'm not going with you.

—You have to go somewhere, honey. Hmm?

After every sentence she adds a soft questioning hum, not

expecting or tolerating dissent from her instructions. —Go home for a little while to cool off, she says. She sits with me, while I look at flights. Pushing a credit card under my nose when I begin to lose interest, she whispers, —What we're going to do is this: tell your ma you saved up and wanted to surprise her. I can't find the words to tell her that home isn't going to fix this. Home is the problem. How will I face Danielle and Aisling again, pretending at normality? And Andy hanging around like a bad smell, and when he's not, Ma is asking how he's getting on and how his ma is doing. I feel sick, the room spins. Kate pulls me close into her.

—Come here, duck. It's alright.

She sends Hannah to grab me a water, anything for me to sip.

## 34

I've packed up my bags already, so now all there is to do is to wait on the sofa for Mrs Cooper to return from doing her messages. She is already an hour late. I try not to watch the clock. I put off making a cup of tea, for fear she'll arrive back while I'm sipping and include that in a clean-up fee. After another half an hour, the front door creaks open. Mrs Cooper enters slowly, weighed down with a variety of shopping bags.

—Are you going out? she says.

I have to remind her that today is the end of my stay at her house. Bags ungraciously dropped at the bottom of the stairs, before beginning to ascend. Arm on the banister pulling her knees up each step. She inspects my room like she's looking for diamond dust to sell. Every fibre of the space is closely inspected, with some areas photographed for proof. She points to the curtains, telling me they've gone threadbare. She scribbles down a note on the inventory. Testing the bed for buoyancy, she presses down, pushing her weight through her arm. Vigorously testing the springs. It's not a bouncy castle, love. It's added to the list. She carries on tallying up the antiquities of the room. Each new addition reduces my deposit.

—Let me just work this out. Then we can settle up.

Bashing her finger on her calculator, she says aloud, —You paid £200 deposit ... I'll have to take a hundred for the cleaning and repair of this room ... And, unfortunately, because I had to rearrange my schedule to carry this out, I will have to charge you for my time. And then there's the leaving early fee. Fifty quid. That brings the deposit to ... twenty quid.

She reaches into her purse to retrieve the single note, freshly pressed from the cash machine. My throat is too dry to speak. Mrs Cooper is already on her way down the stairs by the time I've shaken the shock from myself. I take the stairs slowly and find my case outside the open front door.

—On your way now, she says as she shuts the door behind me.

As I disembark the plane, suitcase in tow behind me, I begin to concoct how I will spin this to Ma and Da. Last night, I had rung the house. Da answered. Quiet as ever. Words spluttered down the line asking them to pick me up. I tell him I'll not be coming back to Liverpool. About the course unenrolling me. He only agreed to be there at the airport. No more, no less. It'll be a surprise to have me home, no doubt. When I make my way through the arrivals hall, they are raging. The pair of them with faces like smacked arses. Furious. But still, public relations management kicks in for them, as they're opting for calling it my decision as opposed to me being kicked out. We're monastic as we get into the car. Pure silence. The motorway zips past a new arena, behind it two big yellow cranes stand tall over the city. In the distance, the mountains rise out of the ground, as if coming up to meet me. The disappointment is palpable the whole way home.

When we get in the door, she can't help herself, following me around the house, giving a monologue, as if the shame isn't buried deep into my bones already.

—All that money wasted! And weren't you set up with the place in Mrs Cooper's? Handed to you! Back in my day we would never have got handouts like that. And what are you going to do now for work? Sure, the coffee shop won't be taking you back after your performance at Christmas! You'll need to get your act together. Start acting your age.

My teenage bedroom is a sanctuary. With practiced care, the lock turns without any noise. The walls in my childhood room feel smaller now. Chloë and Hannah are continuing to text me, filling me in on the latest news, mostly about Hannah riding the ould lecturer. I can't even bear to reply.

On Facebook, I notice that I have been 'unfriended' by a few from my course. Even Gary, for fuck's sake. I bet my plane hadn't even landed by the time they did that. Twats. They were fucking boring anyway. I roll over on the bed, examining the ticket stubs Blu-Tacked onto the wall. Ma had been raging about that at the time. She was worried that the paint would come off. I showed her though; they're going nowhere. The wristbands were a whole other kettle of fish though, raggedy from rainwater and pints. Hardened into a grey-green colour. Absolutely rotten when I think about it. Those bands remained on my arm for months, well into the school term. I would wash and wank with them on. The smell would knock you sick. She was so confident that I would grow bored of staring at the mud-stained cardboard and crusty festival wristbands.

# Part Four

# 35

Potted hyacinths have blossomed. Soaking up the late spring sunshine. They look like little trumpets, rendered in petal. Every one tooting from the stem, a burst of colour where sound should be. These days at home I'm mostly lying on the sofa, eating soda bread, wishing I was dead. Haunting the gaff, I float from fridge to sitting all day. I tag along with Ma when she drives to the shop for a pint of milk. Anything to get me out the house. Sometimes it's all I have to look forward to. I try to round up the troops for a couple of cans up in the park. But the girls both make jokes about how it would be 'ironic' to go and have some park drinks. Instead, they insist we go out out to make up for the complete lack of contact from them on my birthday. I've put on make-up for the first time in ages. Viscous gloop gathers on the rim of the foundation bottle. Two shades too dark now that it's exposed to the air. The mascara feels like it's crisping up on my eyes. I try not to rub them. Big panda eyes would only make this whole thing more desperate.

The taxi driver drops me at the door. Only three steps has me face-to-face with the bouncers. They don't even bat an eyelid at me. Inside, Danielle has found a bench under a heat lamp in the smoking area. Like an eighties' music video, a cloud ghosts around our faces, shining in deep oranges and reds from the lamp. We set up camp there, smoking feg after feg. As a birthday treat, Danielle's bought the chic long and thin fegs. The ones the wee girls smoke in Paris. She's been incessantly referring to this as the 'Welcome Home Slash Birthday Party'. Her arm cuts karate-chops for the 'slash'. In reality it's a 'We'll talk to you now you're back' mope-fest. We take it in turns to get some rounds of white wine topped with lemonade in. Classier than pints, Aisling tells us.

There's nothing new with Danielle and Aisling. It's same old, same old. Not even a new haircut between them. The big news they have to share is that they had talked about getting matching tattoos but decided against it. In the end, the cartoon cherries weren't something they thought would age well for them. They say I'm rolling my *rrrs* now, a guttural rattle to the back of my voice as I pronounce certain words. I can't hear it myself, but people say it often enough that they can't all be liars. I take huge swigs of wine spritzer, crying out for the sugar to provide some sort of buzz.

I break the ice by going to the bar first, get a round in to sweeten the deal. I've just ordered our pints, with a wee tequila chaser for courage. The shot has barely slid down my neck when I see him. Our eyes meet in the mirror behind the bar. Fuck's sake. This city is miniscule, I swear. I dart away as quick as I can while balancing three pints in two hands, spread out like a web. When I get back to the smoking area, I tell the girls who I've just seen. Flat voiced. Mouth pulled down. I could boke. I don't have the words to explain, especially not to Aisling.

Aisling reaches for her phone. —Ah, I'll give him a text. See where he is!

—So, did any of you see any good movies lately? I say, trying to change the subject.

Aisling is still looking down at her phone. A wee smile simmers on her face. She'd make you sick with that look. When he arrives, Andy waltzes towards the table, sitting down beside Danielle. His legs spread wide. He doesn't even look at Aisling, though she's staring right at him.

I stage whisper to her, but she ignores me. —For fuck's sake, girl. You're making me cringe.

Andy looks directly at me. —Well, long time no see, Fiadh. What's the craic?

—Nothing much, I suppose. This and that.

—And how's your ma? I haven't been round in ages. Might pop in and say hello.

My head says, *don't you fucking dare*. While my mouth says, —Awk, I'm sure she'd love to see you.

He doesn't extend the invite for me to come see his ma though. Coward is frightened of what I'd tell her. Aisling glares at me across the table. Her eyes begging me to be polite. I can't do this, so take myself to the bar. I order two vodka Red Bulls for myself. Knocking them back fast, leaving empty glasses on the sambuca-sticky bar.

Blue light sweeps across faces, the wave ripples over bodies moving against each another. The music pulses through me as I am thrown across and between the people around me. We move as one like cilia in the back of my throat, like seaweed on the bottom of the ocean. It doesn't really matter what is playing over the speakers, we move. The boys pump their fists, throw their arms around their friends. They're touching each other as if it's the first time they've hugged. Maybe it is. I dance with Aisling, though her eyes stray over my shoulder. I'm trying to entertain her with more elaborate gestures, hitting every person around me with my flailing. She is so distracted that I may as well not even be out with her. Ah, fuck it. I do the international hand-signal for 'drink?' and walk away.

Just as I reach the bar, the lights come on. Fuck's sake. I can't see Aisling or Danielle anywhere. I go back towards the toilets to search, but a bouncer steers me towards the door.

—Go on now, love, we're closed. Drink up.

I'm not even holding a drink. The crowd slowly shuffles towards the back alley behind the bar. The bouncers try their best to move everyone along towards the public road, shifting liability from themselves for any goings on in the drunken masses. Out on Shaftesbury Square, I call Aisling and Danielle. Dial tone rings off. Robotic voice welcomes me to the mobile messaging service before I hang-up.

By the time I get through to them they've walked to the Holylands to a house party. The name means nothing to me. Somebody in Danielle's class. Clarice. For fuck's sake. I storm off towards them stopping for a cheesy curry chip on my way. The server gives the wee polystyrene box a light tap on the lid as he passes it over to me. Steam swirls out of two poked holes on top. I stuff the box into my bag. Heat radiates from the chips into my torso as I trundle up to the students' area of the city. It's not until I'm at Damascus Street that I think I should have been checking the road signs as I went. Doubling back on myself, I pass Jerusalem Street, then Palestine. Finally, Carmel Street. On the right track. When I arrive at the party, a stranger answers the door. This is her gaff though, so I'm the alien here. Scepticism pushes one of her eyebrows up as I tell her I know Danielle. She goes to double check before letting me in. There's no more than ten people inside. All crammed in. Aisling cosied up with Andy on the sofa, Danielle off in the kitchen with somebody I don't recognise. Everybody in the gaff is paired off. The whole scene would make you sick. I'm flicking through my contacts in my phone looking for literally anybody who would be better craic than this.

I go to chat to Danielle but she's tonsil-deep in some bloke. Fuck it, I'm off. For consolation, I grab the tins beside her and head back out to the street. I take my time dandering through the Holylands, looking in the bay window of the terraced student houses. Every third gaff is having a party, but they all look stale as hell. Big lights keeping nothing in darkness. Three people congregated to dance. Facing each other but not interacting. I stumble on, can in hand, swigging as I go. A group of girls cross the street to avoid me as they walk past. A dribble of curry has leaked from my bag down my legs. I lean one leg on a gatepost, and scoop the mess up before licking my fingers. The girls have stopped in their tracks to watch me. I punctuate this with one long swig of cider. Eat your heart out, babes.

# 36

My mind turns these objects over and over until they blur into the tapestry of my failures. Formal photographs, my hands outstretched to some now forgotten boy. A heavy flowered corsage weighs me down, anchoring me to him. The dress remains pressed and sealed in its dry-cleaning bag in the wardrobe. Paper application forms stacked neatly on top of each other: provisional driving licence; part-time work at the supermarket near Danielle's house; a dance school. The 'personal statement' box partially scrawled over, but mostly blank. An unemptied bin containing a Tupperware box, the inside grey and dusty with a disintegrated tuna sandwich. Old tampons. Hardened with time and blood. A metallic taste floods my mouth as the skin on my cheek breaks. My teeth work over the fleshy sore until it bulges, soft and tender. Fingers corset into my stomach. Holding it in. Puncturing flesh. One sharp crack of the floorboard stops me, as Ma's footsteps near the door.

# 37

Soon as I got back from Liverpool, Ma nagged about me paying my own way. As if the thought didn't haunt me every living moment. I've been called up by Her Majesty's servants to come collect my jobseeker's allowance. Handily the town planners put the dole office beside the shopping centre, so you can kill two birds with one stone and get your messages while you're signing on. It's the only silver lining in this scenario, it has to be said. I've come prepared. In a little paper booklet I've scribbled answers to *ten activities I took this fortnight to try and get a job*. I've gone with the classics: *searched on Get a Job website* and *dropped my CV into nondescript place they'll never check up on*.

My hair is thrown up on the top of my head in a high bun. I didn't even bother to brush it this morning. Sure, who would I be trying to impress down the brew? Inside the gates, the there is a water feature shaped like metallic globes, allowing for a distorted look at yourself – like looking into a pond – before you take the Queen's coin.

Heavy doors act as a deterrent. Any barrier to try and keep some cash in the government's coffers. The woman behind the desk is brisk with me. Avoiding eye contact at all costs. She asks about whether I'm a student. I'm not, I tell her, though she looks doubtful. I consider treating her to the blow-by-blow action account of my fall from The Student Dream. A whistle-stop tour, all trains arriving at Suicide Attempt. Before I can a machine spits out a little numbered ticket. She tells me to sit, I'll be called soon. Thirty minutes pass and I've read every poster on the community board. Stages of Change: Tackling Addiction. Preparing for Your Future. Family Planning Services. Samaritans.

At the forty minute mark, my number is called. Number sixty-three to desk F, please.

Desk F, being the longest walk away, is like all the others. Partitioned. Grey. A man hunches over his keyboard, as if trying to defend it from attack. His shoulders knit towards his face. I pass him my little booklet and watch as he reads my *jobseeker actions*. He's not as impressed as I thought he would be. I put effort into that work of fiction, though to be fair he's not to know that. While he is typing at a glacial pace, my eyes wander around the room. Desperation drips from everything: the ticket machine crying out for an upgrade; the carpet in want of a good hoover; the broken and dejected people all lining along the walls, waiting for their time to be called forward.

I'm half-zoned out of the whole scene, I'm not really there. It's as if I'm viewing my body from above, seeing each movement a slight moment before it happens. I have the distinct feeling that I'm being watched; I'm aware of him before my head turns and catches his eye. David is slouched over one of the hard-plastic chairs, a feat in and of itself as the engineering does not exactly lend itself to reclining. He raises his eyebrows at me in recognition.

The man at the computer coughs, —Are you back with us now?

The prick thinks that he's in cahoots with the British government, and we the paupers are here to grovel at his feet. Begging for pennies. I make a show of checking his name badge. Craig. I stare up at him. His gaze breaks first. It's always the same with men like this. His eyes dart down to look at my tits. Unsatisfied, he goes back to his computer, and then without looking up from the screen asks, —And how have you found the job hunt?

Jesus wept, give me fucking strength. I grumble though I could say anything. Fucking brilliant. Not got out of bed in a week. Sheets reek. Covered in period and sweat. He doesn't see me as a real person, though. He scratches his signature in the box. Approving my efforts. Releasing my money. I'm good to go once my little booklet is in hand. Free as a bird for the next fortnight. Ready to hunt for my dream job in no less than ten actions.

Outside, the cloud of smoke grabs my attention first. He's leaned up against the wall, one leg pushed back against the pebble dash. He's holding his feg cupped inside his fist as if to keep the embers from the cold.

He speaks as if there's an audience waiting on my arrival,
—There's Fee! What's the craic, then?
—Alright, David. I say, not wanting to tell him anything that he doesn't already know.
—Well? What's going on? I hear you're back round our way. You avoiding us or what?
—Been busy, I mumble as I hoke through my bag for my cigarettes. They're always in the furthest corner, hidden under the spilled contents of my make-up bag.
—Aye, you look it, he says nodding to the dole building behind me.

I raise my eyebrows as I light up. Inhaling to escape any need to respond.
—So, what is it then? You got a boy, or what? Think you're better than us now?

I take a long draw of my own feg, hoofing it into my lungs, wishing it was a joint.
—You know our Andy's riding Aisling now.

Again, I inhale, and make to walk away. He follows behind me.
—She's a wee tart that one. Always has been.
—Awk, away and fuck off, David. Leave Aisling alone.
—It's not really about her though, is it? When you've been avoiding us since. You fumin' he's no longer dickin' you?

It happens quicker than I can register in my own head. My hand, feg and all, shoots out and smacks him on the cheek. His own feg now lies in a puddle. We're both standing there, in disbelief. I'm waiting for him to react, and he's probably waiting on an apology, or at least his face is asking for one: his eyebrows nearly kissing his hairline. He may keep waiting; I'm not for saying sorry. On the other side of the road, a bus splashes a tsunami over a group of schoolgirls skiving off. They scream like they're on a rollercoaster. All except one who erupts into a fit of laughter. The silent girl is covered, her white school shirt translucent with the rain. No doubt for the first time that year, she wraps her blazer around her shoulders. While I'm watching this, David has intensified.

—You serious, love?

A laugh bubbles. I hear it as if it didn't come from me. His mouth winds up the muscles in his face before he shoots spit right into my face. Through the goo, I can just about see him walking away. His limbs spread wide, as if trying to escape himself. I scoop the gob from my eyes and dry off with my sleeve.

The rain is coming down sideways in sheets, so the bus shelter is for show more than anything else. Nothing to be done but stand out in the elements, allowing the water to clean away the hawker David spat at me. It's the kind of coldness where the top layer of your skin feels like it's fusing with your jeans. Soaked to the bone. I dance from one foot to the other, trying my best to shake the numbness away. I don't even want to take my iPod from my jacket to change the song for fear it'll be destroyed in this torrent.

I hear it before I see it. The bus trundles along, its brakes screaming as it slows. Before I step on, I shake myself like a dog, water droplets flying from my nose and hair. There's little point in this, as I still have to queue in the rain before boarding. There's no escaping the weather here.

The seats up the back are the warmest. The engine will keep me warm.

Aisling's aunty, Julie-Louise, gets on a couple of stops later outside the massive church. She announces her presence with a loud 'FEEEE-AH'. Arms spread like Christ the Redeemer. I pop my earphones out and obligingly give her a hug. Head turned to the side to avoid my face being buried in her tits. Shifting over my bag, I make room for her to sit. On any given weekend after a few drinks are taken, she insists that everybody calls her Aunty J-Lo. It's yet to catch on, mind, but not for want of trying. Julie-Louise is Belfast's answer to J-Lo insomuch as ex-paramilitary Gordy from down the butchers is our answer to George Clooney.

She announces that her Aisling has been making moves, *in a romantic sense,* she adds, for clarity which was not required.

—Have you anybody on the scene, love?

I tell her that I haven't.

—A girl of your age should be making the most of her singledom. Do you know what I'm trying to say? There are a lot of frogs out there, and truth be told, that doesn't mean you can't have fun while looking for your prince charming, you know? You've got to experiment, love. Kiss all the frogs. You never know.

I know too well what she's trying to say. I have images of her husband, Big Deezy, a balding man who is forever reminding every woman within earshot that his hair fell out due to his 'high testosterone levels'. For avoidance of doubt, after a beat he would add that it meant he was extremely virile. Sluggy eyebrows dancing over his baldy bap.

I stare ahead, a little grunt every so often to let her know I was there in body at least.

—Our Aisling has only gone and tied herself down with this young one. I think he's your pal? He seems alright, mind, but she's wasting her best years on that boy. Lord, what I would do to be back out on the lash with the girls. All the boys in Belfast lining up to get a go on any of us. We had the pick. That's the life you should be after, Fiadh.

This last part she says while standing up to get off the bus. Half shouted back at me. Finishing her sentence as if she's a fairy godmother fading out of my dreams, offering advice I didn't ask for.

## 38

At night, I can fool myself that I'm anywhere but here. Ibiza. The Caribbean. Australia. Somewhere warm. Skin bronzed. Blonde highlights gifted by the sun. I wake up and remember that I'm at home. It's more miserable than when I was in sixth form. Every interaction comes with a layer of pity, a high-pitched query of concern for *my future*. Da is forever asking what I'll do next, as if what I've done before constituted anything at all. I've walked away from an unfinished degree with debts, right back into my childhood bedroom. The teddies line the top of the wardrobe, a chorus of beady eyes judging me while I rub one out to forget where I am. It's all so depressing.

After my morning routine, I check my face in the mirror to see if I can get away with pushing yesterday's make-up back into place. Grey clouds round my eyes: the smoky eye look, I think to myself, before deciding to not bother with the face wipe. I grab my go-to clothes, the ones that if I wear them any more often will disintegrate into dust on my back: my grey trackies and an oversized Truffle Shuffle T-shirt, which I wear for its ironic use of my favourite childhood characters: Strawberry Shortcake, the Care Bears. Sure, if it's good enough for Paris Hilton, it's good enough for me.

Downstairs, I boil the kettle and throw some toast on. Ma has left a pan of bacon on the hob, covered loosely with kitchen roll. That'll do nicely. Sat down with my quick bacon sandwich and a cuppa, I flick through the TV channels. There's never anything on at this time of day. Repeats of *Gladiators*. *All Star Mr and Mrs*. *Dinner Date*. Adverts for funeral costs. I settle for a show about searching for antiques in big fusty warehouses. They always have fleeces on, so you know it's Baltic in there. Money wouldn't pay you to be there.

There's only so much of that I can stomach. It's like God's waiting room. I down my first brew, and check my laptop. First port of call is always Facebook, to see the news. It's where the best drama happens, who's out with who, who has changed their status to single. It looks like Natalie Gillen from school has got married to her boyfriend already. Some people are awful keen around these parts to have the church give the go-ahead to their riding. I could never. The priests in primary school were enough to put you off the church for the rest of your days. They would be puffing about in their capes, billowing in the wind as they stormed down the aisles. The soles of their shoes clacking as they bound towards their target, invariably one of the younger kids who hadn't learnt the art of silent messing around. Through the grill at confession, the musk of whiskey and dust would waft through, before they mumbled something to absolve me, a small girl, of my shallow pool of sins. Imagine if I went now, you could dive right in and swim in all my sins. They'd love that, no doubt.

Danielle posted six hours ago. Christ what time of the night was she uploading photos at? It's her and Aisling out with their new university friends: two girls decked out in bodycon skirts and neon T-shirts. Looks like a rave night. Aisling and Danielle both have on brighter colours than usual. But there's no glow sticks in sight. I investigate by going through every photo in the album. I pause at each photo, looking at the background, trying to piece together the scene for clues, though I'm not sure what for. I have an insatiable desire to know everything about their night out, but not enough to message and ask. I don't want them to know I'm interested. That would be scundering. Their new girlfriends look so boring. I can tell from the photos that they're no craic. *Click.* A photograph of them in a living room drinking. *Click.* Back of a taxi. Aisling's face squished into the corner. Beaming smile. *Click.* Then I come across one of them all smiling and laughing, eyes creased at the corners, unaware of the nightclub photographer taking a photo of them as they dance. At that moment, I miss Chloë and Hannah; a deep ache to hang out with them again. I'm dying to text them. I've four messages from Chloë, all unanswered. The last reads: **Good luck with everything x** The caffeine hits my veins enough for me to entertain the day ahead: filled with housing related shows and job hunting on my laptop until Ma cooks dinner.

Cooking dinner is an event for Ma. She pulls spices and tins older than me out the cupboard, lining them up before deciding to do pork chops and spuds. A pan of water boils away, steaming up the windows. I reach for a lid tucked away under Tupperware in the depths of the cupboard. She tells me it's grand without, sure I'd get lost in there with all the detritus accumulated over the years. Untouched culinary wedding presents, the good china, plastic dining sets for eating outside when the weather's nice enough once a decade.
 —If you're looking for something to do, pop the kettle on for the gravy.
 I scoop out gravy granules into a jug. Water swirls it into a tarry liquid. I beat out the lumps with a fork before testing the consistency. It's thick enough to hold the fork. Ma begins clanging the cutlery on the table. She stops. Leans her arms on the table, locking her eyes on me.
 —Sit down a minute, love.
 I don't like the sound of this, but I do as I'm told. Taking my seat, the one which is closest to the radiator, I make myself as comfortable, as relaxed, as possible.
 —Love, are you doing OK? You've not seemed yourself since you came home. We're worried about you.
 Everything is fine, things are just different now, I tell her. She leans in, as if to coax another answer from me. I let her know that I'm adjusting to life at home at a slower pace. She watches as my hands arrange and rearrange the forks. Ma sighs, returning to cooking dinner. The atmosphere is thick with the unsaid hanging between us.

## 39

All the students are tucked into the south of the city. I'm on the bus over to that side of town. It's far enough away from our neck of the woods in North Belfast for Danielle and Aisling to feel they're *getting away from it, starting afresh,* but close enough that they can run their laundry home for washing on the weekends. I bet they don't even know how to work their washing machines. Their house has that dusty unaired stagnancy. It's choking.

The way this city is built I have to get two buses for around an hour. If I'd been hooped learning to drive it would be a quick fifteen minutes in the car. Terraced houses march past the bus windows at a crawling pace. The brake lights on the cars ahead reflect in the puddles streaked up the road. Moving at tectonic speeds.

When I arrive, Danielle and Aisling are pantomiming at being domestic goddesses: the kettle is just boiled; one is folding a tea towel over the oven door handle; something is crisping in the oven. They're both hovering around, weaving between each other.

I speak mostly to their backs, —Alright, girls. What's happening?

Like a cuckoo clock, they both turn at the exact same time. Their mouths move as if in sync, a gasping laughter begins.

—Sorry, love. Your accent's fucked.

Aisling imitates what she reckons is my new voice, —Sap-ennin?

My head bobs back as if guided by my moving eyebrows, an involuntary jerk. I don't have the patience to give politicians' answers tonight. I direct the conversation away from anything to do with Liverpool. How have they been? Who have they been having drama with on nights out? Even asking about their mas.

I settle myself at what is passing for a kitchen table at their gaff. It's a writing desk pushed up against a radiator. Danielle and I sit at the ends, our legs turned sideways for lack of space. Aisling is the lady of the manor, getting the chair which allows for a normal seated position. I lightly rip her about the luxury she's living in. I love what she's done with the place, I tell her. The décor is to die for.

When the timer goes off, Aisling goes to lift the tray from the oven. She sets it carefully on a tea towel on the table. The edges are burnt, black and flaking onto the material. It looks like it was once possibly a cheesy pasta bake, but it's now dusted in a light ashy crust.

—Tuck in! Aisling says, oblivious to the reticence from around the table. She rubs her hands before dishing it out in heaped spoonfuls onto our plates.

It tastes almost metallic, the charred edges of the cheese sharp on our tongues. Without needing to confer, Danielle and I are bouncing the conversation off each other to avoid diving our forks in for another bite.

—So, what's the score then? What's been happening? I say this last part in the Queen's English to alleviate any bad taste left from their jokes.

—Go on, love, Danielle says, nodding over to Aisling. —On ya go. I'm sure you've some craic to be telling, no?

—Awk, shush you.

My head is bouncing between the two of them. I've always been able to read their faces. But in my absence, they have worked up new ways of communicating with each other without words. Gestures passed between the two in a language I can't understand.

Aisling speaks at me, —It's nothing, really.

Danielle doesn't even attempt to stifle her laugh. She throws her head back and it chimneys out of her throat. —Aye, pull the other one. You're a spoofer, I swear, love.

—Wise up the pair of ya and just tell me what the craic is!

I speak while holding a mouthful of borderline inedible pasta in the hollow of my cheek.

I know it's coming, I can just feel it in my bones. And sure David practically said as much earlier on at the dole office. Even though I know the words that are going to be said, I feel like the ground beneath my chair has liquified. I don't dare look down, for fear the floor will be moving. Danielle says it: not official on social media yet, but they're serious enough for Andy to be visiting Aisling's parents. She says this last bit with half a downturned mouth, as if the movement gives weight to the formality of the announcement. So that's it: Aisling and Andy got it together. Exclusive. Fucking fabulous.

All I can muster up is a flat, —Ah, great news!

I shovel the pasta in, fork after fork arriving at my mouth before the last has been swallowed. My cheeks are filling like a hamster's. My throat dries as I try to swallow. I can feel the retch coming. Not even water can stifle it.

—I think I have to tell yous something.

The hostility in Aisling's voice is sharp, acidic. —What do you mean you think? Either you do or you don't.

—Andy and I are no longer friends, as you know.

Aisling says, —Oh, we've noticed. The whole world has seen you freeze him out.

—Yeah, well, there's a reason.

The air in the room feels thick. As if I'm trying to breathe in soup. I start and stop several times. Beginning a sentence before retracing the path back to where I started, hoping that the right words will come. I tell them about what happened, or at least what I remember to have happened.

Cynical laughter shakes from Aisling. She accuses me of always wanting to ruin everything and make it all about me. She asks how much I had drunk that night; I couldn't be sure. That's enough to seal the fate on that, for her at least.

—Why can't you be happy for anybody? It's always just pure jealousy with you. And then she says towards Danielle, —I told you, she's not been right since Liverpool. Here it is. You can't deny it now.

The look on Danielle's face is one of pitying resignation; it's the facial expression equivalent of a shrug of the shoulder. The 'I tried' look of it all. Danielle eventually offers, —It's hard, Fee, you know. You never said anything at the time, and now suddenly he's the worst because . . . because he's with Aisling? It's tough.

—Are you joking?

They both look at each other instead of at me, denying me the dignity of a returned look. I get up from my chair and put my coat on, keeping my back to them both. The tears are warming my cheeks. I'm careful not to make a noise. It takes all my effort to leave that student dive without showing the front of my body, but I manage it. Neither Aisling nor Danielle say a word. As I'm about to close the door, I shout, —Your pasta bake tastes like shite.

Fury boils under my skin. I'm walking as if about to break out into a run. There's nowhere for all this rage to go. As I make my way to the bus stop in town, the embarrassment settles on me: I shouldn't have said anything, especially not the last part. Sat on the bus, I don't take my eyes off the window, for fear of noticing the other passengers seeing me cry. An old woman sits next to me, takes out a little packet of tissues. She carefully unfolds one, then refolds it into a little square. She doesn't say anything as she passes it over into my hand.

# 40

Spidery threads have developed around my eyes. Crinkly across the forehead. I pull the skin taut, until the pink flesh under my eye pops out like a fish's mouth. Gaping. My hands worry over the material of my skirt, slightly too small, pressing into me. All my clothes pull too tight on flesh. Scissors slip through the fabric, buttery under the blade. I can't take my eyes off my reflection, watching as the point of the blade dips into my stomach. It looks like dough, pushing back to meet the metal. Deep red snakes its way out of me, glooping, sliding.

# 41

I didn't set out to do it, but that's the way of it. It's pishing out. The rain feels like needles, the icy coldness of it is burning my cheeks. My top is sopping through by the time I get there. Fat drips fall from the hood onto my nose and cheeks. I'm watching.

The gravel crunches under my feet as I take a step closer to the window. The light on the inside hides me from view. I rotate my body square on to the glass. Stock still. I stand and stare. I want him to feel watched. Goad him into seeing me. I tilt my chin to my chest. *Go on then*. He's only able to see his own reflection. His eyes dart up to the window. He must have that feeling of being seen. Being caught in a trap. Good.

He turns his back to me, concentrating on the television. *The Sopranos* is on. The set lights up the room in shades of blue and bright white light. His face takes on the appearance of a clown, the beams from the circus lights hiding the crevices under his cheekbones.

I take a step back into the darkness, lift a rock from his front garden in my hand. I bounce the weight of it. I don't take my eyes off him.

The sound fills up the street. A sharp crack. Glass twinkling onto the floor. He recoils back to the other side of the room. Shouting for his da. Dee. Anyone. I slowly walk away, taking a left down an entry, snaking its way back to my house.

## 42

The taxi bounces along a rain-slicked road. It could be any road. By this stage of the night, I'm so deep in the drink that it doesn't matter the destination. All I know is that I'm headed back to a house party. I'm piled into a car with a girl I met in the toilets earlier on. We bonded over our mutual dislike of some other random girl's boyfriend. Leaning over the sinks, we'd locked eyes in the mirror as we caught the sounds of sobbing from a cubicle. A clique was assembled to coax her out into our care. Cheating with her best friend, she said. She stood gurning in a yellow raincoat, her bag tucked under her arm, as if she was ready to head out into a storm. We wouldn't be able to pick Storm-coat's boyfriend out of a line-up, but she was having a meltdown and that was enough for the jury to be out.

—He's a dick. You can do better, love, we incanted beside the sinks until Storm-coat's tears dried, or at least until she needed a wee.

It was only when we were left on our own that I fully took in the other girl: she stood tall above me, easily over six-foot without her platforms on. Her hair was long, hanging slick like oil, flowing like liquid around her face. She was slathering lipstick on to hide red-wine stains. A deep concentration on her face as she looped the red on her mouth, circling over and over until it had hidden all she needed it to. Earthy perfume filled the room. Patchouli or possibly bergamot. I never could tell the difference.

We moved on to gossiping over goblets of gin. I spilled inconsequential insights into my life to this stranger, who I find out is called Niamh. Now, I'm sat next to her in the taxi as she texts. Her face lights up from the phone's glow. It reminded me of when, as children, somebody would hold a torch to their chin while telling a ghost story. Clear as day I remember the raspy tone these stories were told to us in. *And then there was a knock at the door!* Imprints of my nails scallop along my palms at the memory.

Terraced houses stand prone like a row of soldiers. Streetlamps stripe the buildings as we drive past. Street after street zips by with nothing discernible to tell one from the other. The taxi slows, waiting for a sign for which house we are for. This information is not forthcoming from either of us in the back. The road ends. That's it, he says. We've gone the whole length of the road. My new mate hands him a fist full of pound coins. Chiming like a pinball machine, as they drop onto the handbrake then the floor. He's fucking fuming. Giving out that it won't be enough. But sure we're out and running before he's gathered himself.

Niamh doesn't stop for ages. Jogging us a few streets away before she walks us down a new road, studying each house front with the attention of a butterfly collector. As if at random, she shouts—Here! Found it!

It's the one with the door open, of course. The entrance is like a gaping mouth, screaming out for us to come inside. So, we do. I follow her lead, as she takes an exaggerated step into the house, as if jumping off a cliff. Her breathing is stunted. Kind of like Darth Vader.

Inside, she leads me to the kitchen, and out through the back door. We walk across the garden. Roses lit by moonlight line the fencing. We take a turn down a gravel path, until we arrive at a shed. Just short of our destination, Niamh's arm blocks me from stepping any further. She shakes out her purse, sifting through coins. A small bag of pills lands in her palm. It'd be no craic not to. We swallow them dry.

—The Palace!

She speaks as if there's somebody hidden in the hedges. Her eyes scurry from bush to bush. Aye whatever you say, love, I think, while looking at the clapped-out hut. The wood looks like damp cardboard, as if it would disintegrate in your hands. The planks sag as we step inside. An electric heater projects light into the space. Music swims out of a phone balanced over a glass, as if it is playing from under water. In the corner, one fella is sat with his arms crossed, his chin sunk into his chest. He looks like he's just finished up his Christmas feed. To the back wall, a guy is sandwiched between two girls. They look like they're plotting in Churchill's war room. Heads knitted close. It's best to leave them to it, or maybe, depending on how the night goes, to join them. Nobody looks up as we take them in.

Niamh and I sit next to them, hovering as close to the heater as we can. There's a magnetism to the man holding court with the war room women. I can't stop myself from staring at him. His face is striking in a way that I can't put my finger on; he's neither attractive nor repulsive, his clothes lack any sort of distinction: grey jumper, blue jeans, white trainers. I can't stop stealing a glance over in his direction. If he notices, he doesn't let on.

The conversation trickles on with what's-her-name. My head spins, unable to concentrate on the words she is saying. Every so often, she'll say something like 'You know?' or 'What do you think?'. The only truthful answer to both of these is 'Yeah, I don't know'. The only sentence I seem able to muster. Still, I stare at him. He seems to be listening intently to the two girls. Parting his lips every so often. Trying to find a moment to speak. He is looking at his own hands, and then up to the girls who flank him. He goes out to the garden. I seize my opportunity when I see him move. Fucking bingo. Smooth as butter, I count a full sixty seconds – timed in my head – before I follow in his tracks.

Out in the garden, my eyes take a few moments to adjust to the dark. I stand there waiting for the world to come into focus. It takes longer than usual with all the drink taken this evening. He calls me from where he's sat, directly in a flower bed. Chrysanthemums crushed under his arse. He softly pats the planter, offering me a seat. As I go to park myself, he tells me not to sit so far away. Romantic, I think, before he says he has just pissed up there. We get chatting, about where we've been earlier that night. He's been here only. All night in this dump. He asks if I'm single as he's rolling a feg in his hands. Tobacco drops onto the grass. I am a mere accidental consequence in his night. He takes a draw, exhales through his nose, then leans in to kiss me. It's all very mechanical. Clinical almost. The shed door screeches open, and he pulls away from me. It's the Christmas dinner snoozer heading through the garden towards home.

—Thought that was my missus for a second.

His body eases, moving back into position. Head titled. Eyes closed long before he's close to my lips. We lower down onto the grass, settling into our crossed legs. He takes his hand and massages my thighs. My dress is splayed around me while the rain needles my face like little pins. Pushing away from him I lie back, feeling the mud soaking into my hair. I rotate my head into it, pushing my scalp into the soil. Like bedsheets in the throes of passion, my hands grab the grass. My back arches. I can hear my breathing echoing around my head. When I open my eyes, he's gone. At first, I think it's Andy standing there. For a second, my brain tricks me that yes, it's him; I'm home safe. Their eyes are the same, but the nose gives it away. Andy's is delicate. Unbroken. It's David there at my feet, watching me stare at the stars.

—Fucking state of you. Up, now.

I don't; instead I wriggle around on the soil. Snaking my hips as I move. A tingling rush.

He's holding his hand out to me. I don't take it. The world feels like it's vibrating around me. With a sharp rip, he grabs me by my top. Up like a ragdoll, he throws me onto his shoulder. My head bobs up and down as he walks us out of there and out to the street. I'm dropped down onto the pavement. It's as if my whole body is jelly: my feet give way under me. My back flops against the wall. David is gabbing away on his phone, his back to me. I can't hold my head up; it's lolling towards my chest then to my back. My cheeks feel like they're melting into my shoulders. It's bliss.

Everything feels like it's swirling around in deep waves. My skin is exposed to the elements and shimmering with every breeze. David is still speaking, but I only catch a few words. I hear his name. Andy. He's talking to him. Dee is watching me now. He crouches down, one hand outstretched on my calf. It feels like it could go through me. My legs are like dough. I try to stand up. Slurring words at him that even I can't follow. Dee turns towards the house. Facing the War Room fella from before. Stood in the doorway, he shouts —Everything ok? It's as if they're speaking in tongues. I can't pick out the words. They smile at each other, before War Room guy disappears back into the gaff's gullet.

All Dee's attention comes back to me, —Andy's on the way.

The next time my brain checks in with my body, I'm tearing off, the ground is unsteady beneath my feet. Beyond the gates, the houses look the same: a bay window, curtains pulled, a gated garden. My body stumbles left, so my legs follow suit. Staggered breath hurricanes around my head. Much further up the road, I stop to spew outside a gate. When I look around, there's only me in the street.

My eyelids peel like a wax strip from the surface of my eyeball. The inside of my mouth has dried out, sticking my tongue like Velcro to the roof of my mouth. The headache arrives next. Fucking hell, this is a bad one even for me. I've not had the drunken sense to leave out a glass of water.

I force myself up out of bed, dragging my feet towards the bathroom. The tap clunks on, rattling the pipes in the walls. I put my head under the faucet. The sharp, coldness stings my temples. There's a throbbing behind my eye sockets. Water pools on the tiles around my feet.

Down the stairs, I settle into the sofa for the day. *Grand Designs* is on. I'm not confident that even King Kevin McCloud can ease this hangover for me. The laptop roasts my legs as I click between tabs for various job sites, never really committing to one for too long. Each description is like the last: Exciting new opportunity!

Fast paced! Competitive salary! It all amounts to nothing. A complete absence of meaning. My head hurts too much for this. I palm two paracetamols into the back of my throat, washing them down with a sugary tea. Just as I struggle to swallow, Ma walks into the room.

—You were home so late it was early! Where were you? I was worried sick.

The thumping inside my head intensifies. I can feel the blood moving around the back of my eyes. Floaters appear in my vision, dancing between Ma and me. A small groan escapes from my throat.

—Hah! That good? Well I have to say love you must feel as fresh as you look. And all self-inflicted too so there'll be no moping about my house. What're you going to do with yourself today?

I gesture grandly towards the TV, like an emperor showing off all the land they reign over. The grandeur of satellite TV. Hundreds of channels to pull me through this day.

—Love, you need to be doing something. You know Gordy down the butchers is looking for somebody for the tills?

I gag at the thought of meat hanging around the shop like lanterns. Even the imagining of the smell makes me feel lightheaded.

—Nah, you're alright, Ma. I'm fine.

—Beggars can't be choosers, love. You're not above work.

# 43

Chinese takeaway night is always the best round our gaff. Ma signs off her duties and lets Da and me order in. Salt and chilli chicken. Curry sauce poured over the top. Powerful stuff. A real death row meal. I'm fit to burst as I'm cleaning up our dishes. My phone drills against the kitchen counter. There's a steady stream of texts arriving from Danielle. Notifications fill my home screen. She can wait. I go pop the kettle on, taking my time before opening the messages. The buzzing continues, waking the beast as Ma bursts in from the other room, her glasses balanced on the top of her head.

—You not going to answer that?

Her head dips towards the phone; the glasses fall to her nose. She's over like a shot, the phone is in her palm, outstretched to me. It vibrates again in her hand.

—It's Danielle, love. What's going on?

—Awk, just give me it. She can wait two minutes for fuck's sake.

—Fiadh Donnelly. You watch your mouth in this house.

My bottom lip tucks up over my tongue, a cradle to stop me biting through it. In a sign of surrender, I put my hands up. I take another mug out of the cupboard. The tension in Ma dissipates as the tea brews. With my back to her, I check the messages. Danielle is after a late-night coffee. So desperate for it that she's sent a dozen messages. It's the first I've heard from her since our dinner date. Butterflies tingle in my stomach. There's nothing else to be at this evening, other than watching shite on telly with Ma. I text back: **Sure**. My Christmas clothes are in need of an outing. I throw them on and head out.

It's as if this city's public transport is designed to keep you in the house at all costs. The buses are few and far between, and you'll be sardined the whole journey. Standing back to front with strangers, whose arms hold the rail above for dear life, pushing out their sweaty armpits to eye level. On the second bus, the air is close. Long legs of raindrops dance down the windows. Streetlights zip past the window, kicking through the streams of rain.

Getting off the bus, the streets look molten after the downpour. Huge onyx craters appear at the side of the road; the darkness so deep it looks bottomless. The only image I catch is my own on the surface of the water. The mirror of my face dapples as rainfall reaches a crescendo outside the café. Danielle is already there, wrapping herself around a coffee, steam swirling up from the mug.

—Awk, love. Did you swim here?

I wring out my hair, a shower flowing off the ends onto the cement floor. My shoulders perk up in an offer of apology to the barista. He shuffles over, taking my order, ignoring the new lake at our feet.

Danielle is talking at a hundred miles a minute, about her coursework, about festival tickets she's got us, about some wee fella she's been texting who sent her a picture of his wab. It looks like it's wrapped up in a parka; good for this weather, she tells me. I hope he's not going out in just that. She only stops for sips of her drink.

The barista pops my latte in front of me just as the door chimes. I see her coming in the reflection on the coffee machine. She's walking up towards us, long strides begin to shorten as she realises just as I do why we're there. For fuck's sake, Danielle.

Aisling takes her time. Shaking out her umbrella. Uncoiling her scarf. Each finger on her glove released with precision. She jumps out of her skin when the barista comes over. Ever the risk taker, she orders a decaf.

The coffee machine whistles as milk is heated. Danielle spoons another sugar into her half-finished drink. It rings against the cup, before she settles it on the table.

—Right, this needs sorted.

My head drops to one side. Aisling jumps in before I can say anything. The words whip out of her like a machine gun: We've been friends for so long! We shouldn't fall out over a boy! What about the good times! We're meant to be mates! She misses me.

—OK.

Danielle, playing the diplomat, asks if I have anything to add.

—I don't. You're right.

As if strings cut from a puppet, Aisling lunges over the table first, capturing me in a hug. I hold her, lightly.

# 44

Ma has signed me up for one of these 'wellness days' down at the leisure centre. A bloke from the estate is putting on a yoga sampler class. Ma reckons it'll be good for me to try something different. Before I can protest, she's bundled me into the car. As I'm buckling in, her arm thrusts towards me, gym kit hanging limp as a faint. Ma natters on about the health benefits of yoga. Great for destressing! And sleep! I'd kill to be put in a long coma right now. A car crash would do it. Blood. Mushed limbs. Hot metal mashed with bodies reduced to meat. Anything to not be here.

Inside the leisure centre, a woman sporting a blown-out eighties haircut asks through a smile why I'm there. Her arms are knitted in front of her on the reception desk. On a page, tallying numbers for each of the classes. Needless to say, Yoga with Brian is not oversubscribed. But still, I can't resist asking if she can *squeeze me in*. Eighties-Wig doesn't seem to notice or care.

—It's in the big hall, love. Down that way, second door on your right. Changing rooms are straight ahead.

The changing room cubicle stinks of bleach and toes. Tiles clogged with fluff and muck from the playing fields complete the ambience. I've never changed so fast in my life. In the hall, my fellow yogis are all in their seventies: three ladies palled up together. They huddle together and giggle at their adventurousness. They don't even notice me as I stand near them. Brian booms into the room, long strides as he claps his hands together. The ladies eat it up. Chuckles bursting out of them.

—Well, ladies!

He bellows to the almost empty hall as if he's just come on stage at a sold-out stadium tour. I can't believe I'm here. We roll out mats, sticky with other people's sweat. He instructs us to fold ourselves over, touching – or trying at least – to bring our hands to our feet. Not one of us can do it, so yogi Brian shows us how it's done. Bending over, he touches his toes, before pushing his hands to the floor, raising his whole body off the ground. The ladies *oooh* at him. Lifting their hands to their chests. Gasping.

He dials it back a notch, showing us the much tamer move of lying on your back and thinking. Corpse pose he calls it. Above, the overhead lights look like alien spaceships descending from the sky. I wish they would beam me up. When I zone back in, Brian's voice has become raspy, but no less Belfast, as he guides us through 'the forests of our minds'. Man must be baked as hell.

—First, relax your cheeks – not those ones ladies! Relax your jaw, your mouth, and your eyebrows. Really relax your eyebrows.

The skin around my eyes is clenched tight as a fist. I'm concentrating on my eyebrows: what do they have to be stressed about? Not got the star treatment with a wax appointment? Having to make do with the quid tweezers from the pharmacy, the ones which inevitably do the ingrown pubes too? Fucking hell, this hasn't relaxed me at all. If anything, it's given me a laundry list of other things to be concerned about. My poor fucking eyebrows are having a nightmare of it.

A mat slaps down next to me. I peek one eye open and see Ma folding herself down onto the floor. Her legs and arms jutting out unnaturally, like she's discovering she has limbs for the very first time here in this room. She gives me two thumbs up. I close my eyes, concentrating on unravelling the knot of my brows. Brian gets us back on all fours, to the delight of the women in the room. Guiding our bodies into the downward dog pose. Ma's face contorts as if she's heard the dirtiest thing on earth. Christ.

In our gym kits, we convene in the leisure centre café. We drink teas poured from a hot water urn. It tastes like a metallic watery soup. Ma blows the surface of hers, cooling down the molten liquid. She pulls it away quickly, the first sip burns her lip. —What are we doing here? she asks, giggling like the schoolgirl she must have been. Her chin buckling into her chest as she mimics the instructor. Holding her hand to her heart, she says, —Nah Ma says ommmmm.

She repeats each word through heaving laughter. It's infectious. People around the café are beginning to stare, which adds fuel to the fire for both of us. Tears gathering in our eyes as we try not to look at each other. Having an audience compounds our joy. A transgression, mother and daughter acting the maggot like two teenagers.

—Awk, there you are. I missed this, Ma tells me.

I've not been myself, I'm told. She was worried, but here I am. A glimmer of my old self. The relief on her face cracks something in me. I hold her hand and cry laughing.

## 45

It's happening. It's boiling up inside me.
   Rising.
A tide up to my neck.
   I can feel it what's about to happen.

# 46

My days at home are sucked dry by the shite I'm getting up to all day every day. Ma's friend Tracy has got me a trial shift at her son's restaurant. Flipping bacon on a grill, serving teas, and mopping up spills and baby spew. I tried to tell Ma that I'd be fine getting work eventually. I was still processing moving from Liverpool, I told her, settling back in at home. She snapped, —You're going.

Now though, I wish I had avoided taking that final pill last night but God forbid starting on a come down while still out. Watching people haunt a party, chewing the bake off themselves, while the fear starts to settle in on me. Nah, fuck that. So, I did the only thing I could have done in those circumstances: slap another pill into me and grab a beer from a bath filled with lukewarm water. When I got home, I lay buzzing in my bed all night, listening to Tiesto on my iPod. Didn't sleep a wink. Couldn't. Just wrapped up, staring at the ceiling's plaster dimples.

My alarm goes off after having my eyes closed for a second. Fuck's sake. It would be easier to just hide forever. When I eventually haul myself into the bathroom, I stoop into the shower and hope the water will burn away The Fear. It doesn't. If anything, it makes me hyper aware of every ache in my body: my legs are throbbing as if in competition with my head. A tension in my jaw. I've eaten up the inside of my lip. I would give a kidney, a limb, fucking anything to be going back to bed and not to this greasy spoon with Tracy's son, Shane.

Out of the shower, the water drips from my hair straight on to the floor. I don't mop up the puddle I create after I leave the bathroom. I know Ma will be raging, but I can't even face the thought of her annoyance.

Downstairs, Ma has the tea waiting, and a sandwich wrapped up in tinfoil.

—There's your lunch ready, love. Do you want a bottle of juice for it too?

If I open my mouth, I'll regret it, so I just shrug. Ma goes to the cupboard and produces one of the little sippy bottles of blackcurrant juice that kids get in their meal deals at burger chains. The doorbell rings in three short, sharp bursts, followed by one long drill. Ma dusts off her hands on her thighs, patting any dirt from her hands into her jeans. By the time we get to the door, he's already back in the car. Buckled in and ready to go. He must have sprinted back.

My body deflates as I get inside the car, as if melting into the fabric. Coldplay's 'Viva La Vida' is pumping through his souped-up radio. I want the car to swallow me whole as I clock his beaming eyes. He looks possessed.

—Are you ready to have a great day?

Christ. I don't have the stomach for this. I make a sound, but not quite words. He asks again, more animated. Arm pumping.

—Aye.

—You can do better than that! I always like to start the day with a big smile!

The car groans into gear. It's not even that far; I could have walked. At the lights, I think about opening the door and making a run for the hills. I could live off the grid up Cave Hill. Or on the run on the Camino. My dreams are drowned out as his left hand turns up the radio talk show. Three ould blokes are arguing over the pub closing hours.

—Too much, too late, one man wheezes, like his soul is leaking from his body, ready for whatever waits after this mortal existence.

Shane is nodding along. He yanks up the handbrake, shaking the whole car. He parks a mere few paces from the door. Close enough to make a leap from car to café.

He throws open the door, —It's a new day!

Swear to fuck. I can't cope with this. I'm treated to the grand tour of the kitchen: the mop bucket, the giant dishwasher, and where the new cloths can be found.

—Stop me at any time if this is too much.

I pop the kettle on, showing him that I'm settling in rightly. He hides his glee with a downturned smile, tucking his chin into his shoulders to conceal the unwarranted pride. Eyeing me like his protégé.

# 47

I'm up early the next morning. Laundry, I told my ma the night before, which isn't a lie really. She's got hearing like a bat; it's a talent how she can decipher who is responsible for floorboard creaks from the sound of our footsteps. If Da or I pause too long on the stairs, she knows exactly where we have stopped. What we're likely to be doing. I take the bedsheets from the wash. Freshened by the scent of 'tropical dreams', or so the packaging says. I bury my nose into the material and take a deep breath. It smells like all the other detergents.

The ironing board clangs onto the kitchen tiles, bouncing like a tuning fork. I let it sing through the house. Sure, it's all part of the charade. My palms run along the material, smoothing the swathes of it under my hands. The heat radiates through me, up my arms and into my bones.

Then I'm elbow deep in detritus under the kitchen sink, plastic bags stuffed with more bags spill out onto the floor. Empty bottles, bleach and sprays are next. Ma keeps them all in case she ever needs to spritz something. To date, the occasion has never arisen, which to her mind means the day is drawing ever closer. Then it's in my hand. The power of it is electrifying. Then the lid is off, popped somewhere on the floor. Who knows where. Who cares? I hold the marker like a dagger and scrawl the words.

I fold the sheet up, then place it inside a tote bag. The morning is Baltic when I step out. A misty fog hovers over the roads. In a couple of minutes, I'm stood at the entrance to the estate. It's so still. Nobody seems to be up yet. It being a Sunday morning and all. My skin prickles, with sweat or cold: it's hard to tell. Dawn is beginning to break. There are cars driving past, headlights shining on my back. No rest for the wicked. Looping the corners through the wire. A crucifixion in cloth. Rain is soaking through my hoodie. I hope it doesn't smear the ink. I pull the sheet's corners sharply. There it is. It's out in the open.

Andy Garrity: Predator.

The black crumbs fall down Ma's chin to their final resting place on her nightie. I've already received texts from Danielle and Aisling asking me what's going on. I plead ignorance, telling them I'm just out of my bed. What's happening, I ask?

—Somebody has poor Andrew terrorised, Ma says between mouthfuls of burnt toast.

Her elbows are perched up on the table, holding a slice in one hand and her brew in the other. —Terrible, she inhales the words before slurping her tea.

I say nothing.

—What has poor Andrew done to deserve this treatment?

I play on my phone, scrolling through unanswered texts. Clicking into old photos of flowers, the girls, anything.

—No doubt someone's jealous of him and Aisling. Have you spoken to them? They'll need their friends around them at this time. It can be hard. Sure, what will the people who don't know him think, the blow-ins in the town? Terrible, terrible. We're living in awful times, love, where whatever's said goes. She looks off towards the wall. Very, very hard on a young man to come up against this sort of gossip. And what of his poor mother? Deirdre's head must be away with it all. I must give her a call. What's Andrew's take on it all, love? Before I go and ring Deirdre, it'd be wise to know what the Garritys are thinking of it all.

At this point, she stops and takes me in for the first time. Looking at me as if she's just noticed I'm there.

—Well? How is he?

—Oh, he's grand, no doubt.

—Grand? Love, he's being branded a pervert.

As she says this her chin thrusts violently into her neck. She could make an easy claim for whiplash.

The plates clatter as I stack them one on top of the other, sandwiching in the flakes from the pastries and toast. Ma scolds me for not brushing them off into the bin first. I sweep the crumbs with a theatrical flick of the wrist, making a show of the domestic servitude. I complete the act with a bow to my ma.

The kitchen is warming up with the heat radiating from the oven. Ma always has the roast on early, allowing enough time for the meat to settle into itself. The vegetables are stacked high in their pots and pans, ready for boiling water to be chucked on top and set on the stove. I don't know how she does it, but every Sunday dinner is approached with a religious vigour. A commitment to seeing off the week with the grandest meal. It's like she spends all year preparing for the big one: Christmas lunch. At the end of every meal, she rates her efforts through an inhaled few words. Along the lines of 'Grand enough', 'Very good,' or most ominously a long humming noise as she thinks of adjustments for next week's dinner, possibly a different cut from the butcher, parsnips honeyed before roasting.

# 48

Half asleep outside a big Tesco, we hover around waiting for the bus to pick us up. Our rucksacks poke out over the top of our heads. Danielle's hoking through hers, pulling out drink for the journey. Something to get us started. A rickety bus straight from the early nineties pulls up. The doors open like nails on a chalkboard. The bus careens down the motorway, tyres knocking off every bump on the road. I'm throwing back a vodka coke, pre-mixed in a washed-out milk carton. There's a milky residue stinking up the rim. Aisling is minding all our tickets in a poly-pocket, tucked behind a schedule of all the bands she'd like to see that weekend. The Prodigy. Justice. Amy Winehouse. She's running through estimated stage times. I'll never know how she can be holed with all that, but it's easier to let her take the reins.

Several hours of holding in a piss later, we arrive at a big muddy field. A crush of people in wellies wade through the dirt towards the festival campsites. Danielle and I take it in turns lugging our tent. It's a bulky cheap one. Pure shite. Wouldn't hold back a sneeze. Aisling lets Andy carry theirs, while her hands fumble with the paperwork to get us in. Inside the chain-link fenced field, we hunt out the perfect spot to throw up our tent. When all set up, it looks like it's quaking at the knees. A slight breeze threatens to send it off to the skies. Danielle bucks our bags in; we're both satisfied that what will be will be.

Our wristbands are fresh, bright weaves against our skin. We waste no time before bombing over to the stages: there's a singer there who has infamously returned from a stint in rehab; more bands with T-shirts and waistcoats than I can count; and a DJ playing remixes of songs from our childhood. The four of us move as a pack between every stage. Andy keeps his distance from me. Not saying a thing. Danielle clicks a disposable camera every twenty minutes or so, capturing us pushing through crowds, arms held pints in the air. The mud sticks to my bare legs, flicked up by my wellies, not quite far enough to reach my denim cut-offs. There's a stench of stale beer and muck.

We pair off, Aisling and Andy doing their own thing as Danielle and I make our way to somewhere discreet. The security staff were checking people for drinks as we were coming into the fields. Danielle's sister had warned her about this but said that the fellas on security wouldn't want to get too handsy with a wee girl. She took her chances and stuffed a coke bottle filled with vodka in her kecks. She'd been practising for weeks the art of walking somewhat naturally with her legs clenched. We find a spot near the first aid tent. It's quiet around there at this time of the day. The bottle was warm when she first whipped it out of her trousers as we entered the field, now it's flat and covered in dirt. I shut my eyes as I take a swig. It burns my throat on the way down, but it's better than paying festival prices for a pint. We take a few gulps before she manoeuvres it next to her foof again.

The masses of people seem more bearable now, floating by as we make our way to whatever stage is straight ahead. It doesn't really matter who's on; we'd lost our wee printed timetable long ago. It was never really about the music for either of us. We were there for the experience. The boys from all over the island! A fresh pool for us.

—So, are you and Andy just going to blank each other all weekend or what?

—He's pretty preoccupied. I'm sure he'll be grand.

—Everybody's talking about him, you know. After that message round your way.

We keep walking, neither of us speaking. People scream at the top of a Ferris wheel, waving down to their mates. Some fellas are shaking their pods. It spins slowly back towards the ground. Danielle's eyes are filling.

—Was it you, Fee?

—Danielle. When have you ever known me to be up early? Never mind up and out the gaff.

—I'm being serious. You've had it in for him.

I'm sharper now. —No. I didn't.

—OK, is all she says.

Sawdust lines the floor of the tent we enter. The singer mustn't be able to see a bucking thing with his sunglasses. The lights are dimmed for a slow song. Lighters are raised up in the air. Danielle hokes into the bottom of her bag and takes a photo of us in the crowd.

I wake up in a booze-blurred haze. It doesn't get dark here, with the floodlights and guard towers watching over the campsite. The organisers say it's for safety, but most of the people up there are on the cans too. A beer-can hiss lets my brain know that my body has decided to have another. The night passes, but I can't get back to sleep. I'm sat up in my tent, watching the shadows of people float by. Their limbs like drainpipes, their voices supernatural. Danielle is snoozing beside me, face down and hugging her backpack. I shake my sleeping bag out and pull it around my shoulders, wrapping myself like a caterpillar. I slightly unzip the tent, and smoke feg after feg with my head half-hanging out of the flap. Just one hand poking out from my sleeping bag cocoon.

It is fierce cold out when I decide to brave it for a piss. Light comes through the blue plastic walls, giving the portacabin a blue luminescence. Toilet paper is sopping with piss or vomit. I don't investigate further, and hoke out tissue from my hoodie, taking a mental tally whether I have enough. There are two squares of bog roll at the most. It's pish-soaked in seconds. Nowhere near enough. I shake and drip-dry. The stench in here is thick, noxious. I hold my breath in huge gulps, reducing the number of inhalations while inside. I burst out with a new appreciation for the mud stink.

My feet slurp in the ground as I head back to the tent. I see a light coming from Aisling and Andy's tent, the shadows showing them knitted together, laughing. In something akin to somnambulance, I walk over. I hunker down and listen for their breaths. I hear Aisling purring into him. Insufferable. In my tent, I zip into my sleeping bag and try to settle back down as the crowds walk past, their shapes darkening the tent. I must have fallen asleep, as I wake up a few hours later. I'm half in and half out of the tent, my face pressed on the damp grass. A squashed quarter smoked feg lying beside me. I open another can. It's too early.

In the morning, the whole campsite has an air of one big hangover. Eerie. Silent. People shuffle to the water fountains with little washbags, in an attempt to clean up before presenting themselves back home to their mas. The other festival goers are packing up their rucksacks, double checking that nothing has been left behind in their tents, before they finally set them alight. Danielle is away to find a stall still selling food, to set her up for the two-hour journey back up to Belfast. I think it's just me with the tents. It's so still that I nearly don't bother popping my head into their tent to check they've taken everything. He's there. Lying there like a corpse. Andy's out for the count, but he's a big boy, I think, he can fend for himself.

Aisling's rucksack is leaning up against mine outside my tent. When I see her, she's weaving her way back towards me. I drag her bag as I make my way towards her. Danielle and Andy have gone on, I tell her. They're away on to the bus. Tents are all clear.

We amble our way to the pick-up point, stopping at a coffee van for a tea to tide us through the day. I'm tapping down my pockets, searching in my bag.

—Fuck, love, my purse. I've left it in the tent.

I run off, telling her to meet me at the bus.

—I'll be back.

Back at the tent, I dive my hand in, feeling around in the litter of disposable baby wipes for my purse. The theatre of it all settles into my guts. I side-step to Andy's tent, unzip it an inch, peer inside. He's still sleeping off the hangover: dead to all the world.

He doesn't even raise his head. The campsite is nearly empty now. With the last remaining people running from their tents, as they begin to go up like little bonfires. Anything to avoid packing up. The flames throw their arms out to the sky, swallowing all around them. I steal a look inside again. No movement.

He's on his own now. I take a couple of steps away from the tent, rummage around my pockets for a feg. My hand shakes as I imitate striking, once, twice, before I light the end of it. As I inhale, the embers blaze. I return the match back to its spot in the box. Lighting each of the other heads. I throw the box into the tent. It hisses as it bursts into a ball of light. Crackling plastic catches the sparks. I don't look back as I walk away.

Back at the coffee cart, the barista looks ready for murder. His eyes dead in their sockets. Dull. Red rimmed. I'm the last order for the weekend. The relief is palpable when I order a tea. Two thimbles of milk and three sugars should do me, given the state of this hangover. I'm fumbling with my purse in my hands, watching the field light up. Candescent polka dots in ochre. Hot tea warms my hands as I walk to the pick-up point. Up beside the bus, the three of us watch over the pyres. Aisling has her phone out texting away. Her ma. Andy. It is as if her body knows before she does. Her legs bounce. The whole of her body electrified.

—Is this the right bus?

The tea comforts me. Heating my chest with every gulp. I close my eyes as the screams are carried on the breeze up from the campsite. Blue lights bounce off the bus window. It dawns on Aisling first, then it ripples out to the rest of the passengers waiting to board. Screams. Now closer.

# 49

Nobody makes a peep on the bus up the road to Belfast. Aisling's in bits, her shoulders are rattling. Danielle is texting away; she hasn't raised her head since we got on the motorway. My adrenaline is pushing up against the silence. Waiting is making me itch. My thumb clicks through songs on shuffle: Arctic Monkeys; one line up or another of the Sugababes; Daft Punk. Jitters won't let me settle on any song for longer than the intro before I'm onto the next. A shake has developed in my leg. I'm dying to walk it off. There's nowhere to go. I'm trapped. I take a can out of my backpack. It's crushed the metal ring pull bubbling out like an asshole. It buckles gently as I open it.

I'm half-rightly by the time we pull into the petrol station off the Shore Road. Pure silence as we pour out of the bus. A queue of parents wait to pick up whichever one of us belongs to them. They break ranks as soon as they spot their kids, rushing towards them, thankful that they've returned unscathed. Ma's arms pat me down as if to check that I'm not concealing any injuries. Her lips quiver as she scans my face. The final assessment is I just need a good shower and a hot meal.

It's only in the aftermath when the dust has settled that the horrors can be seen. *Choked words. Broken skin. The pressure.* The phone rings and rings and rings. I don't move to answer it. Da is pretending he can only hear the movie he has on. *The Silence of the Lambs.* It keeps ringing. A metallic drilling. Ma is the first to crumble: throwing her hands on the sofa as she pushes herself from her cushioned groove. Footsteps so heavy they could break floorboards as she makes her way to the phone. Once the receiver is to her ear, a smile is pulled from her, lifting her voice. It doesn't last. Her hand cradles over her mouth, for what feels like minutes the only words are sucked in on her breath.

—And is it serious?

The rest of the call passes slowly, as all the details funnel into the room: *third degree burns, yellow and red oozing wounds, intravenous drips, creams, gauze, liquid food*. All the details retold to Da and me as she pulls apart the two sides of a chocolate bourbon.

—Could have killed him.

She whispers, her eyes turned down towards the biscuit.

—How could this happen to that poor wee pet? Julie-Louise was saying his mother's head is turned. And no wonder! The shock alone.

Her voice trickles away from her. Da and I are still staring ahead. What escapes from her next is like a balloon deflating. Her shoulders folding over the rest of her as the tears shake out.

Three hard knocks on the front door announce their arrival. They come in flak-jackets, scraping their boots on Ma's wooden floor, leaving dark scars. A radio beeps every few moments, before the officer twists the receiver down to a mumble. Both Ma and Da watch them wordlessly as they settle in front of me at the dining-room table. A mug of tea sweats in my hands. The questions come: *Tell me about the day you came back from the festival? Who was there? Was he drunk?* I rattle through monosyllabic responses. Playing the moody teenager. Da signals an end to the chat, by standing up and holding the door open.

When they leave, Da sits opposite me, and asks with words dripping in sincerity if I'm OK. I am. I really am! Red rag to the bull, Ma is up and guldering. Emotion boiling out of her. The skin on her face is crimson, damp with sweat or tears. My hand finds the TV remote.

—Do you have no shame, Fiadh?

A whisper of a smirk slips over me. The muscles on my face working in tandem to get me in trouble.

—Have you no empathy? You're a heartless wee bitch. And him being your oldest friend!

She leaves as I erupt. Da witnesses the mirth.

—He's no friend of mine.

## 50

When the doors open, first the smell wafts, sweet and thick. A honeyed stench of spilled beer. Inside the lights are dimmed as if by candlelight. It would be awfully romantic if it wasn't four in the afternoon. The regulars are holding up the bar, their shoulders hunched in on themselves. They're silent except for their orders. I make my way to the bar. Order two vodkas, then sit in the booth in the back. The first drink is a warm-up, easing my muscles into the evening. The second is a more languid affair.

As the day slithers away from me, I take stock of the men who arrive: after five is when the working world crawls in, looking for something to help them forget their days. Men gather in twos and threes, little swarms. I stare into the backs of their skulls, hoping for one – any really, it doesn't matter which – to feel my gaze. It takes time. It always does. Then, he looks. Catches my eye. A quick raised eyebrow then, I return to my phone. The bait is set. When I go to the bar next, he sidles up beside me.

The booth feels cosier now that there's two of us. Legs graze under the table. The brief electric shock of touch vibrates its way up my body. He's picking the label from his beer, gathering the papery remains into small piles on the table. They're pushed around as we talk incessantly about nothing. It's all just window-dressing before the main event. He wants to talk about the news, but this is dangerous territory: there's nothing less sexy than politics. I steer the conversation as best I can, tell him I've recently gone through a break-up. He places a hand on my knee. —There, there. It'll be alright, he hums.

We leave the bar together, our arms threaded around each other's backs. He jangles his keys. A nearby car's headlights flush the street in a golden glow. He opens the door for me, bowing as I make my way into the passenger seat. The car splutters as his hands fumble to turn the engine on. Impatience or an internal safety gauge throws my body into motion, climbing over the car, straddling him. My back crushes against the steering wheel as he struggles to locate my tits. One rasping shudder lets me know he's done before we start.

The streets are eerily still at this time of night. It's not quite letting-out time for the bars, so there's only stragglers. I pull a feg from my bag to keep me company on the walk home. Night sky shimmers above me, lit up by streetlamps across the city. Cars drone past. Cats are fucking or fighting somewhere nearby. Footsteps. David is closer than I expected when I turn. With him, it's always hard to tell what's next. He's shaking.
—Alright?
His lips are rigid as he speaks, forcing the word into sharpness. He's taken a step towards me, close enough to smell his breath, sharp with sickness or drink. Under his breath, he's repeating Andy's name to himself. Over and over. I inhale deep into my chest.
—Oh, fuck off, Dee. He was a mess all weekend. Pinged out of his nut.
His eyes are searching my face for any signs, a facial twitch, a flush of emotion. Fancies himself as Belfast's Columbo. I return the stare, until his eyes begin to fill.
—He won't even speak anymore. Fucked up.
—Terrible, I say through a stream of smoke.
—Aye, it is. It's a fucking nightmare. Aisling reckons he went back to the tent, forgot his fegs or something. Couldn't wait to light it and the tent went up.
—It's all such a shame. All so needless, isn't it?
He's shaking. Fingers flex into a fist, bouncing off his thigh.
—She must be beside herself.
—You not seen her?

Grief will do that to a person, I tell him; it tears you away from the ones you're closest to. I'm giving her time. She texted me incessantly in the days after. Checking and double checking that I was sure he wasn't there. It came easy to me, the lying. I told her he wasn't. Maybe he was still out of it, she countered, filling in the gaps herself, looking for a reason, anything to explain it all away. I tell him this just as I told her.

Dee is standing there, weighing up whether I'm a spoofer. His eyes searching for answers. To what though? I'm not sure he knows. I feel nothing for him. No pity, nothing where shame should be. No sorrow at all. A quiver wobbles over his bottom lip. He stymies it by squaring his shoulders out. His chest puffed. Shaking all over. When he walks away, the streetlamps drape their light over him. His shoulders begin to shake just before he turns the corner.

# 51

An Indian Summer makes it a warm morning, but I'm layered up in jumpers. All the essentials are stuffed in my bag: socks, extra knickers, my passport. The stroll to the café is gorgeous. Sunshine swims through the leaves, a psychedelic astral projection on the tarmac. It's as if the roads are melting with the heat. The row of shops almost looks appealing in this weather. Shane's café is open already. Door's open. Smell of freshly cooked bacon drifting out.

—Awk, what about ya? He says, ignoring the fact I've not been in for a single other shift since my first.

—Your ma sent me down for a shift, I tell him.

A balled-up apron is passed between us. It only has one noticeable stain, so I'm in luck. I tie the straps loose around my neck, then my hips. The mopping needs doing, he tells me with a wink as he disappears to the back. As I'm swilling out the bucket, the regulars appear. Old dolls wheeling their bags in. Newspapers tucked under arms. Powdery perfume clouding around them. They order cups of chino, extra hot lattes, cheese and ham toasties. My thumb catches on the corner of the till as I'm closing it. It bounces open an inch. They're where they are always kept. Shane's predictable if nothing. The twenties and tenners are tied up in an elastic band at the back. I shout over my shoulder to him that I'm nipping out for a feg. Grand, he shouts, just as I'm slipping the bundles into my front pocket.

It begins to rain just as the bus pulls into the airport. Bag overhead I tear off to the check-in hall. Scan the boards for departures. Queuing up, all the people around me chatter excitedly about reunions and holidays. Sunglasses on the tops of their heads. I buy the only ticket I can afford. Cash from the till covers it. A last-minute trip to visit my fella, I tell them. A text pops up on my phone from Ma asking what I fancy for dinner. Unclipping the back of my phone, I slide the sim card out, place it between my teeth and bite. I drop it in the liquids bin at security.

Hidden in the corner of Starbucks, I keep my head down. Everyone and their ma seems to be off on their travels today, fuck's sake. Last thing I need is to bump into anybody now. I don't even have my phone to distract me. On the runway, planes park up and take off. High-vis blokes run around waving neon batons. Over the loudspeakers, my flight is called. It's time.

Everywhere in this city reminds me of change. A fresh start will do me good, to be unfettered. Freedom. Fucking shitting it now though, as the doors close. Locking me in. I'm frightened of flying, but too scared of what will happen if I don't leave. The stewardess passes out a bundle of necessities for the flight, every item new and wrapped in cellophane. I sit in the cattle class seat for my journey, pull on my in-flight socks, tuck in my thin blanket. The selection of movies is roughly a decade out of date. I select two or three to sustain me for the journey, knowing I will probably opt to watch the plane icon move its way around the globe. My eyelids feel heavy. I dream that I am home. Over the clouds, I wake up, not sure where that is or what it means yet.

# Acknowledgements

Huge thanks to everyone at John Murray Press, especially Becky Walsh for guiding me through the debut novel process and for being such a wonderful editor. *Exile* has undoubtedly been made a better book because of your feedback and support. Thank you.

To my agent, Eleanor Birne, for believing in this work before it was completed, for the thoughtful conversations on the manuscript before it went out on submission, and for being a champion of me as a writer.

My unending thanks to everyone at the Irish Writers' Centre who, along with the Arts Council of Northern Ireland, awarded me an Emerging Writer's Bursary that enabled me to take Conor Kostick's 'Finish Your Novel' course. It is no exaggeration that this work would not exist without that award. Thank you. And to the group of writers who, during those workshops and after gave feedback on early drafts of *Exile*, particular heartfelt thanks to: Marlene May, Mary Meaney and Fiona O'Rourke.

Thank you to Heather Parry at *Extra Teeth* for publishing my fiction for the first time.

Thank you to the Irish writing community who has been so kind and supportive; particular thanks to: Rachel Connolly, Jan Carson, and to Lucy Caldwell for her encouragement and feedback during the Faber Academy. To Nathaniel McAuley for friendship and reading this novel in its (very messy) draft form. To Darran Anderson and Jill Crawford for putting wrongs to right while I was writing this book. To Maggie Scull for being an all-round inspiration and brilliant friend. To Grainne O'Hare for cheering me on to the end.

To my Belfast besties, for long nights in each other's gaffs as teenagers, for the gossip, for the fun and love and warmth. Thank you doesn't quite cover it, but here's to the best mates I could have hoped for: Katherine O'Doherty, Marcus McAlister, John Gillen, Paul O'Neill and Daniel 'Titney' McMullan.

The biggest of all thanks to my family. To Mum for being my number one supporter no matter what. To Dad for always being there when I need it. To Rory and Megan, for kindness and love.

To my husband, James, who gave me the confidence to put this work out in the world. To say 'thank you for everything' does not quite cover it but to put in words how much I love you would be to fill another book. So, for now: thank you for everything.